CONFESSIONS FROM A NAUGHTY NANNY

PIPER RAYNE

About Confessions from a Naughty Nanny

When a famous music producer moves to Lake Starlight it can't just be a coincidence. It's the universe helping to move things along in the right direction so that Griffin Thorne can discover me.

I have to confess—I'll do whatever it takes to make that happen.

Confession #1: I may have overhead that he was in search of a nanny. What can I say? My brother has a big mouth.

Confession #2: It's possible I helped along the assumption that I had nanny experience. Hey, babysitting my nieces and nephew counts, right?

Confession #3: There's a good chance I oversold my qualifications. But my Grandma Dori backed me up, so it's not completely my fault.

And it worked. He hired me. Only for me to find out that he left the business.
I guess it's on to Plan B.

When he accidentally overhears me singing, I expect nothing from him. Then he asks to work with me on a song

for our town's Founder's Day Parade and it feels like a
dream come true. Until...

Confession #4: I've fallen for him.

Confessions
of a
Naughty Nanny

The Baileys

Austin Bailey - 35 years old
(Biology Teacher/Baseball Coach)
Savannah Bailey - 33 years old
(Runs Bailey Timber Corp)
Brooklyn Bailey - 30 years old
(Runs Essential Oil Company)
Rome Bailey - 28 years old
(Chef)
Denver Bailey - 28 years old
(Bush Pilot)
Juno Bailey - 27 years old
(Matchmaker)
Kingston Bailey - 24 years old
(Smokejumper)
Phoenix Bailey - 22 years old
(Finding Herself)
Sedona Bailey - 22 years old
(Student)

ONE

Phoenix

"Did he just pick his nose?" Sedona asks.

"Yep. Welcome to Rome's life now."

"Ew, gross."

Dion pulls his finger from his nose and inspects the booger on the end. His mouth slowly opens.

"Phoenix, stop him."

Dion sticks his finger into his mouth.

"Then I'd have to touch his finger," I say.

"You cannot let our nephew eat boogers."

Sedona is much like Savannah. I think they share a Pinterest page on organizational techniques.

"Can and did. If you want to stop him, get on a plane."

My bitterness toward my twin sister living out her dream can be heard in my voice. I'll admit, I am a little stubborn.

"How many times do I need to apologize for not making it to a two-year-old's birthday?"

I can hear Sedona's exasperation toward me in her

voice. Now I feel like a shitty sister for not jumping up and down because she's about to graduate from college with the English degree she has always wanted.

As I'm about to respond, Grandma Dori puts her face in front of the iPad.

"Hi, Grandma," Sedona greets her for the fifth time so far today, and we haven't even had the cake yet.

"Technology." Grandma Dori shakes her head. "You look tired, dear. Naps are great, but no more than fifteen minutes." She wiggles her finger.

"Maybe it's Jamison keeping her up at night?" I say.

Grandma Dori looks at me with her grey eyebrows raised.

"Stop it, Phoenix. It's not, Gram. Don't worry about that."

Sedona's quick to diffuse any rumors that she may not be a virgin. This family would be shocked to know she lost her virginity well before I ever lost mine. I can picture their gasps and covered mouths—"not our perfect Sedona"—if they ever found out. But me? I'm the black sheep, the bad pea in the pod, or whatever idiom one might use for the person who isn't like the others in their family.

"Don't let her fool you, Grandma. I heard her birthday gift from Jamison was a threesome."

"*Phoenix!*"

Sedona's so loud, all the partygoers turn and look our way. They don't ask for a reason why Sedona's cheeks are pink with embarrassment. They'll all assume I'm the cause.

In truth, I think Jamison got her a necklace with his picture inside a heart or something pathetically cliché.

"I'm kidding," I say.

Grandma Dori smacks me on the back of the head. "What am I going to do with you?"

I shrug and pop another shrimp tart Rome prepared into my mouth.

"How's the food?" Sedona asks after Grandma Dori heads over to talk to Juno.

"Awesome as usual."

She groans. "All I have is a stale bag of Cool Ranch Doritos."

"Why doesn't Jamison bring you something?" I can't even count to two before she's making an excuse for him.

"He's in Chicago."

"Doing what?"

"Playing professional soccer." She rolls her eyes and blows out a breath. "I should probably go. I have a final to study for."

I roll my eyes.

"Cake time!" Rome yells, and Harley walks in with an elaborate dinosaur cake.

"Did you just buy one in every color of these things?" Denver asks Rome, touching the wrap contraption Rome has Phoebe in on his chest. At only five months, she's the spitting image of her older sister, Calista.

Dion jumps up and down and digs his fingers into the cake.

"Glad I'm not eating the cake," Sedona says.

"There's a whole other good side," I say, eyeing the side Dion didn't get his fingers into. I plan on devouring that chocolaty goodness to bury my depression over my lack of forward motion in my life.

"I miss Sweet Suga." Sedona sighs, and I bet if I looked at the iPad screen, I'd see a bit of drool falling down her chin. The one thing I have that she doesn't is that I get to eat cake from her favorite bakery.

"You're still coming back after finals, right?" I ask.

"Um... yeah."

"For good?"

The silence on her end makes me swivel the iPad to face me. It's then that I see the hesitation in her eyes.

"Sedona." I clench my jaw. I knew Jamison would make her change her plans when they got back together.

"Well, Jamison asked me to move in with him."

"He what?"

Austin interrupts us. "Hey, girls, mind actually singing for your nephew's birthday?"

I turn the iPad back toward everyone while anger festers inside me. My mumbled "Happy Birthday" song is drowned out by the rest of my siblings and guests. My eyes remain on Dion. His smile is so big, you'd think all the characters from Paw Patrol were surrounding him.

I remember the day he was born. Harley's text came through right after I finished a gig that paid me only twenty dollars because the bar was so empty. She announced that she was in labor with Dion, and my phone blew up as I walked out of the dingy bar in Los Angeles that had treated me more like a glorified karaoke singer than a professional singer.

I sent the obligatory congratulations with a sad emoji that I wouldn't be there. And I meant that text. I love my niece and nephew. If only for the fact that they make Rome's life hell at times. I mean, Calista and her whole "Baby Shark" obsession last year brought me weeks of happiness. But as my family seemed to be thriving here in Lake Starlight, my dream was on its deathbed back in LA.

The twenty dollars in my pocket wasn't going to help me make rent. Savannah and Austin helped the first year, but after that, I was on my own. Once the eviction notice landed on my door and my bank account went negative, I used the credit card they'd given me for emergencies to purchase a one-way ticket back home.

I live rent-free with Denver and Cleo at Savannah's. I hop from job to job, each of my family members taking a chance on me when all I really want to do with my life is become a famous singer.

"Phoenix," Sedona whispers, and I reluctantly turn the iPad back my way. "I'm coming home after I graduate. I promise."

I nod. I miss my twin like crazy, but she's not going to ruin her future because I lack one. "No, you're not. You're going to move in with Jamison."

A small smile lands on her lips and she stares at me so hard, I wiggle in my chair. "You know it's going to happen, right? One day, whether it's tomorrow or five years from now. You're meant to be a singer."

The rest of my family has decided I tried and failed at a singing career, so their belief is that I need to fall in line with a boring job. Not Sedona though.

"Move in with us. New York needs singers too. I know you're all about the pop star idols, but there are a lot of options here too."

I chew on my fingernail. She's been making the offer ever since I returned home, but it's hard to put yourself out there again when the chance to fail outweighs the chance to succeed. And I'm not going to mooch off my sister who hasn't even graduated from college yet. I already feel bad enough mooching off my older, successful sister.

"Hey, Sedona. See you in two weeks!" Juno hands me my cake. "I'm going to book us a Broadway show."

"Oh, okay!" Sedona says.

Only a few of us are going to New York for her graduation. And thanks to our moneybags brother-in-law, Wyatt, and his Whitmore status, we get to take a private plane there and back.

"*Mean Girls* is playing," Sedona says.

Juno's eyes light up. Great. Another expense I'll need money for.

"Which side of the cake did this piece come from?" I ask.

Juno looks at me, her forehead wrinkled. "What does it matter?"

"I just need to know."

"I don't know. Are you allergic to the right side of the cake now?" Juno shakes her head at Sedona, who rolls her eyes.

"It's gonna be so much fun." Sedona names everything we can do and talks about how much she needs to have fun now that Jamison travels for soccer so much.

Then Denver's conversation with Kingston becomes my focus as they move closer.

"Griffin Thorne, the music producer?" Denver says as if Kingston is an idiot for not knowing who he's talking about. He kinda is. "Remember when my plane went down?"

Kingston nods, picking up his second piece of cake. Little does he know what surprises might be waiting for him in that layer of frosting.

"He's moving up here. Just built a house, and he's looking for a nanny. Anyone you went to school with still around who you think might be good?" Denver asks.

After Denver told me about Griffin Thorne's nanny-seeking at Cleo's birthday last week, I tried to find the agency he was using, but no one gives out client information. Apparently, there's some sort of privacy concern with stuff like that. Using the few connections I still have from high school, I found the house he built, but after stalking it for four nights in a row, there was no sign of him.

"Are you listening to me?" Sedona asks.

Without asking Denver point-blank for Griffin's number, I'll never find a way to reach him. And if I ask Denver, he'll probably give Griffin a picture of me and say, "If you see this girl, call the police." He's so worried I'm going to embarrass him.

"I could be a nanny, right?" I ask Sedona.

"Do you like kids?"

I look at Dion with green frosting all around his face and his hands in his hair. I cringe. Harley approaches him with a wet nap, and he runs, smearing the frosting along the wall of their new house. Maybe boys are more work.

Calista has her baby doll and is pushing her around in a stroller, constantly stopping to fix the blanket or feed her a bottle. She's sweet. Then she takes a pillow from the couch and shoves it under her shirt, patting her stomach as though she's pregnant. The whole room laughs, and she cries.

Okay, this isn't a good sign. I'm no good at keeping a kid clean or dealing with their emotional pitfalls. But sweet Phoebe is sleeping in her wrap, nuzzled into Rome's chest. So content and quiet. I could handle her.

"Yeah, sure. I like them enough," I finally answer Sedona.

"They pick their noses and eat their boogers. They have meltdowns for no reason, and if you think that cute baby in Rome's arms doesn't wake up every night wanting to be changed, feed, or soothed, you're wrong. It's work."

Sedona knows me the best out of everyone in this family, so I'm not too happy about her pinning my exact thoughts of the scenario in front of me. And who knows, maybe Griffin Thorne's kid is one of those gifted ones. He could be super smart and only want to play with his science kit in his room or something. I could nanny a kid like that no problem.

Now I just have to figure out a way to bump into him.

"I know it's work, but I'm out of options. Plus, did you hear what Denver said? Griffin Thorne, the big music producer, is looking for a nanny."

Her face pales and she shakes her head. "Don't do it. This is not going to turn out well."

"How can I accidentally-on-purpose run into him?" I ignore her objection.

She's used to it after twenty-two years. "Go somewhere kids hang out. Parks, ice cream shops, zoos."

I love Sedona. "I'll look creepy if I'm at the park by myself."

"Hence the bad idea thing."

"Okay, guys." Rome claps, and everyone quiets down. "Harley and I are finally ready to go get married, but we need some amazing aunts and uncles to babysit for us while we're away. Who's up for some quality time with their nieces and nephew? It'll be short since I have the restaurant, so a long weekend or five days, tops."

"Don't do it, Phoenix." Sedona's teeth look as if they're wired shut as she speaks.

I raise my hand. "I'm in."

Sedona sighs.

Everyone looks at me as if they're waiting for me to say I'm joking, then Rome looks around with a plea in his eyes for someone else to volunteer.

"Come on." I stand. "I can handle three kids."

"Maybe we can spread out the responsibility," Holly says. "We have to work during the day, but Austin and I can do nights."

"This is ridiculous," I mumble.

"Phoenix, turn up the volume for me," Sedona says. I put the volume to the highest it can go on the iPad. "Listen, guys, give Phoenix a shot. She deserves it, and her nieces and nephew love her. She'll be fine."

As if we choreographed it ahead of time, my sweet niece runs over to me and raises her arms to be picked up, which I do.

Harley looks at Rome, and he nods. "Okay, Phoenix, you'll have days, but I'm telling you right now, you better answer the phone when I call, and I want pictures of my kids every day."

"Deal."

I give Sedona a look of appreciation and she smiles back at me.

Obstacle one figured out. Now I have to run into Griffin Thorne so he can see what a perfect fit I'd be as a nanny. Which shouldn't be too hard. Lake Starlight isn't very big.

TWO

Griffin

Maverick sits in the back of the brand new SUV we drove off the lot an hour ago. Our stuff won't be here for two weeks, so I grabbed us a suite at Glacier Point which seems to be the best resort close to town.

"'Welcome to Lake Starlight. Your new home, you just don't know it yet,'" Maverick reads the welcome sign to our new town with contempt.

He's less than thrilled about this abrupt change in his life. I did spring it on him at the last minute, but sometimes when you hit a breaking point, drastic measures need to be taken.

My gaze veers to my laptop bag on the passenger seat. It holds the magazine with the article that opened my eyes wide. A sellout? I'm not a fucking sellout.

"Turn this up, Dad," Maverick says.

I groan, hearing Tyler Vaughn's voice through my speakers. Maverick sings along to the mediocre lyrics that hold no emotion or truth. Back in the day, a song brought an artist healing, it meant something. There was a rawness in the lyrics you felt bone deep. But what do you expect when you try to turn a YouTube sensation into a star?

There might be a total of ten different words in Tyler's entire song. And I'm ashamed to admit my name is attached to it. The last time Maverick looked at me like I was his idol was when I introduced him to Tyler. How pathetic of a father am I? I haven't even taught my son the true power music holds when it speaks to your soul.

They say there are artists who change your career. Tyler Vaughn changed mine, but not for the better. He took a song I hated and released it with my name attached to it, then he stole the other song we hadn't finished, put it out, and didn't give me credit.

I could've stayed in LA. The list of artists who want me to produce their albums is long enough for me to bounce back from a shit article some post-grad who learned how to master a thesaurus wrote. I'd come back bigger and better. But that article hit more than my ego. It was a wake-up call for me to question what direction I was taking my career.

I tune out the song, soaking in the new town I've visited a few times over the years. Maverick hasn't spent much time downtown, so I park along the curb in front of a bakery. Surely something sweet will cheer him up.

"Why are we stopping?" he asks.

"I want to show you downtown." I turn off the ignition and Tyler Vaughn's voice cuts off. A smile creases my lips as I exit the truck.

"Do we have to?" Maverick whines.

I open his door and shut my own. "Come on. You need to see where we're going to live now, soak up the culture and people."

"What's next? You gonna have me sit on a log and wait

for a moose to stroll by?" He unclips his seat belt and shoves his phone into his pocket.

"Come on. Have an open mind."

"Mom said this is just a phase for you." He jumps off the running board to the ground and looks around. "It's cold." He pulls his arms into his body through the sleeves of his shirt.

"I told you to put on a sweatshirt."

"Back in LA, it's eighty degrees."

I rustle his hair. "We're not in LA anymore, Toto. The faster you get used to this place, the happier you'll be."

"Mom said she'll take me back to LA when she gets back."

I nod but don't respond. Maggie is as reliable as a politician's campaign promises. She means well, and her love for Maverick isn't a question. But her acting career comes first, plain and simple. I can't say much though, because until six months ago, my career came first too. Unfortunately, Maverick is used to the two of us being somewhat absent parents and buying him whatever he wants to make him happy. That's all changing now though.

When I push open the door to the bakery, a door chime rings out and a woman comes up to the counter from the back room.

"Whoa, look at all these, Maverick." I motion toward the glass cases filled with sweet treats.

He looks unfazed by the rows of decorated cookies and cupcakes piled high with frosting in the display case.

"Welcome to Sweet Suga," the woman says and waits patiently behind the case.

"Thank you. Look, they have cookies and cream." I point.

"I don't like cookies and cream," Maverick says, stepping farther down the row. "Donuts?"

She smiles politely. "Sorry, I already sold out."

"Sold out?" His face contorts into what I read as a "where the heck did you move me?" expression.

"I only make so many every morning and, not to brag, they go pretty fast," she says.

"And you don't make any more?" Maverick asks.

The woman is nice, her gaze flickering between Maverick and me. "I don't. I run the bakery by myself most days, so I wake up early every morning and make what I can. If I made more, I'm not sure they'd sell out."

I nod slowly. I understand. But Maverick cocks an eyebrow my way. He has no idea what it's like to go without something. What it means to not waste money.

"Which ones go the fastest?" he asks.

"Well." She contemplates his question for a second. "I'd say the everything donut. Which is funny because it's all the different cake flavors mixed together—chocolate, strawberry, vanilla, orange, marble. Then it's glazed. But once a month, we have a green tea donut that Wok For U features. That's very popular as well."

Maverick looks at me and I nod.

"We'll be back for some tomorrow," I tell the woman.

"I'm sure you won't be disappointed. Is there anything I can get you today?"

I look at Maverick. He peruses the bakery cases a little more seriously now. I suspect that in his mind, a store that sells out of a product must be the best of the best and worth bragging about to his friends back in LA. Just shows the long road we have to take to get him back to an average eight-year-old kid.

Maverick picks out the cookies and cream cupcake, and

I don't say anything. It's better to leave it alone. He knows. I know. No need to draw attention to him purposely being difficult minutes earlier.

"Here you go. Remember, once I'm sold out, I'm sold out." She smiles, handing the box to Maverick.

I place a five dollar bill on the counter and tell her to keep the change. "I assume there's no putting any aside?" I ask, because I really wasn't thinking I had a wake-up call tomorrow morning in the form of a donut.

"I'm Greta." She puts her hand out over the cash register, ignoring my question or answering it by not answering it, I guess.

"I'm—"

"Griffin Thorne. I know."

I shake her hand. "Oh, you do?"

"Denver Bailey." She raises her shoulders in a "you know how it is" gesture. "The whole saving your life thing."

I nod. Of course. "Right."

"I heard a rumor you were moving here, but I didn't know anything about—"

I put my hand on Maverick's back. "Maverick."

"Maverick," she says with a welcoming smile. "It's very nice to meet you both. I think you're going to love Lake Starlight."

The door chimes behind us.

"Greta! Help. We need sugar before a meltdown occurs."

I turn to find a woman who has a toddler boy by the hand, a baby attached to her chest in a carrier, and a little girl whose face is now plastered to the cookie case, her arms extended in a hug over the glass.

"Hi, Phoenix," Greta says.

My gaze drifts back to the dark-haired woman. She's

attractive and young. Much younger than me. And she looks exhausted, as if she's in a wrestling ring and desperately stretching her arm out to her partner for a tap-out.

Her head turns in my direction. She blinks and her eyes widen. Quickly, she straightens the baby in the wrap. She squats next to the boy, licking her finger and wiping his face. When that doesn't work, she lifts the hem of her shirt, giving me a great glimpse of her bare stomach. Tattooed script runs along her ribcage, but even when I squint, I'm unable to read it.

"Cookies," the oldest child sighs before kissing the glass.

"Calista, do you know how many people have touched that glass today?" the woman—Phoenix, I guess—asks.

"Excuse me," Greta says and moves down the counter to the opening with two cookies in wax paper in her hands. "Calista. Dion."

The little girl lets go of the case and grabs the cookie. "Thank you, Miss Greta."

The boy pulls away from the young woman. She doesn't look old enough to have three kids already.

"Hold on, Dion," she says, sneaking looks at me. She probably recognizes me since Greta did too.

"No." He pulls away from her, but she grabs the neck of his shirt.

Maverick and I stare at the scene as if they're paid actors.

"Dion." Her voice is strained through gritted teeth.

"Cookie!" He escapes and her weight shifts, tipping her backward. She clings to the baby strapped to her chest right before she falls on her ass.

She doesn't get up. She sits there and stares at her son and daughter eating their cookies, chatting it up with Greta.

"Here." I approach her and put out my hand.

She stares at me as if I just teleported into the bakery. With a deep inhale, she places her hand in mine and I gently pull her to her feet.

"Thank you," she mumbles.

"You're welcome. Are you okay? The baby?"

Her hands run up and down the baby's back. "Oh, this one could sleep through a hurricane."

"You've got your hands full. I'm Griffin, by the way."

"Phoenix," she says.

"What's your name?" The young girl approaches Maverick with the boy in tow.

"Maverick," he says, sitting in a chair because he can't stand for more than five minutes at a time.

Turning away from the kids, I study the brunette. Could these be her kids? There's no way she's old enough.

"Are they all yours?" I ask. I'm desperate to find a nanny for Maverick, and so far, I've had no luck with Denver asking around for me. I really wanted to avoid leaving Maverick with a stranger, but if this girl is the nanny and not the mom, maybe she works for an agency in town.

"God, no." Before I can ask anything else, she says, "I mean, I'm the nanny."

I nod. Perfect. "I thought you were a little young to be the mother of these three."

Based on the small lines on her forehead, she's insulted. "I'm not young. I mean, I've experienced life. I can drink and smoke if I choose to."

I chuckle. "I didn't mean to offend you."

I glance at the kids when I hear a chair scrape across the floor. Maverick is on one side of the table, Calista on the other, and Dion is up on his knees, practically pressing his face to Maverick's.

"Oh, you didn't. I just meant, I'm not *that* young."

"Gotcha."

We stand in silence for a moment, our gazes shifting to the kids' table again.

"So are you with a nanny service?"

She doesn't answer.

"I'm only asking because I had a buddy who was trying to find someone for me, but I'm getting down to the wire and I'm thinking I'll have better luck with an agency instead."

She blinks. "Well..." She glances at the kids again. "I can do it."

I rock back on my heels. Her eyes have dark circles under them. She looks worn down. Maverick can wipe his own butt, but he can be a pain in the ass attitude-wise. "I think you've already got your hands full."

She looks at the baby in her arms and jolts. "Oh no. I mean, their parents are coming home in two days. Then I'm done."

I nod. "So you're free for overnights?"

Her tongue slides across her bottom lip and her gaze dips down my body.

Shit. That made me sound like a pervert. "I mean, if I needed you."

"Definitely. Overnights are no problem."

"Great. Can I send you an application, and then I can do a background check..."

Her face pales as I keep talking about the steps I take to make sure I'm not hiring some random criminal with a record. When the door chimes, we both turn toward the entry.

"*Yay!*" Calista runs over, and the woman standing at the door swoops her up in her arms.

"Hey, kiddo," the woman says.

"Can I have your phone?" Calista asks in a sweet voice.

Without saying anything, she kisses Calista's cheeks, puts her back down, and hands over her cell phone. "Rotten to the Core" from that *Descendants* movie plays, and the little girl dances. And yeah, I only know that because a friend of mine helped produce the music in that movie.

"How was today? I came right from school. Austin's got baseball..." The woman finally catches on to my presence and stops talking. "Oh... hi."

"Hi. I'm Griffin." I extend my hand.

The woman looks at Phoenix and back at me. "Hi. Holly Ba—"

"Will you excuse us for a moment?" Phoenix asks. She snatches the woman by the arm and drags her down the hallway toward the bathrooms.

"Hey, Holly, I made some dog treats for Myles and Daisy." Greta's words are left unanswered as the women are now gone.

Maverick stares at the little girl dancing around the bakery. I think maybe it's about time I hightail it out of here.

THREE

Phoenix

"You found him. Maybe you should go back to school to be a private investigator or something." Holly sneaks a peek down the hallway.

Griffin is standing right by the opening.

"Shhh," I say, not wanting him to overhear.

"Give me the baby," Holly says. "My plan is to let the kids pick up all the balls from baseball practice to exhaust them."

I pull Phoebe from the holder, and Holly gets the cloth off of me and puts the wrap on herself. By the time she has her own baby, she'll be a pro.

"I didn't find him on purpose. I wasn't expecting to find him right now at all. Otherwise I would've maybe brushed my teeth and showered this morning. Yesterday I had Calista in a dress, Dion's face was clean all day, and Phoebe had one of those pretty ribbons in her hair. Of course the day I run into him, Phoebe will only sleep attached to me, Calista is on a sugar high, and Dion is a mess."

Holly can't even argue. She hands them to me in the morning all neat and clean and happy. I hand them back to her in mismatched clothes, dirty, and cranky.

"What were you guys talking about when I came in?"

I smile. "He asked me if I was a nanny."

"Jackpot," Holly says. Have I mentioned how much I love her? It's like she gets me. "So is he going to hire you?"

"He just mentioned doing a background check when you came in."

She cringes while we get Phoebe into the wrap now attached to Holly. The baby fusses for a second but calms down when Holly pats her bum.

"Yeah. I guess I didn't think this through because hello, he's going to find out I'm a Bailey. And then Denver will find out and..."

She looks down the hallway again. Griffin waves, and we both wave back.

"The two of us hiding out in this hallway looks suspicious," Holly says.

"Will you vouch for me? Maybe he won't insist on a background check if the school principal says I'm legit."

She releases a long breath. "Phoenix..."

I get it. She's the principal of the high school. She has to stay on the moral high ground. But a girl's gotta try.

"Please? It's not like I'm a bad person. I'll keep his kid safe."

Holly's hands run over Phoebe's back as she shifts her weight side to side. "I don't want to lie."

"You're not lying. I *am* a nanny right now for Rome and Harley."

She gives me a look that says I'm stretching the truth. "You'd better figure something out because he's talking to Greta now."

I look down the hall and see that she's right.

"She's going to spill who you are."

"Damn it." I speed walk down the hall. "Griffin."

He turns toward me. "Hey, I had no idea you were a Bailey? I know Denver. Well, you probably know that with what we went through a few years back."

"Greta, I need four cookies. Two dinosaur and two sunflowers." Holly doesn't join our conversation. Guess she's pretty firm on the not-lying thing.

"Yeah, Denver is my brother."

Holly stays a safe distance away. "Dion and Calista, we need to get going. You get to help Coach pick up the baseballs after practice today."

"*Yay!*" Dion falls off the chair.

Holly sighs after she sees him get back up with no visible scratches.

"This is great," Griffin says. "Denver's good people."

I nod.

"Let me introduce you to Maverick."

"Thanks, Greta." Holly takes the bag of goodies and turns to the kids. "Say goodbye to Aun—Phoenix. You'll see her tomorrow."

Dion and Calista each hug me.

"You'll pick them up at seven again?" she asks, her hand already on the door handle.

"Yep."

"Nice to meet you, Holly..." Griffin waits for her to fill in the rest of her name.

She waves. "You too." I'm not sure if she pinches Phoebe, or it's just great timing, but Phoebe wails and rocks her head back. "Gotta go. Welcome to Lake Starlight."

Holly practically pushes the kids out the door. She might not lie for me, but she'll omit information. Still works.

"That woman has her hands full," Griffin says with a smile.

He's really attractive. Much more so in person than on television or in a magazine. His dark, shoulder-length hair is lighter on the ends and looks thick and shiny, while his deep brown eyes hold a bit of mystery, but they're kind.

"She does now," I say.

"This is Maverick." He holds out his arm, but the kid doesn't bother leaving the table and his eyes don't leave his phone. "Maverick?"

The boy sighs dramatically like I used to. Okay, like I still do. He pockets his phone and comes to stand next to his dad, still not making eye contact with me.

"This is Phoenix Bailey. She's Denver's sister."

Maverick nods.

"Hey, Maverick," I say with a huge smile because I'm channeling my inner Nanny Jo.

"Hi."

"We're staying at Glacier Point right now. Maybe we could meet for coffee tomorrow. You can fill out an application and back—"

The door chimes again and I hold my breath because one of these times it's going to be Denver. He'll out me as not being a professional childcare provider right away.

"Griffin Thorne. I heard you were moving to Lake Starlight." Grandma Dori walks in with Ethel on her heels, fresh from the beauty shop I'd guess, since their hair is nicely styled, and Grandma Dori's blue gleam is brighter than normal.

He circles around and puts out his hand. "Hello."

"Dori Bailey. Denver's grandmother." She shakes his hand. "This is Ethel."

Ethel waves but puts her finger on her hearing aid and

walks to the other side of the shop to talk to whoever about her podiatrist appointment.

"Nice to meet you. I feel like I might meet the entire family today."

Grandma looks at me and slides her arm through mine. "Oh, you've met our ever-reliable Phoenix. She's the best. Who else have you met?"

She pats my hand with her free one. I strain to smile when I really want to remind her that it was just a few weeks ago that she said she didn't know what to do with me.

Griffin smiles. "Just Phoenix."

So he never caught on to Holly being a Bailey by marriage. That's good.

"And who are you?" Grandma bends as much as she can and gets in Maverick's face.

Griffin elbows him, and Maverick has to catch his balance to right himself.

"Maverick," he mumbles.

"Maverick. Like Tom Cruise?" Grandma Dori says.

"What?" Maverick asks with disdain.

Surely this kid knows about *Top Gun*?

"The character Tom Cruise played in *Top Gun*," Griffin says and smiles at both of us like, 'Kids, am I right?'

"You'll need to come over to my granddaughter Savannah's house. We have eighties movie nights," Grandma Dori says.

Maverick looks at his father. Griffin smiles and nods. Even I know eight is too young for that movie.

"Dear, what brings you to Sweet Suga? Ethel and I were coming back from Clip and Dish and saw you talking to our new Lake Starlight resident, thought we'd pop in."

"I had Calista, Dion, and Phoebe. Holly's taken them though." I'm trying to tell her with my eyes not to out me.

"She's so good with those kids. I mean, if their parents could maybe spread them out a little more, it'd be easier, but they do love Phoenix."

Griffin smiles at me. His teeth are so white, so straight, so alluring. And when he smiles, there are these crinkle lines at the corners of his eyes that do something to me. Damn, everything down south is saying screw the nanny position and screw him instead.

No, no, no. I will not be detoured from my goal. I'm lying for one reason only—to have this man see how talented I am and skyrocket me to stardom.

"I hope they won't get mad if I steal Phoenix away," he says.

Grandma widens her eyes at me. "Oh, you better snag her before someone else does. She's a hot commodity in Lake Starlight."

Thanks, Grandma, for refraining to mention that you fired me yourself.

"Really? I was going to do a background check and an application, but—"

"Background check? Dear." She touches his arm. "You're not in LA anymore. This is Lake Starlight. And Phoenix is a Bailey." She lowers her voice. "I'm the matriarch, and I would never tell you to hire my granddaughter unless I knew she was the perfect fit for you. You can trust me on that. Right, Ethel?"

"Right. Someone was just asking about Phoenix at the salon."

What did these two do? Rehearse this before coming in here?

"Geez, I had Denver looking, and he never mentioned Phoenix."

Grandma waves him away and rolls her eyes. "Oh, he's

so forgetful these days. All his attention is on Cleo. You know what a new relationship is like."

Surprisingly, Griffin nods as though he does. Obviously, I've googled the man, but other than his wife, there's been no one serious. Sure, there have been some rumors of him with different artists, but even I know those aren't always true.

"I'm enrolling Maverick at school tomorrow and I have to get working on the house if we're going to move in. Maybe we can meet tomorrow over coffee to discuss salary?"

"Why wait?" Grandma Dori drags me over to a table, pulls out a chair, and shoves me into it. "Talk now. We can take Maverick down to the park. You can see it from the window. Right by the library."

Griffin follows the direction Grandma Dori's finger is pointed and nods.

Maverick doesn't appear to be jumping for joy about it, but he doesn't say anything.

"That'd be great," Griffin says.

"I'm sure you have a million things to do. Securing the nanny should be the first." Ethel puts up her pointer finger as if she's the wisest one out of all of us.

Grandma Dori pulls out a chair for Griffin and he sits down, running his hands through his long strands. I hope there's no drool dripping down my chin. He's completely gorgeous. Why on Earth would his wife cheat on him with his ugly-ass partner?

Before I can blink, the three of them are out the door with the chime ringing and I'm sitting alone in front of Griffin Thorne. I had a plan. All these things I intended to tell him. But I clam up and sit there silently instead.

He bites the bottom of his lip. "I'm not prepared for this."

I laugh nervously.

"Do I make you uncomfortable?" he asks.

"No," I say in a rush. But the truth is, he does. He's Griffin fucking Thorne. He's worked with some of the biggest names in the business. Of course he makes me nervous.

"You obviously know what I used to do?"

"Used to?"

He inhales. "I was a music producer back in LA, but I'm putting that behind me now. But I still need someone to watch Maverick while I finish working on the house. I'm going to do a lot of the work myself, and hopefully by the time I'm done, I'll have figured out what I want to do with this next stage of my life."

"What?" My voice is no louder than a whisper, but he hears me.

He nods slowly. "I've decided to step back. I'm sure you don't follow the music scene, but..."

I listen to him talk about an article in a music magazine. I've read the one he's talking about—the one that said he sold out. He tells me how the business has changed and what used to inspire him feels like work now. My heart breaks while he speaks. I know what it feels like to be passionate about something, and I can't imagine him losing that.

I should walk away. I should tell him the truth. But for the first time in my life, I feel sorry for someone who isn't my family.

How could he not want to fill his days creating music? He's produced huge artists who might never have become who they did without him. He's lost the spark. The same spark inside me that I hope never dims. I might be down right now, but I'm not out.

"Phoenix?" He touches my hand to gain my attention.

I pull away, placing my hand in my lap. "I'm sorry, what?"

"Is that good then?"

"Yeah," I agree without processing all the details. "Wait..."

He chuckles. "I thought I lost you for a moment. Until we move into the house, you'll pick him up after school and watch him until dinner. After we move in, you can have the spare room. Take him to school, pick him up from school, run the house errands, and cook us dinner?"

I nod.

"I'll pay you..." He seems to think about it for a moment, then says a figure that makes my eyes widen.

I've never had a job that paid that much a week, and I can't pass up money like that. It doesn't matter if he's left the business. With money like that, I can probably be back in LA and pursuing my dream by summer's end. I can handle hanging out with his kid and picking up his dry cleaning. No problem.

I hold my hand out across the table. His slides into mine and I ignore the rush of electricity when our palms meet. "Deal."

"Perfect. This is gonna work out great." He winks, and I have to remind myself that I'm here for his son, not him.

FOUR

Griffin

The next day, I sign Maverick up for school. I might've seen the smallest of smiles on his lips when he found out there was no uniform at his new school. This will be the first public school Maverick has attended.

After school is all sorted, I decide to run over to Lifetime Adventures to let Denver know the search for a nanny is off and I hired his sister.

"It says I need all these supplies, and why are they giving me a Chromebook? I have a Mac." Maverick must have fished out the school welcome package from my bag.

"Because the Chromebooks have the school software. You won't need your Mac for school." Surprise, surprise, he zoned out during the principal's tour.

His grunt says he's not pleased. "I have to do a test tomorrow?"

"Yeah."

"Why? I'm coming from a better school."

I glance at him in my rearview mirror. I hope he isn't a

condescending snob to the kids at his new school. Sometimes I think I did a piss-poor job of raising him. But I have to remind myself where he grew up. The boy has never had a chance at a normal life. That's all about to change now.

"They want to see where you fall compared to your classmates."

"Um... I'm smarter."

I blow out a breath, thankful when I spot Denver's SUV outside Lifetime Adventures. We can table this talk for the time being, but eventually I'll have to sit Maverick down and talk to him about not being a pompous ass to his classmates.

We get out of the SUV, and I stop to look at the mountains. Lifetime Adventures has had a remodel since the last time I saw it. The building no longer looks like a rundown cabin. It's been cleaned up and has new windows and a new sign.

I give the guy credit. I pegged Denver as one of those forever bachelors, but it looks like commitment has been good for him.

Maverick sits down in the gazebo and pulls out his phone.

"Are you staying out here?" I ask.

He nods without looking up. Please tell me this kid will become an actual kid at some point.

"If a mountain lion comes to feast, run in and get me, okay?"

That garners a look from him. "I'll come in."

Finally, one sign that he's actually eight and not thirteen. LA makes kids grow up too damn fast.

He follows on my heels, sliding in front of me to get into the building first.

"I was kidding about mountain lions," I say, pressing my

hand on his shoulder and squeezing. "Maybe a bear though."

"Where did you move me to?" He seeks out the first chair and plops down onto it.

"Griffin!" Nancy stands from behind her new desk. There's no longer an ancient computer at her workstation.

"This place looks great," I say, hugging her and kissing her cheek. My gaze falls to the large picture behind her with Chip Dawson's name on the bottom.

"Would you like a cold brew?" She rushes over to the coffee station and opens up a mini fridge. "I'm a master at it now."

Her excitement has me saying okay even though cold brew isn't really my thing.

She hands one to me then bends down to Maverick's face. "Do you want some candy?"

"No."

I kick the bottom of his foot with my shoe, and his gaze flickers to me.

His shoulders falter and he looks at Nancy. "No thanks."

She doesn't give me the look of 'you should be a better father.' Instead, there's sympathy in her eyes.

"What the hell are you doing here?" Denver's leaning on the door frame with his arms crossed.

"I live here now."

He shakes his head and already has his hand out before he's halfway to me. "Someone should examine that head of yours."

We shake hands and lean in for a hug.

Maverick blows out a breath. "True story."

Denver gives me a look, and I non-verbally confirm that yes, my kid is still being a little shit about this move.

"The place is looking good." I take in the new waiting room filled with pictures of the previous owner—Chip—Denver, and Cleo. There's even a poster of us on the *Uncovering America's Beauty* reality show I did with them a while back.

Denver shoves his hands into his pockets and follows my gaze around the room. "Yeah. Business has been good."

"And Cleo?"

A smile lights up his face, and I'm kind of jealous seeing how happy the bastard is.

"We're good. Really good."

I'm not sure I ever looked that way about Maggie. Everything moved fast, and before we could process if we wanted a serious relationship, Maverick was born. Then it was all juggling schedules and flip-flop-parenting. Sometimes I think I drove her into Adam's arms.

"That's awesome. I came by to tell you that I found a nanny."

He signals to the table in the corner, and we pull out the chairs. Opening the fridge, he grabs himself a Powerade. "Mav?"

Surprisingly, Maverick looks up. The kid hates his name being shortened. Denver holds up a Powerade, and Maverick nods, holding up his hands. He catches it.

Denver whistles. "Watch out, shortstop. You play baseball?"

"No."

"You should with hands like that. Maybe football. My buddy Liam—"

"I don't like sports." Maverick unscrews the top of his bottle and leans back in his chair.

"Sorry," I say.

Denver waves him off. "I get it. You took him away from all his friends. You're a bastard."

"Thanks?" I chuckle.

Denver laughs. One of the reasons I love Denver is his happy-as-shit attitude. Nothing gets the guy down. Even when we were stranded on the mountainside, he was as positive as ever. If you put shit on his doorstep and lit it on fire, he'd probably either tell you how to do it better or slap you on the back and say good job. *Then* he'd kick your ass.

"That's great about the nanny thing. Sorry I wasn't much help. I even asked my brother, and he didn't know anyone."

I lean back in my chair. "I hired your sister."

Denver chokes on his Powerade, sitting straight up in the chair, grabbing his throat.

"You okay, man?"

He nods and sips the drink one more time. "Did you say you hired my sister?" He wipes his chin with the back of his hand.

I nod. "Yeah. I ran into her and the three kids she's looking after right now. I met your grandma too. This really is a small town."

"Please tell me it was Juno you met?" he asks.

"Juno? No. Phoenix. She's the nanny, right?"

Denver's happy mood disappears and his jaw clenches as if it's turned into granite. Did he not want me to hire his sister? I study him as he pulls out his phone.

"This one, right?" He shoves a picture of Phoenix in my face.

I smile. "Yeah."

His chest rises and falls.

"Shit. Did you not want me to hire your sister? Is that why you never mentioned her?" I'll feel horrible if I overstepped. Then it dawns on me that maybe it's not a boss/employee relationship he's concerned about. "Oh, you're not worried? I mean..."

Denver pockets his phone. "Cleo!"

"She's in the garage, remember?" Nancy says.

"Right. Page her please," Denver asks and puts his head in his hands.

I lean forward. "You okay, man?"

"Uh-huh," he mumbles.

"You're not worried I'm going to hit on her, or something are you?"

"Nancy!" His voice grows louder.

"She's attractive, that much is obvious, but she's young. Way too young for someone like me." What could I possibly have in common with someone that young?

He peeks at me, his face pale.

Cleo comes in through the door and smiles when she sees me. "Griffin!"

I stand up and hug her.

"Hey, Maverick," she says, and he picks up his head and actually waves to her. "So it's official. You're here now?" I nod, and her gaze flickers to Denver and back to me. "What's up?"

"I hired Denver's sister, and I think he thinks I'm going to hit on her or something."

She glances at Maverick, but he's put on his head-phones. Our chatter is probably interrupting his game or something. What am I gonna do with this kid?

"Which sister?" Cleo licks her lips and slides the chair out from the table. Her hand disappears under the table when she sits, and I assume it's on her boyfriend's leg.

"Phoenix."

Her lips purse and she nods. What am I missing here?

"Denver's grandma said she's a hot commodity, that if I didn't snatch her up right away, I'd miss my opportunity. Since she's a relative, I figured I could trust her to take care of Maverick."

Cleo nods as if she understands why I would do that, but her eyes shift to Denver, who's now finished his Powerade. He tosses the bottle into the trash can but misses and the bottle travels across the room. Nancy stands, picks it up, and puts it in the trash can.

"Thanks, Nance," he murmurs.

"I'm sorry if this upsets you. I'd retract the offer, but that's kind of a dick move."

"Oh no." Cleo shakes her head. "Definitely don't retract the offer." She examines her boyfriend again. "Denver is a grown man. He understands that you'd never cross that line."

Denver stares blankly at her, and I know I'm missing something here.

"You know how brothers are. Overprotective." Cleo slaps his leg hard and he jolts. "Right, Denver?"

"Okay, just tell me," I say.

"There's nothing to tell. Denver worries too much." Cleo smiles, but I've been around her enough to know it's not one hundred percent genuine. "But Maverick will love Phoenix. She's fun... really fun. Always lots of fun." Cleo's toothy grin is still hiding something.

"I figure if she can handle the three kids she's watching now, then Maverick should be easy. To keep her busy, I figured she could do some housekeeping and maybe cook some meals."

Denver rolls his eyes and a guttural sound erupts out of him. Cleo stares at me as if she didn't hear anything.

I let it go. I need a nanny, and I'll prove to Denver that I can keep my hands to myself. In the end, he won't have to worry about anything. Once he sees things will be fine, he'll be good with the arrangement.

"Would she be moving in with you?" Cleo asks.

Another sound leaks out of Denver's mouth.

"Yeah. Once the house is done enough to move into. Easier for me since I'll be working on the house. Plus, no sense in her driving home too late just to come back in the morning."

"Makes sense. She's been staying with me and Denver, so..."

She looks at Denver with an expression that says 'now we'll be able to do whatever, whenever.' He rolls his eyes.

"I'm sorry, man, I don't want this to affect our friendship," I say.

Denver shakes his head. "It's okay. It won't."

His words are cold and curt though, and I feel like a jackass for blindsiding him about this. Does he really think I can't keep my dick in my pants?

"You can trust me with her," I say and lock eyes with him.

He nods.

Cleo pats my hand. "We know that. We just hope... that it works out." Her speaking for both of them says it's time to go and let Denver process the information.

"Okay, I should go. I have to go school shopping."

Cleo and Denver both stand.

"Don't worry. I'd never piss off the man who saved my life." I hold out my hand, and Denver puts his in mine. Maybe I'm imagining his grip is a little firmer this time around.

"Let me know if she causes any problems," Denver says. "I'll handle her if need be."

"Problems?" I ask.

Cleo giggles. "There's that overprotective brother thing again." She slaps his stomach. "They're both adults, babe."

He says nothing, and I hug Cleo then Nancy before leading Maverick out of Lifetime Adventures. I hate that Denver's not cool with this. First I move to his town, and now I steal his sister to work for me. Maybe I'm taking too much from him.

He'll see though. Having Phoenix work for me will work out beautifully.

FIVE

Phoenix

I eat a taco while bingeing *New Girl* on Netflix. Hey, I deserve it after watching Rome's kids for the past five days. He and Harley returned last night with wide grins and matching wedding bands. I'm happy that they finally found time to sneak away and tie the knot, but I was ready to be done with babysitting duty.

My phone rings and Denver's name lights up the screen.

It was only a matter of time, but I'm not in the mood for his lecture, so I let it go to voicemail. Five minutes later, he calls again, but I still don't answer. Ten minutes later, it's the same thing. After twenty minutes, the front door opens, and I cringe.

Should've answered the phone.

"*Phoenix!*" Denver yells.

"Can we please talk about this rationally?" Cleo is right behind him.

I press Pause on my show.

His feet stop at the edge of the hallway. "Too busy to answer the phone?" His gaze shoots to the television.

"I don't wanna hear it. I'm twenty-two. I can do what I want. Plus, I just watched Rome's kids for five days, so I *am* qualified." I ball up my taco wrapper and sip my water.

"You're lying to Griffin, and now you've put me in a shit position." He runs his hands through his hair, pacing in front of the television, blocking any chance of me seeing the show.

"Let's just talk," Cleo says, rounding the couch and sitting down. Her gaze holds a silent reproach I think is aimed at both of us.

"Talk? If she was Kingston, Rome, or Austin, I'd have her pinned to the ground by now. Shit, Phoenix, what are you thinking?"

He's way too emotional about this, and I look at Cleo, silently asking her what exactly his problem is.

"Listen." I cross my legs on the chair. "It was a coincidence. I wasn't expecting to run into him. I had the kids with me, and *he* approached *me*."

Denver stops and drills me with a hard gaze. "You honestly expect me to believe that?"

I look at Cleo again. "It's true. I'll admit to maybe trying to run into him because you wouldn't do me a solid and introduce me, but that didn't end up happening. Are you embarrassed of me or something?"

He groans, and his vision shifts to Cleo. I have to admit I love that he looks to her for answers. It's kind of cute. I'd mention it if he wasn't already pissed at me.

"I'm not embarrassed, but if you kept up with the industry, you know he's out. He's left the business. You trying to get him to hear you sing—"

I put up my hand to stop him. "I know. He told me he

left, which is such bullshit because he's so talented. That asswipe who wrote that article has no idea what he's talking about. Griffin didn't sell out, he became successful and artists came to him. He helped them find their own sound, whatever it is."

Denver and Cleo remain silent, staring at me.

"What?"

Denver shakes his head, staring at the floor. "He's my friend, and you're not some hot commodity in Lake Starlight even if that is what G'ma D told him." He looks up. "Yeah, he told me. So she's in on this scheme too?"

I hold up my hands. "I never asked her to be. I'm being completely honest when I say it really was a coincidence. And I believe in signs. Just like with you and Cleo."

"What?" The anger spout opens up again. "Why on Earth would you compare you and Griffin to me and Cleo? Tell me you aren't going to try to sleep with him." He falls on the couch and Cleo taps his leg.

"I'm sure she's not. Right, Phoenix? I mean he's older, a father..." She widens her eyes for me to reassure my brother with the words he desperately wants to hear.

I could add to Cleo's statement that Griffin's also hot as hell and sex on a stick. He's the type of man that you know if you allowed yourself just one kiss, you'd be ruined. But that's not why I want the job.

"Listen." I sit up straighter. "I don't want to fuck him."

Denver groans, pressing the heels of his hands into his eye sockets.

"You're right, I wanted to get him to hear me sing, work his connections, get his opinion. But when he told me he was out of the business, I detoured from the original plan."

"And what is your new plan?" Denver asks.

"He's paying me good money. I suck at everything else."

Cleo pats my arm. "You don't."

"I do, but thanks. Grandma fired me. Rome fired me from the hostess gig. I'm not a waitress, a librarian, an assistant, or a store clerk. I'm a singer, and I know deep down in my bones that's what I'm supposed to do with my life."

Cleo smiles and side-glances Denver, who now sits up with his head in his hands.

"I can work with an eight-year-old. Hell, we probably have the same mind-set. This is something I can do, and Griffin is going to pay me extremely well. I can save money and then go back to LA to pursue my dream."

Cleo runs her hand over my forearm. I'm not sure if it's because we've lived with one another for over a year now or if it would have always been this way, but without Sedona here, Cleo is my closest friend. We click, and she doesn't have the "Phoenix is such a disappointment" mentality.

"I promise, Denver, I won't ruin this friendship for you. I'll do my job and keep out of his way. Come the end of the summer, I'll put in my notice and he can find the next nanny for his son. It'll be like I was never there."

He looks up and nods. "No sleeping with him."

I roll my eyes. "Those who screw their co-workers shouldn't cast stones at others."

Cleo laughs and Denver bolts to his feet.

I grab his wrist before he can flee the room. "I'm kidding. Come on. Griffin Thorne would not be interested in a twenty-two-year-old misfit. You're worrying over nothing."

He nods, and I release him. "Let's go, Cleo, we have to get back to the office."

She stands and holds her arms open for me. I climb out of the chair and she hugs me fiercely. "You're growing up so fast." She pretends to sniffle. "Seriously though, please refrain from becoming the cliché nanny who slept with her boss. I'm not sure your brother would ever recover."

I laugh and she does too.

"He's super hot though, right?" I say just to needle my brother.

"He's also in his thirties and has established his life. But yeah, he's hot." She giggles.

I nod and say nothing else. I'm not looking to sleep with Griffin Thorne. I strictly want his money.

"*Cleo!*" Denver yells.

She draws back and shakes her head at him. "Calm down before you give yourself an aneurism. My God, it's not like Griffin is your best friend."

"Yeah, my best friend already fucked my other sister and now they're living together."

Cleo covers her mouth and laughs. "Shit, you might be oh for two soon."

He fists his hands at his sides. "Not making it any better, babe."

"You're overreacting," I say.

He shakes his head and spins on his heel. "I am not."

"Are to."

"Okay, kids, let's stop fighting," Cleo says and follows Denver out of the room.

A second later, the door shuts and I sulk down into my chair. I told Denver the truth, but what I failed to tell him was that it's not inconceivable that Griffin would have some music friends over at some point. If I happen to be introduced to them and they ask me to play karaoke or something... just saying.

My phone dings before I have a chance to unpause the TV.

Griffin: *Want to meet for dinner at Glacier Point to talk over logistics?*
Me: *Sure.*
Griffin: *Perfect. Six o'clock okay? I know it's early, but Maverick has testing tomorrow.*

Oh yeah, of course Maverick would be there. It's not like this is a date or anything.

Me: *That works. See you then.*

I set down my phone and inhale a deep breath, placing my hand over my stomach. It's going to have to stop with the butterflies every time I interact with Griffin. We're on a mission, and no matter what Denver thinks, it's not to get laid. At least not until after I quit. A farewell fuck wouldn't hurt anyone.

SIX

Phoenix

I pair my jeans and T-shirt with a leather jacket and a pretty kickass pair of boots I stole from Sedona the last time she was home. She's got all the good shopping in New York.

"Hey, Mac," I say, walking past the bellhop at Glacier Point Resort.

"Phoenix. Looking good as always." He eats me up with his eyes. Mac was always a flirt.

"Thanks. I love the little hat."

He touches his head as though he forgot he was wearing it and his smile dims a bit.

I'm so busy looking over my shoulder and laughing that I run into a hard chest. When I look up, it's my brother-in-law.

"Phoenix," he says with his arms crossed.

"Wyatt," I mimic his brooding tone.

"What brings you to my hotel?"

"You need to update the bellhop uniform. Mac looks

like he could be one of those dancing bears with the cymbals."

Wyatt glances over my shoulder. "You might have a point. But again, what brings you here?"

I pat his shoulder. "Oh, don't worry. I have a dinner date."

"With who?"

I lean forward as if we're in LA and the people around here would actually swarm Griffin if they knew who he was. "Griffin Thorne," I whisper.

"You know I can't let you through. Denver gave me strict instructions that you aren't to be in contact with him." He stands there like a bodyguard. Wyatt might be the size of a bouncer, but he's a gentle giant.

"Griffin's expecting me."

He arches an eyebrow.

"I swear. I'm his new nanny."

He chuckles, but when I don't laugh, he stops. His smirk says he might be impressed. "You scored the nanny position?"

"What? Did Denver have some secret meeting with all the guys in the family to keep me away from Griffin?"

"Just me, because he knew Griffin was a guest here. I agree with him though. I don't want my guests uncomfortable. Especially one who could refer wealthy guests to my hotel."

I pat his shoulder again. "No worries then. Like I said, I was invited to dinner by the man himself."

He looks me over. "Okay, but I'll be watching. Brooklyn's coming by to have dinner with me."

"Great." I force a smile knowing Brooklyn will interject herself into the dinner with Griffin now too. "Maybe a private dinner in one of the suites is what you guys need."

He shakes his head. But hopefully he's thinking I'm a brilliant sister-in-law and is now piecing together a plan to get my sister into bed somewhere far away from where I'll be.

"Be careful, Phoenix." He steps to the side, letting me through. I could've gone around him, but we'll pretend he's a big, bad brother-in-law.

I walk backward away from him. "What's fun about being careful?"

My smug look strips away when I run into another solid chest. I'd bet money it's my dinner companion because that is just my luck.

Wyatt laughs, and his perfectly arched eyebrows shoot up. I bite my lip and he nods like "yep, it's Griffin." Then he spins on his heel and heads to the office, laughing the entire way.

I turn around to find Griffin. His hair is pulled back tonight, and it looks good, but I really wish it was down. I love it down. But with it pulled back, I see the strong jawline he hides under his long strands. His eyes are lit with humor, not annoyance, which is a good sign.

"You should watch where you're going. You could have toppled me over," he says.

I laugh. No way in hell could I do that. "It's probably safe to say that you put a gym in that new house of yours."

"How'd you guess?"

Because I felt your abs through your leather jacket, so I know working out must be high on your priority list. "Just an inkling."

"Do you work out?" he asks innocently.

There are so many spins I could put on my response, but I do love my brother, so I'll play nice. "Sometimes, but I don't enjoy it."

He nods. "I think the majority of people don't enjoy their workouts."

Is he purposely trying to goad me into saying something crass? Because there are definitely certain workouts people enjoy immensely.

"True enough," I say instead.

"Maverick is at the table." He motions for me to go in front of him.

I do, hoping like hell he's staring at my ass. Crap, less than five minutes in his presence and I want him ogling my body. Not a good sign. Not at all.

"Hey, Mav," I say, sliding into the booth. He's already got a plate of mac and cheese with a side French fries in front of him.

"Maverick," he mutters.

"So no to Mav then?" I wiggle to get my jacket off.

"No."

Griffin grabs the edge of my sleeve, and I look over my shoulder in surprise to find him helping me. He's a gentleman too.

"Thanks," I say.

"Of course." He folds himself into the booth across from me and eyes Maverick's plate, which sits mostly untouched.

"Do you play sports?" I ask Maverick, since diverting my attention to him stops me from obsessing over Griffin's beard and wondering what it would feel like going down my stomach. A surge of electricity bolts down my body right between my legs.

"No."

"What do you like to do?"

He holds up his phone. "Play games."

"He likes those role-playing games," Griffin says, and the waitress comes over.

"Phoenix." She touches my shoulder.

"Hey Molly, how's Katie?"

"She's good. Thanks for asking. What can I get you?"

I look across the table and see a beer in front of Griffin and a Coke in front of Maverick. I probably shouldn't drink alcohol. Wine would be a bad idea. "I'll have, um... a kiddie cocktail."

Molly starts to write it down but stops and looks at me. "Kiddie cocktail?" Her expression asks what the hell is wrong with me.

I shake my head, laughing. "Sorry, no. I was thinking Maverick might want one."

"I'm not five," he sneers.

"Maverick," Griffin bites out his name with zero patience.

"Sorry. Um... I'll have iced tea."

"Sweetener?" Molly asks.

I want to tell her to get me whatever. I'll drink whatever she thinks is appropriate because my mind is focused on the fact that Griffin's leg is pressed against mine under the table. I'm definitely talking to Wyatt about how small his booths are. "Sure, that'd be great."

"I'll be right back," she says and leaves the table.

Griffin leans forward and his leg disappears from mine under the table. "You know you can get a cocktail, right? And not a kiddie one."

Maverick peers up from his phone, watching our exchange.

"Oh no. I'm not a big drinker."

He leans back and sips his beer. "I just didn't want you to think you had to pretend because I hired you as my nanny—I mean, Maverick's nanny. You're not mine. Obviously."

I giggle and he sips his beer.

Oh, Mr. Thorne, I have a feeling I'd enjoy giving you orders if I was in charge of you. I keep that thought to myself. Obviously.

"Jesus, I'm sorry. I'm just flustered," he says. "We were shopping for school stuff all day, and Maverick has to go in for some tests tomorrow. I have a lot of balls up in the air right now."

Do not picture Griffin's balls. Do. Not. I nod. "No need to apologize. I'm nervous. I mean, I don't usually order kiddie cocktails. But my brain went right to wondering what you'd think of me if I ordered a beer and the words just kind of fell out of my mouth."

He laughs. If he has dimples, they're hidden under his beard, but his eyes portray everything I need to know. He's not judging me at all. "I wasn't going to say anything, but please, order a cocktail. You don't have Maverick tonight."

Molly returns to the table with my iced tea and a container of sweeteners. Maverick steals one right away.

"I'm sorry, Molly, can I have a beer as well? Whatever is on tap is fine."

She smiles at me like she knew I was acting differently and walks away.

Maverick opens the sugar packet and pours it in his mouth. Griffin says nothing, and Maverick reaches for another one.

I put my hand over the container. "How about you finish your dinner first before you have another one?"

Griffin's eyebrows raise as high as Denver's did earlier. Shit, I overstepped. Maverick's father is here. I don't need to dictate what the kid can and cannot do. But I just copied what I've seen Harley do with Calista. Then again, Calista is four. Maverick is eight. Maybe he's allowed to have all the sugar he wants.

But Maverick picks up his spoon and piles the mac and cheese into his mouth.

"I would've hired you for that alone," Griffin says. "Maverick is…" He looks at his son, and I get that he doesn't want to talk in front of him.

"Have I told you I'm the youngest of nine?"

He brings his beer to his lips again and sips. "No."

"I am. I have a twin, Sedona. You probably know Denver has a twin, Rome."

He nods. I'm not surprised he doesn't know much about our family. Denver's not big on rehashing our life story. He doesn't like the pitying looks.

That's where we're different. Not that I want to be the kid who was orphaned at eight and whose brother raised her. But it's my life and there's nothing I can do about it.

"Our mom was a travel writer, so we're each named after the place we were conceived," I say.

"Conceived?" Maverick asks.

I bite my lip, shooting an *I'm sorry* look at Griffin. *You're really blowing this.*

"It's where you started to grow in your mom's belly," Griffin tells his son.

When you become a mother or father, can you just word things perfectly for a kid? That was impressive. I was about to say mommy and daddy have sex and…

"Wait then. If there're twins, how does that work?" Griffin asks.

I laugh. "Denver was the layover to Rome. And they visited both Sedona and Phoenix with me and my sister. Anyway, my entire point of telling you I'm the youngest is that I'm probably the most spoiled." I look over to find

Maverick staring at me as he dips his fry into ketchup. "I'm kind of the brat of my family. The difficult one."

Griffin's smile says he thinks I'm lying, that I made this up to tell him I'm similar to his son, but it's the truth. It's the reason Denver is going ballistic on me for being his friend's nanny. If it was Sedona, he would've recommended her for the job right away, whereas I had to go behind everyone's back.

I hold a chip on my shoulder and my family isn't shy to tell me how annoying it is. But I welcome the chip. It lets people know I'm not a hugger. I'm not a "sit down and let's talk out your problems" kinda person.

Molly swings by and places my beer on the table.

I thank her then return my attention to Griffin. "So no worries, Mr. Thorne. I can handle this job."

"Griffin," he says.

"Okay, Griffin." I smile, and he smiles back.

His leg stretches out under the table and presses against mine again. I'm not sure if he knows it's my leg or thinks it's the pole. Regardless, I'm not moving, because I'm never one to shy away from something that feels good.

SEVEN

Griffin

It took me until right now to figure out why all my friends looked at me like an alien had abducted my body when I told them I was moving to Alaska. I'm under the sink, and the wrench falls out of my hand and misses my eye by a hair before falling to my shoulder.

"Shit!"

Maybe not having the contractor finish the house completely before we moved in was a bad idea.

How have I forgotten how to use my hands? My dad was a carpenter and taught me to build things, fix things the entire time I was growing up. Something like this would've been easy for me fifteen years ago.

The worst thing that can happen to someone is to skyrocket into stardom. Don't misconstrue what I'm saying. When Cammie Sanchez's album hit platinum and her song sat at the number one spot for half a year, it was one of the best moments of my life. It was definitely the most surreal thing to ever happen to me. I went to bed a man waiting for his big break and woke up with a voicemail box full of people seeking me out.

I let the fame and the money get to my head though. Which brings me to where I am right now. Trying to reclaim some part of myself by installing a sink when I have enough money in the bank to pay a plumber to install it a million times over.

One part of me that never changed is my incessant need to do something when I put my mind to it. Right now, I want to get this damn sink installed by myself without the help of anyone else.

My dad would be pinching the bridge of his nose, shaking his head and watching me fumble my way through this though.

Grabbing the wrench, I wiggle back along the hard wood under the cabinet to get in a better position. This sink will not win.

When I clamp the wrench along the fastener to the pipe, the doorbell rings and I close my eyes.

"Maverick!" I yell and hear his feet on the floor a minute later. "Get the door, bud?"

"I'm in the middle of my game." He doesn't move, his feet remaining in my peripheral vision.

"Maverick, go get the door."

He huffs, but I no longer see his legs. Hopefully, that means he's on his way to the door. The doorbell rings again.

"Maverick!" My tone holds no patience now.

"I'm getting it!"

Which he must because it's Phoenix's voice I hear next. "Hey, Mav."

"Maverick," he corrects her.

She giggles and snaps her fingers. "That's right. I really like Mav though. It has an edge to it."

I smile as I crank the wrench. One thing she's bound to find out soon is that Maverick isn't a cool or trendy kid. He's a snob and thinks money can buy him out of anything, but he's not the fashion kid or the sports kid. He's the gamer kid.

"Maverick is my name."

"Okay. Okay. I relent." A short pause. "Is your dad home?"

"Under the sink."

"I'm in here," I say right before the elbow of the pipe hits me square in my nose.

Her legs appear a few minutes later, and I see that she's wearing a pair of workout pants. But the kind that are like a second skin.

I inwardly groan because Phoenix isn't just attractive. She makes my dick drunk to the point that it doesn't give a shit why it needs to stay away from her. It wants her, and it lets me know that that desire isn't going anywhere until it's deep inside her.

"Do you need any help?" She bends down.

Jesus, her shirt dips and I see directly down the neckline to her bra-covered breasts. As though I needed a visual of her cleavage to give me more beat-off material.

"No. I'm almost done." That's a lie. "You have your stuff?"

The elbow part clinks on the other part and I get to the same spot I was at minutes ago. This time around, I crank and crank. Thankfully it doesn't hit me again.

"Mind turning on the water?" I ask.

"Sure." She straightens up. "One. Two. Three."

The water shoots down the drain and another part of the pipe falls off.

"*Damn it!*" I scream. "Turn it off."

She does, but not before I'm completely drenched from

the waist up. When I wiggle out, I see that she's biting her lip to keep from laughing.

"I've been on this project since lunch."

"Why didn't you get the builder to do it?" she asks.

"Because I'm going to install that sink no matter what."

"Why?"

She's not trying to be difficult. One thing I've noticed in the little conversations we've had since I hired her two weeks ago is that Phoenix isn't afraid to ask questions.

"Because I came here to..." I let it hang there because I don't really know Phoenix and I definitely don't want my reason for coming here to end up in some tabloid. "Griffin Thorne went to Alaska to find himself." I'd be more of a laughingstock than I am now. "You want to get your stuff?"

She points at my shirt. "Did you want to change first?"

I look down at myself. Stripping it off in front of her would be a bad thing. Unprofessional. "Yeah, I'll meet you outside."

"Sounds good."

After climbing the stairs two at a time and exchanging my wet shirt for a dry one, I head outside to find her bent over the trunk of her car. I might as well get used to having blue balls for the foreseeable future.

She turns around, probably feeling my eyes on her and thinking how creepy her new boss is.

"I'll show you to your room." I grab two suitcases, and she follows me with a box.

This time, I'm not the gentleman I should be because I go inside first. I'm going to have to resort to self-preservation techniques so I don't cross a line and give her brother a reason to kick my ass.

LATER THAT EVENING, I'm fixing a dinner that resembles something in a college student's repertoire—six packets of ramen noodles and a loaf of bread.

I sip my beer as Phoenix rounds the open staircase and walks through the dining room to her right and great room to her left. Maverick is watching YouTube on television. She looks at it for a second before joining me in the kitchen.

"You all settled? Do you need anything?" I crack an egg and add it to the noodles.

"It's all great. Thank you."

I look over my shoulder at her and smile. "I made dinner tonight, but feel free to say no. I'm as good of a cook as I am a plumber." A rush of anger zaps through me when I glance at the sink and see the damn thing in pieces.

"Ramen is good, but what are you doing with the egg?" She rounds the island and peeks into the pot.

"A friend of mine was appalled I allowed Maverick to eat this because of the sodium level and said at least put an egg in it. I did it once and he liked it. It gets some protein into him."

She nods but says nothing.

I sip my beer and put it down quickly. "I'm a terrible host. Did you want something to drink? I have wine, beer?"

She takes a moment to think it over. I can see she's uncomfortable.

"Listen." I turn off the burner for the stove. "I'm a pretty easy boss. I mean, I'm drinking and I'm his father. I'm not opposed to you having a drink as long as it's not overboard."

"Okay."

"So if you want some wine or something feel free."

"Okay." She heads to the fridge, opens it, and pulls out a diet soda. "You've had live-in nannies before?"

I put the ramen in three bowls and slice the bread. "I

have." *Never as hot as you.* "But our house was bigger in LA, so they had their own kitchen and living area. Pretty much kept to themselves."

"Oh. Maybe... would you prefer if I..." She raises from the stool, but I wave her back down.

"No, no."

"Am I imposing?"

I laugh and look out at the family room. "Yeah, Maverick is a big conversationalist, as you can see."

She giggles.

"Truth is, I was so busy back in LA that I was barely around. This is new for me. You're probably more comfortable than me."

A look crosses her face that suggests I'm wrong, but she sips from her can and says nothing.

"I was thinking after dinner, when Maverick is getting ready for bed, we could talk about the rules and the schedule and stuff."

"Sure thing."

"You're very agreeable." I raise my eyebrows, and the cutest smile creases her lips.

"Give me about a week." She winks. It's more playful than flirtatious.

"Good. I hate overly polite people."

"Then hiring me was a smart decision."

Just like that, the uncomfortableness between us drops away, and it only increases my attraction toward her. There's no pretense with this woman—I get the feeling that what you see is what you get, which is a huge change from the people I'm used to dealing with.

After dinner, Maverick goes up to shower. Once I get him into bed, I return downstairs to find Phoenix in front of the television with a glass of wine.

Grabbing a fresh beer, I join her but sit on the other side of the sectional. "What are you watching?"

"Oh nothing. It's your house. Here." She holds out the remote to me, but I wave away the gesture.

"I haven't watched television in ages unless it was sports. Feel free to watch whatever you want."

"I can watch TV in my room if you'd rather me go upstairs after Maverick is in bed at night?"

I shake my head. I guess the uncomfortableness between us hasn't evaporated completely. "No. You're more than welcome to watch TV here. So let's lay out the rules, shall we?"

She mutes the television and positions herself to face me.

"I'll probably be up with you and Maverick in the morning. You can drive him to school, then I'll leave a list of things I need done each day. Probably just grocery shopping, picking up anything Maverick needs, and cooking dinner. I'll be in my office for the first couple weeks because I have a lot of loose ends to tie up with leaving my company."

"Okay."

Another damn okay.

"I already mentioned drinking. Feel free to add anything to the grocery list and buy whatever food you like. Neither me nor Maverick have any allergies. Do you have any questions for me?"

She shakes her head. "Nope. That all sounds good."

"I'm sure it's clear, but Maverick isn't exactly happy to be here right now. If he gives you a hard time, let me know and I'll talk to him."

"I can handle Maverick."

"You sound so sure of yourself. I love him, he's my son, but he can be difficult."

She smiles and shrugs. "We'll manage just fine. I'm not worried about it."

Good to know *she's* not. I'm worried in two days, she'll quit. "Okay, but if he—"

She puts up her hands to stop me. "Don't worry about it. The kid is in the middle of a huge change. I get him. A pretty big change happened to me when I was eight and here I am."

For some reason, the pain in her eyes tugs on my male ego to try to heal the wound that still lives inside her.

"And Lake Starlight isn't so bad. My entire family loves it here. Maverick will too." She winks.

I think about her words. I want my son to love Lake Starlight. To give it a chance to feel like home, but my thoughts are soon preoccupied with what happened to Phoenix at the age of eight to add that dimness to her eyes.

It doesn't escape me that she said her family loves Lake Starlight but never said that she does. Now I have to decide if I want to become invested enough to find out why.

EIGHT

Phoenix

I distract myself with Tyler Vaughn's new song while I wait in the kiss and ride line to pick up Maverick after school. The YouTube sensation turned certified star courtesy of Griffin. If anything, that should've proven to Griffin that he was the best of the best. Tyler's got a new beat he never had when he only covered other people's songs. Part of me would love to convince Griffin where he belongs, but I would never put my opinions on someone else since that's what's happened to me my entire life.

Phoenix needs to... Phoenix should... why won't Phoenix listen to us? I love my family, but there isn't a blueprint of what a Bailey should be. I thought they realized that when Savannah convinced Austin to let me go to LA after college, but ever since I returned, they've been trying to shove me into a box I know would suffocate me.

My eyes catch Maverick approaching the car. His shirt is askew with a small rip at the collar, and his perfectly gelled hair is messed up. Did the kid actually play at recess?

After climbing into the back seat, he puts on his seat belt.

I turn down the radio. "How was school?"

He stares out the window. "Fine."

"Did you play with the kids at recess? Looks like you did."

The traffic line crawls forward and someone honks behind me. Normally that would mean flipping them off, but I have to be mindful of Maverick and the fact that all my wrongdoings will probably be reported back to his dad.

"No."

"Well, you look like you had fun."

"Some kid cornered me in the playground."

"What?" My foot slams on the brake, and I turn around in my seat to look at him over my seat. Another honk from the car behind me, but I stay turned around and examine his appearance closer. No visible markings, except the tear. "Who was it?"

This town isn't that big. I can find his parents' address. A protectiveness I've never felt for a child I barely know consumes me. Maybe it's because I know what it's like to be the different one.

"No one. Can we go?" The plea in his voice pulls at my heart.

I turn around and drive, but I go the opposite way of his house and head into downtown Lake Starlight instead. There are only a few ways to get over a shitty day. Since he's not old enough to drink, comfort food will have to do.

"Do you want to talk about it?" I ask.

He sings along with the Tyler Vaughn song and shakes his head. "You know my dad hates this song."

"Really?" I look at him in the rearview mirror. "Didn't he produce it?"

He nods. "Every time I ask him to play it, he gets the same look as when my mom cancels plans with me."

My ears perk up at him referencing his mother. Other than her being the famous actress, Maggie Cooperton, I don't know much about their situation. I have no idea how Griffin was allowed to bring Maverick up here to live.

"Well, I love Tyler. I think your dad is uber-talented for what he did for him." I turn up the volume and we sing along to the pop song.

Maybe food isn't the way to get Maverick to open up. Maybe it's music, like me.

During the high pitch area that technically isn't Tyler's best, I sing over him because I'm lost in the song.

"Whoa. Phoenix." I catch Maverick's eyes widening when I glance in the rearview mirror. "You can sing?"

My cheeks heat, which is strange because I've never in my life been embarrassed for anyone to hear me sing. "Yeah, ever since I was young. My mom loved to sing too."

It's the truth. My mom sang all the time. While she cooked, especially when she baked. As she did yard work, or in the car. There always seemed to be music filling the walls of our house, which is why I find it odd that I'm the only one from our family who wants to do something musically.

"Like she was a singer?" Maverick asks as I park on Main Street in front of Terra and Mare. Rome is outside, sweeping the sidewalk.

"She was a singer, but not a famous one."

"Then she wasn't a singer." He unbuckles himself.

I forgot how a kid's world is so black and white. I've always considered myself a singer, even if I never make it big. But to Maverick, who comes from the world of celebrities, you're not a singer unless you have millions of followers on Instagram.

"Why are we here?" He looks at the restaurant.

Rome walks over and stands in front of my car.

"That's my brother, Rome. He makes the best I-had-a-bad-day macaroni and cheese."

His shoulders slump. "I don't wanna talk about it."

Turning around in my seat, I hold up my finger to Rome. "And I won't make you, but it's my job as your nanny to make you happy. I'm hoping you love it as much as I did on bad days."

He looks at me as though he doesn't understand why I care. I've seen that look in the mirror. Then that innocent eight-year-old boy disappears, and he straightens his back.

"It's not going to work, but I'm hungry so..." He opens the door, gets out, and slams it shut.

Little does he know I'm familiar with having a chip on your shoulder too.

MAVERICK SITS at a table near the corner, doing his spelling words while eating a bowl of mac and cheese courtesy of my big brother. Rome sits at the bar with me and we stare on as if he's a science experiment.

"So what happened?"

"Some kid cornered him on the playground. That's all he's saying."

Rome crosses his arms. "I'm afraid when my kids get to that age, I'll be in prison for beating the crap out of some little shit."

I put my hand on his shoulder. "I fear for you too. You need to relax."

He side-glances me with a "you're out of your damn mind" expression. It's cute how protective he is of his kids. I can't fault him for it. The way I was ready to pull Maverick into the principal's office and demand retribution makes me think I wouldn't be much different.

"How much for you to make me a dinner to bring home?"

He laughs. "You're supposed to cook for the guy too?"

"Yeah, it's not your typical nanny gig since Maverick is in school most of the day. I cook, clean, take care of any household chores, plus Maverick."

He stands from his stool. "You do know this is going to end badly, right? Like, once it all comes out why you took the job. The fact G'ma D lied. All of it."

"I didn't take the job for the reason you think. Besides, I'm doing a pretty great job right now." I look over at Maverick, who has a small smile on his face.

Rome follows my gaze. "You did good today. That's the first dish I perfected."

We share a look, and for a moment, my mind travels to the first time Rome made me mac and cheese. It was the day Jackson Irving told me that my dad killed my mom. The hurt from that day still burns in my gut, but it's like a smoldering ember now, not a bonfire.

"Kids are assholes," Rome says as though his mind went to the memory too.

Eight-year-old me crying at the kitchen table. Rome being the older sibling who had to be home to watch the younger ones, cursing that it was his day. Him not having any idea what to do with me and Sedona, because I'd shared with her what Jackson had said and she was upset too.

A half hour later, he knocked on our bedroom door and told us to come downstairs. There were three bowls of mac and cheese on the table and a photo album of us the year prior when we went to Seward for a weekend as a family.

Of course, even though Rome helped me feel better, I still kneed Jackson in the balls the next day.

He squeezes my shoulder and stands from the stool. "Don't forget the Founder's Day Parade meeting," he calls before he disappears into the kitchen.

Shit. I look at my phone. I had completely forgotten that our family is meeting here to talk about the song we're singing this year. It's Kingston's turn to pick.

I pull out my phone and call Griffin.

"Hey, Phoenix," he answers.

"Hey, I brought Maverick to my brother's restaurant for an after-school snack. I forgot that I have a family meeting to attend. Do you mind if I keep him here with me and bring him home after dinner? I'll bring you a meal as well. My brother is a great cook."

"I can come and get him. You have your family meeting." There's a pause. "I'll be there in about twenty minutes. Let me shower quick."

A vision of a naked Griffin with droplets of water falling down his body flashes through my mind. I mentally slap myself. "If you're sure."

He chuckles. "I'm sure. I told you I'm an easy boss."

"I know. But I completely forgot. I'm sorry."

"Phoenix, it's fine."

I sigh, feeling like a disappointment for not remembering earlier and arranging to get Maverick home. "Okay."

We hang up, and I tell Maverick I'll be right back, then I head into the kitchen. "I need a good meal for Griffin and Maverick, with sides."

Rome's one step ahead of me, closing up a to-go container with what he's serving the family tonight. After putting it all in a bag, he hands it to me. "Here you go."

I rise up to my tiptoes and kiss his cheek. "You're the best."

"*Hello!*" Grandma Dori's voice rings out, and I fall down to my heels.

"Why is she early?" I whisper.

Rome shakes his head. "She's always early."

I leave the bag on the counter, and after I tell him about my phone call, Rome says he'll put it in the warmer until Griffin arrives. I'm on my way out to the dining room when I hear Grandma asking Maverick what happened.

"Chad Billings?" Grandma Dori says.

"The Billings." Rome sighs, following me. "Family of assholes."

The Billings have almost as big a family as us. Since our names are near each other alphabetically, almost every year, there's been a Billings next to a Bailey in the yearbook.

"Chad is nothing. You can take him," Grandma says, and Rome nudges me forward. She finally notices me. "Phoenix, you can't have a Billings boy beating up poor Mav here."

"Maverick," he corrects her.

She stops talking, stares at him, then turns to me.

"What am I going to do, fight his mom? How did you get out of him what happened?"

She smiles like she always does when she gets what she wants out of people. "Fighting back doesn't make it better. And what can I say, I have a connection with Mav." She pats his hand.

"Maverick," he corrects her again.

She doesn't bother responding to him. "The Billings kid plays baseball. Rome can start a team and Maverick can beat his team. Then the kid will stop. It worked for Austin when that oldest Billings tried to bully him."

I look over my shoulder at Rome and smirk.

"Sure, G'ma D," he says. "Let me run a baseball team. You know, with all my free time."

Grandma pats Maverick's hand. "Don't worry, dear, we'll get this figured out."

Maverick shrugs because I'm not sure he really cares.

The door opens and a freshly showered Griffin appears. He looks at the state of Maverick, then at me. "Did you forget to tell me something on the phone?"

Without another glance at me, he heads toward his child, further inspecting him.

My stomach sinks. How did I forget to tell him about what happened to Maverick at school today? Maybe I do suck at this nanny thing.

NINE

Phoenix

"The Billings," Grandma says to Griffin as if he has any understanding of who they are. "They're all bad seeds."

Griffin briefly looks at Grandma Dori then back at Maverick. "What happened?"

"I don't wanna talk about it." Maverick pushes aside his bowl of mac and cheese.

"Why did the school not call me about this?" Griffin seeks an answer from me, but how would I know? "I'm calling them first thing in the morning."

"Don't, Dad. I told them that my shirt got caught on the chains from the swings."

Griffin swivels around and my shoulders sink, hearing the embarrassment in Maverick's tone. He looks at Rome and me for a moment before falling on bended knee in front of his son's chair. "Why?"

"Because I'm not going to make friends by telling on people."

Griffin blows out a breath and runs a hand through his hair. I watch the movement with such intensity I guess that Rome elbows me. Again, the thought of Griffin naked in the shower accosts my brain and a dirty feeling washes over me. I need to stop these thoughts.

"I'm not going to allow kids to be mean to you," Griffin says.

"I can handle myself. Don't call the school," Maverick pleads.

"I told him that to beat the Billings boy, we need to set up a baseball team and kick their butts."

Griffin glances at Grandma Dori, obviously confused.

"I don't play sports," Maverick says.

"Every boy plays sports," she says, her eyebrows crinkling as she looks at me.

Of course she thinks that. All her grandsons played a sport. Hell, all of Lake Starlight heads out to the high school games because there isn't much else to do in our small town. She won't understand a kid who wants to play video games all the time.

Griffin doesn't say anything even if he's thinking it. "We should go. We'll talk in the truck." He packs up Maverick's backpack and swings it over his shoulder. His hand slips into his back pocket and he pulls out his wallet. "What do I owe you?"

Rome holds up his hand. "Nothing."

"Are you sure?"

"Yeah," Rome says. "And I have a dinner for you."

Rome eyes me, and I startle out of my thoughts. "Yes. We have some dinner ready for you guys."

I run back into the kitchen, grab it out of the warmer, and bring it back to them. By the time I emerge, Griffin and Maverick are by the front door.

"I'll walk you out," I say.

Griffin takes the bag, his eyes on Rome only. "Please let me pay you something."

"No. We're good. Promise." Rome shakes his head.

I follow them out of the restaurant, and Griffin puts Maverick in the truck, and the food in the back seat before looking at me. "I've got him for the rest of the night, so enjoy your family."

"Mr. Thorne." I step forward and his hand falls from the handle of the truck.

"It's Griffin."

I nod and bite my lip. "I'm sorry. I was trying to get more information out of him. He was really shut off when I picked him up. I was just doing what used to work for me when I had a bad day at school. By the time I called you, he seemed to be over what happened and I forgot, but I shouldn't have."

He steps up to me and places his hand on my upper arm. A rush of electricity bolts through my body. "It's fine. I'm upset because of what happened to him at school. I mean yes, I do wish you would've called me immediately, but you tried to make him happy and that's not a bad thing."

He squeezes my arm, and I want to step closer and feel those hands run down the length of my body. "All right?"

"Okay. I'll see you at home."

He climbs into his truck and pulls out of the parking spot before the word home resonates a warm feeling inside me. I like that I get to go home to Griffin after a family meeting because all this evening's dinner will entail is a lot of arguing.

"See!" Denver's loud-ass voice pulls me away from watching Griffin's taillights disappear down Main Street. "Look at her."

Cleo pushes down his arm. "She's just watching him leave."

"I've got my eye on you, Phoenix." He does the whole two fingers pointing at his eyes before turning them around to point at me.

"Just go get a beer." Cleo shoves him through the door of Terra and Mare.

The two of them go inside, then it's like a funeral procession, all of my family's cars lining the street parking right in front of Terra and Mare. I wave and head inside to get this meeting over with because the sooner we finish, the sooner I'm back at Griffin's.

THE SONG "What Happens in a Small Town" by Brantley Gilbert and Lindsay Ell finishes playing through the restaurant speakers.

"Kingston, that's not a 'thank you to Lake Starlight' song," Savannah says.

Every year for the Founder's Day Parade, one of us gets to pick a song which all nine of us will end up singing on a float, embarrassing ourselves. But it's a Grandma Dori must and family tradition.

"We've run out of thank you songs. It's about a small town and truthfully"—Kingston turns on his brilliant smile as if it's as easy as flicking on a light—"it reminded me of you and Liam."

"What?" She looks at Liam and his hand disappears under the table. "Let me listen to it again."

Kingston plays it again, and we all eat and listen in silence. I won't mention that the song reminds me of Kingston and Stella, not Liam and Savannah, because I like the idea of going in a different direction than the thank you songs. Kingston is right—they've run their course and we need to switch it up.

The song ends and Kingston clears his voice. "It's still a tribute to a small town."

"It's a love song," Juno interjects.

"What about something with less love in it? There are plenty of songs that are about living in a small town and loving it. This is clearly a breakup song." Austin spins his pasta around his fork.

"I like it. I think it speaks to a lot of romances in this family and in town. It'll resonate with the people of Lake Starlight." Brooklyn shrugs. "I agree that it's time for a change."

Grandma Dori puts down her fork and wipes her mouth. "I'm willing to be flexible, but I'm thinking this means a lot more will be changed than just the song. There's no way nine kids can sing this song."

I straighten in my chair. What is she going to say?

"Kingston and Phoenix will sing this song on the float."

"What? I can't sing," Kingston lies. We all know he can but pretends he can't. He even resorts to lip-syncing most times because he thinks he's fooling us.

Rome throws his napkin at him. "You can too."

"So we have new additions to the float." Dori skips over Kingston because her word is final. Which means I'll be practicing with Kingston to get this right. "Holly, Wyatt, Harley and the kids are all welcome to join the float."

"What about Liam?" Savannah asks. "He's practically family anyway."

"Until you hold a marriage license in your hand, he's not on the float."

"I still do the classic car thing anyway." Liam smiles at Sav.

"Then maybe I ride with you." She leans toward him, and he takes the opportunity to kiss her temple. Ugh, these two.

"As much as I'd love to have you next to me, you know where you belong. I'll be waiting at the end for you." He kisses her one last time, and she picks up her fork, apparently appeased by his answer.

"So we'll have two floats. Kingston and Phoenix will sing on a smaller float in front of the family. The family float will have everyone else. We'll hand out candy and wave and smile," Grandma Dori says.

"I'm not singing," Kingston says.

"Too bad, little bro, you should've chosen a different song." Rome grips his shoulder on the way out of the room.

"I can't sing."

"You're lying. You can to. You forget how you used to sing in the shower." I elbow him.

"Just admit that you're the only Bailey man who got Mom's talent." Denver raises his eyebrows.

Wyatt looks at Kingston. "I have to admit, I'm excited for this. I never would've guessed."

Kingston's jaw clenches and he buries his head in his plate.

"Anything else we need to discuss?" Grandma asks.

Denver's eyes fall on me. "We could talk about how Phoenix railroaded her way into being a nanny for Griffin Thorne?"

"Babe," Cleo says, putting her arm around his shoulder. "You need to let this go."

"Phoenix needed a job. Griffin was hiring. From what I witnessed this afternoon, she's doing a fantastic job."

Grandma Dori winks at me. "Maybe motherhood is her calling."

The elation of receiving a compliment gets doused with a large bucket of cold water.

"He's my friend, and we all know why she's actually there." Then it dawns on him and Denver points at Grandma Dori. "That's why you're okay with this song. Because it'll give her a solo for Griffin to hear."

I can't say the thought hadn't crossed my mind. I get to sing, and even if he's not in the industry, he might feel compelled to reach out to one of his friends. Surely, he doesn't want talent to die in a small town like Lake Starlight. But singing on the family float is an obligation, so it's not like I have a choice anyway.

"Not true, Denver," I say.

"Why do you have such a problem with it?" Austin asks, using the fatherly voice he perfected all those years ago when he was our guardian. "She hasn't done anything wrong."

Thank you, Austin.

Denver throws up his hands. "Griffin is my friend who's now under the belief that she's a 'hot commodity' in Lake Starlight. That he has a qualified nanny working for him. I never said anything to refute that when he told me. Eventually he'll find out that she's lying and only wants him for his connections."

"And his money," I add.

All my family's heads turn in my direction and I bury my head into my plate. Bad timing, I guess.

"She's not pushing her career on him. Otherwise he would've fired her already. She's his nanny and acting as that," Holly points.

I mouth, "Thank you" to her.

"You guys just don't understand. He's done a shit-ton for me over the last year and I'm betraying him by not telling him the truth."

I should've known Denver would feel conflicted. One of his best traits is his loyalty to his friends.

"What are you afraid of?" I drop my napkin. "That I'll embarrass you? That I'll screw up? What? Do you think I'm not that talented of a singer? Because I'm done caring what you all think of me." I stand and tuck in my chair.

"This is getting out of hand," Grandma Dori says.

"I agree," Holly says.

"I never said you weren't good, but we can't refute that you never made it when you went down to LA," Denver says.

Anger burns hot in my veins, and if I don't leave now, I'm going to lose my shit. "I have to get back to my nanny job." I turn to Kingston. "Let's practice this weekend."

He nods in the silence that's fallen over the table. It's uncomfortable now that one of our own just stabbed me with a hot poker right in my biggest wound.

"Phoenix." Denver stands and runs a hand down his neck. "I didn't mean—"

I put up my hand to stop him. "It doesn't matter. I better go."

No one says anything. No one follows me when I leave. No one seeks me out.

Ten minutes later, I'm in the driveway of Griffin's house, debating if going behind my brother's back was the stupidest decision I've ever made. Now when Griffin hears me sing at the parade, the truth will come out.

Maybe there was a reason I couldn't make it in LA. Maybe I'm not as talented as I think.

TEN

Griffin

The next morning, I'm up at five am because the paperwork for Tyler Vaughn came through last night from my lawyer. I'm still deciding whether or not I want to file suit against him.

I'm in the kitchen getting breakfast going when Phoenix comes in to pack Maverick's lunch.

"Good morning," she says. "I could've made breakfast."

"I was up. Hard time sleeping last night."

She sighs. "I know the Billings family, and if you go to the principal, it'll only make it worse on Maverick. I think we should allow him to handle it himself and if it gets worse... I say this knowing I'm not his parent and have no right to offer this advice, but—"

I put the spatula down and approach her, putting my finger over her lips. "Relax. Breathe."

She exhales. I can tell from her rambling that she's nervous.

"Thank you for your opinion, and I wasn't up because

of Maverick. Believe it or not, I know he can handle himself. He and I had a long talk yesterday about dos and don'ts. I won't interfere unless it gets worse."

"Oh."

I smile and remove my finger. "Always feel free to give your opinion. It's just work shit that's got my mind spinning." Heading back to the stove, I flip the pancakes and see that they're slightly burned. "I did want to talk to you about a few things though."

"Oh?" She zips up his lunch bag and slides it into his backpack.

"I have friends coming into town in two weeks."

"That's nice. I can stay with family while they're here."

I laugh. She's always drawing conclusions before I can finish. "No need. There's plenty of room. I just wanted you to be aware that we'd have some guests. If we go out that weekend, I'd need you to watch Maverick, but they're homebodies like me, so I imagine we'll be staying in."

She nods and collects Maverick's folders from the counter, then puts them in his bag. "Great. I'm sure you miss home."

"Truth is, I don't really. I miss my friends, but that's about all."

"And Maverick's mom?" She flushes. "Forget I said that. I'm so sorry. None of my business." She pours herself a cup of coffee in a to-go mug, adding milk to it.

"Are you nervous around me?" I plate the pancakes for Maverick and take the milk from her once she's finished to pour him a glass.

Her gaze is on her cup, rather than on me, as she takes a sip. "A little."

"Why?"

"He should really get down here to eat. *Maverick!*" she yells up the stairs as she passes me.

I grab her wrist lightly to stop her and she freezes. If I was one of those people who believed in the energy between two people, I'd say we have sizzling electricity. So much so that I retract my touch before I get carried away. "I want us to work together, which means being open and honest."

A sigh falls from her lips and she faces me. "First of all, you're my boss. Second, you're Griffin Thorne."

"I get the boss thing, but I told you, I'm easy. Second of all, I'm just Griffin Thorne, homeowner in Lake Starlight, Alaska."

Her shoulders sink. "You're Griffin Thorne, award-winning music producer from LA." As if she has to make her point, her eyes veer to the glass case holding my Grammys in the family room.

"Not anymore." I cross my arms and her gaze dips to my biceps.

"All right. Who are your friends coming in two weeks?" She crosses her arms, mimicking my stance, and my gaze dips down to her breasts. Although Phoenix dresses in a lot of casual clothes, her T-shirts are always a little tight in the breast area, which I love. I shouldn't, but I do.

"Van Brewton and Trey Galger."

Her mouth hangs ajar. "Seriously? Your two friends coming here are the founders of Aces High record label and the judges on that singing show on TV?"

I nod. "You'd never guess it when you meet them though."

She shakes her head. "And you don't want me to be nervous around you."

The sound of Maverick coming down the stairs interrupts us, and Phoenix scurries as far away from me as she can, as though we were doing something wrong.

When Van texted me this morning and said they were coming up, I almost said no. That we're building a new life and seeing my two best buddies from LA would only bring back everything I hate from that part of my life. But Maverick loves his pseudo uncles, and he needs a pick-me-up from them probably as much as I do.

"Eat up. We need to go." Phoenix ruffles Maverick's hair and his hands go to his head to straighten it all back down.

I lean over the counter and whisper to Maverick, "Guess what?"

"What?" he asks, concentrating only on forking the pancakes into his mouth.

"Uncle Van and Uncle Trey are coming to visit in two weeks."

He looks up and his fork drops to his plate. "*Yay!*"

I nod. "Yep. Where should we take them while they're here?"

I finish cleaning up the kitchen, using the small sink in the island since I still haven't gotten the other one together. I'm aware of Phoenix trying to distance herself from the conversation instead of being a part of it. As if she could ever be invisible.

"What do you think, Phoenix? How do we entertain them?"

She looks up from her phone, her keys already in her hand and purse crosswise over her body. "Um. In two weeks you said?"

"Yeah."

Maverick looks at her like he did when he met Tyler.

Like she's won him over already. She mumbles something and her face pales.

"What did you say?" I ask, leaning closer as I dry my hands on the dishtowel.

"Um." She clears her throat. "That's the weekend of..." She swallows again, staring at her phone. "Founder's Day."

"What's that?" Maverick asks before shoving more pancakes into his mouth.

She looks at him, her skin more pale than usual. "It's a day to celebrate when my family's company, Bailey Timber, was founded."

"Oh." I look at Maverick, and he actually smiles and nods as though that would interest him. "Perfect. What do they do?"

Her eyes close for a moment, but when they pop back open, she straightens her back. "There's a carnival. That's the fun part. Skip the parade though. Just a bunch of fire trucks and boring floats." She tucks her phone into her purse. "Ready, Mav?"

"Maverick," he corrects her and stands from the stool.

He grabs his backpack off the counter, and I wait at the hallway opening to give him a hug. "Have a great day."

"Thanks," he mumbles.

"Remember what we talked about."

He nods. "I will."

"Okay, I'll be back around lunch. I'm going grocery shopping afterward."

I glance at the unfinished sink. "The sink and I are going for round two."

She smiles and shakes her head. "Have fun. I always root for the underdog, so I'm sending positive vibes your way."

I watch her walk out the garage door with Maverick in front of her.

Damn, maybe I should've put a long sweater in the employment agreement, so I don't have to stare at that ass all the time. A man can only handle so much.

ELEVEN

Phoenix

We're a week away from Founder's Day. I chop up some vegetables in an attempt to make a meal that Austin gave me the recipe for. He says it's quick and easy, but so far, I've been cutting and chopping ever since Maverick got home from school.

"How is it going with Chad Billings?" I ask.

He puts his pencil to his paper. "Fine."

"Fine? Like in he's still bothering you?" The carrot slips off the cutting board and falls to the floor. Ignoring it, I pull another one out of the package and half it like Austin said.

He looks around—for Griffin, I assume, but he ran out to FedEx. Said it was something he had to do on his own.

"Your dad isn't here."

"I paid him."

Another hot burst of anger flows through me. I'm starting to see why Rome is the way he is with his kids. I place the knife on the cutting board. "You paid him?"

Maverick nods. "He said I was a rich kid, so I should prove it."

"And where did you get the money?"

He looks around again. "My dad has this jar in his closet. He puts loose change and small bills in it."

Of course a penny jar to the rich would mean putting your twenties in it at the end of the day.

"How much are you paying him?"

"Five a day." He shrugs.

"Five dollars a day!" I screech.

Maverick rears back from me. "But he leaves me alone now."

"I know, but you can't be paying him, Mav."

"Maverick," he says.

"Sorry."

He shrugs because the poor kid has gotten used to me shortening his name. I think I keep calling him Mav because I want him to loosen up a little. Get dirty. Be a kid. Isn't that why all the Williams of the world were called Billy as kids and the Richards were called Dicks? Actually maybe a bully came up with that one.

I sit on the stool next to him. "We gotta think of something else."

"No. This is working."

"Believe me, Chad Billings is going to come up with something else he wants. It'll never end until you end it."

"What does that mean?"

"It means we're going to come up with a new plan. Just give me some time."

"Okay." He picks up his pencil and continues working on his homework.

Ten minutes later, I manage to fill what Austin calls a

magic pot with the vegetables and a roast beef. I lock on the lid and press the buttons he instructed.

"If my brother's right, we'll be eating dinner in an hour." I hold my hand up to Maverick, and he stares at it. "You're supposed to slap it."

He lightly taps his palm to mine.

"No, high-five me." I keep my palm high in the air.

He smiles and hits his hand to mine again.

"Good job."

He pushes his papers and pencil to the side. "And I'm done with my homework."

"Time to celebrate then!" I crank my phone to "Truth" by Lizzo.

Maverick jumps off the stool, and we sing the lyrics as I circle him around the great room. We dance to the beat, and although I'm much louder than him, he's smiling and laughing. I've been blessed with a few smiles these past few weeks, but this is by far the happiest he's been around me.

We fall on the couch after the song is over, then Maverick sits up. "Can I play a song on your phone?"

"Sure." I sit up and dig it out of my pocket for him.

He scrolls through it. "You like country?" He positions the phone screen toward me, and the song Kingston and I will be performing is the first song to come up.

"I like a lot of different styles of music. That song is there because..." I look toward the back door to make sure Griffin hasn't returned. "Well, I have to sing it in the Founder's Day Parade."

He presses Play on "What Happens in a Small Town." The song begins and I sing Brantley's part. I have the stronger voice, so I'm carrying Kingston through the song.

"What do you mean you're singing it in the parade?"

He leans down and I peek over to find him looking at the lyrics of the song.

"Remember how I told you and your dad that it's in honor of when my family started the company?"

He nods.

"Well, every year my family gets on a float and sings a song to the town. Kind of like a thank you."

The back door opens, and I scramble to grab the phone, but between Maverick and me, the phone falls to the floor. The song continues to play, and by the time I'm on all fours between the couch and the coffee table, Griffin is staring at me over the edge of the couch.

"What are you guys doing?" He's smiling, so that has to be a good sign.

"Phoenix is singing on a float at the parade," Maverick rambles as if it was a secret we'd been keeping from his dad.

"Really?" He shrugs out of his jacket and lays it over the edge of the couch. Rounding the couch, he sits down next to his son. "Is that the song?"

He nods toward my phone, and I clutch it to my chest for dear life because the last thing I can do right now is broach this subject with him.

"Yeah," Maverick answers.

"Let me hear it? Brantley Gilbert, right?"

Maverick sits up on his knees next to his dad, and Griffin runs his hands through his hair. I wish the ground would open and swallow me. Here is something I want. I could sing for Griffin Thorne and get his opinion on my voice, yet I can't find the confidence to do it.

I press Play, but instead of my phone playing Brantley Gilbert and Lindsay Ell's version, it's the version Kingston, and I recorded two days ago.

"Shit." I look up, horrified. "Sorry. I mean, that's the wrong one."

My phone twists in my hands as if I'm a giant whose hands are too big to handle it. Eventually I press Pause and shut it off.

Griffin looks directly at me but pats his son's back. "Hey, Maverick, go upstairs and wash up for dinner."

"Phoenix said we have an hour before dinner," he whines.

"Okay, then give us a little privacy."

Maverick groans, but one thing I've noticed is that it's a rare occasion when he outright defies his father. He might give him attitude, but overall, Maverick respects his father. After stomping upstairs, Maverick shuts his bedroom door.

"I should check on dinner." I stand, but as I pass Griffin, he lightly touches my wrist.

"It can wait." His voice is serious.

I swallow the dryness coating my throat. I have no idea what he's about to say and I'm not prepared to hear it. Let him have his professional opinion, but if he doesn't like my voice, someone else will. Isn't that how some famous stories go? Michael Jordan got cut from his high school basketball team. J.K. Rowling was on food stamps before she became a successful author.

His thumb runs along the inner side of my wrist and shivers run across my skin. I don't think he's even aware that he's doing it. "Sit."

"But dinner," I say.

He pins me with a stare.

I sit down next to him. His cologne is all I can smell.

"Are you a singer, Phoenix?" he asks.

"I can sing," I answer, dodging the question.

He raises his eyebrows. His dark eyes are so pure and

honest, demanding the same from me. "That was you on that recording?"

"And my brother."

He takes a moment before speaking again. "I need to ask you a question."

I say nothing, because although I don't know Griffin well, I can tell he's concerned about something.

"Did you take this job because you wanted me to discover you?"

There are so many ways this could go. I could put my whole life out on the table for him. All the failure that's come with trying to become a success. But when I accepted the nanny position, I did it for the money.

"I took the job because you're paying me well. That..." I want desperately to tell him that after the summer, I plan on heading to LA, but then he'll probably replace me before I'm ready. Crossing my fingers and tucking them under my thigh, I'm as truthful as I can be. "The money is the reason I took this job."

He nods. "So you have no ambition to become a singer?"

Why, oh why does he have to keep digging?

I clench my fingers over one another harder. "Sure, I do, but I'm not so stupid to think they'd ever come true."

"You know I'm out of that scene now. I can't help you." His honest eyes from moments earlier now appear skeptical. What happened to him to make him so untrusting? This probably isn't the time to ask him since I'm only telling half the truth in order to stay employed. "And when Van and Trey come, I'd appreciate you not hanging your hopes on them."

I shake my head like I didn't hope maybe they heard me singing in the shower or something. "I'd never do that."

He nods. "Now that that's cleared up. Can I hear it again?"

"Why?"

He sits up straighter. "Because you have a good voice from what I could hear."

I press Play and rest my phone on the coffee table. My stomach twists with nerves.

Griffin leans over, his long fingers pressing down on his jean-clad legs as he gets into the tempo and rhythm. I watch him, the song almost becoming background noise as an imaginary spotlight casts over Griffin while he's doing what he's so talented at. From an outsider's perspective, I'd say he still loves it.

He listens to the song in its entirety, and after what feels like an eternity, he picks up my phone and hands it to me. "Thanks for sharing that with me. It's good. Can't wait to listen to it live." Standing, he looks at me. "I have something to do before dinner."

He disappears upstairs, and I sit on the couch as the doubt settles in. Maybe there *is* a reason I never made it in LA. Maybe it's because I suck. Perhaps it's time to think of a Plan Z.

TWELVE

Griffin

I pace my bedroom floor, Phoenix's singing voice running through my mind. There's something there that can't be mimicked and can't be taught. If I was in LA and heard her, I would've invited her into my studio and spent an entire week working with different sounds and different styles, figuring out where she fit best.

The song she played me doesn't allow her to belt it out like I'm sure she can. She's carrying her brother, but he's not that bad.

Which brings up the fact she could've lied to me downstairs. She could've taken the nanny job for the sole reason of getting access to me. There's nothing I hate more than when people use my kid to get to me.

But then again, I approached her, not the other way around. So I'm not sure what to think. My history dictates that I shouldn't trust her, but the way this all came about and how she was obviously doing her best not to let me hear her sing at the parade make me think my instincts are off.

Ten minutes later, I'm still going back and forth in my mind when Phoenix texts me to say dinner will be ready in fifteen.

I sit on my bed and put my head in my hands. I know who I need to talk to in order to sort this out, so I pull out my phone and dial Van.

"What's up, mountain man?" he answers, and surprisingly, it's quiet in the background. The guy has the social calendar of the President.

"Where are you?"

"Office. Why?"

"It's usually never quiet wherever you're at."

He chuckles, and the flick of a lighter and his deep inhale says he's lit a cigarette. "Well, we just lost one of our money-makers. I'm wallowing with a drink and a smoke."

"Who left?" I ask.

"Thought you didn't want to know about the business anymore?" There's a teasing lilt in his tone because he knows how hard it's been for me to leave work completely behind. Especially in my head.

"I care about *your* business."

"Uh huh. Well, it'll be in the press soon enough, but you don't talk to anyone else anyway... LK left."

"Shit. Seriously?"

Aces High made LK's career. Signed him when four other labels said no, gave him a say in his creative, pretty much made him what he is today. But I know there have been a few problems over the years as a result of his entourage.

"Yeah. You know that asshole who likes to act like his manager?"

"Will or something, right?"

"Yeah. He's starting his own record label and LK's going

to invest, which means his catalog will go with him. He gave us the runaround when his contract came up for renegotiation. We rolled the fucking red carpet out for him too. I'm starting to understand why you ran to Alaska."

I shake my head and look at my bedroom floor. "I didn't run."

"You sorta did," he says.

There's some truth there. I could've ignored the bullshit from that article. I had enough people to support me. I could've stalked Third Street Promenade for a new voice or sound. Instead, I decided to put it all behind me because I was so tired of fake people with fake agendas and fake motivations.

But the itch Phoenix's voice has given me tells me that no matter how far away I get from LA, music will probably always be a part of me.

"I have different priorities now," I say in my defense.

Van sighs. "Yeah, but you could work out there. There are lots of artists who'd go to Alaska just to work with you."

Which reminds me of the reason I called. "I have a predicament."

He inhales and exhales—taking a drag off his cigarette, I assume. "Please. Get me outta my head before I decide to put a hit out on LK."

I chuckle because Van would never. He's a teddy bear tucked into the skin of a bastard. "My nanny can sing."

"Convenient."

I nod even though he can't see me. "I know. She says I'm not the reason she took the job."

"Did you think she'd just out herself?"

We've both been used and abused by multiple women who didn't like us for us but wanted us for what we could do for their careers. Get close to us somehow, then suddenly they're singing in the shower or leaving demos on the night-stand after our night together. Phoenix might be one of those women too.

"I don't know what to think. But the bigger problem is that she's good. I can't stop hearing her voice in my head and wondering what I could do with it."

"Like Cammie?"

"Yeah," I say, defeated at the thought of putting all that work into someone. "But... better."

"Better?" The high pitch of his voice says he won't believe me until he hears her. "Are you fucking the nanny, Grif?"

Phoenix's ass comes into my mind, as does the way she licks her lips when she's packing Maverick's lunch in the morning. Or how when her long dark hair is pulled back into a ponytail, the length of her neck is on display. "She's hot, but no. She's more than a decade younger than me."

"So? Nothing wrong with that."

"There is when you're friends with her brother and she's looking after your kid."

"Yeah, yeah. So you're telling me it's not her body making you hear something that's not there?"

"I'm telling you, she's good. And if I worked with her, she'd be amazing. But I'd probably lose a nanny. And besides, that isn't what I came up here to do."

"But you could put your name on her and maybe..."

If I'd known LK left Aces High before I called, I might not have called. Van is going to think Phoenix might be his new artist to replace LK.

"I said she was good, I didn't say she's ready to go."

"You and your perfectionism."

I laugh, because he's not wrong.

Competing thoughts about what I should do rush

through my head. Ignore the fact that talent is sleeping under my roof? Let all that talent waste away in small-town, Alaska? I could refer her to an old colleague. There are bound to be lots of producers who would want to work with her, but most of them would use her up then dump her when the next best thing came along, rather than trying to develop her talent and her career.

"She's a young girl from a small town in Alaska. Work with her a little and go from there. It's not like down here where you have to nail someone down with a contract right away."

I run a hand through my hair. "I said I was getting out of the business."

"And you are. So you found a side project to keep you busy. Music is your passion. Did you really think you'd move up there and not have the urge to create music and nurture talent again?"

I did. And I see now how unrealistic I was. "I guess. There's this parade, and she has to sing on a float next weekend—"

"Fuck. Where the hell are you getting me into when I'm up there? A float? A parade?"

"We're gonna get you donuts, so shut up."

"Donuts?"

"Just wait and you'll see what I mean."

He chuckles. "All right. You got your head on straight again?"

I nod but don't answer, still thinking it through.

"I can see I lost you. Listen, don't overthink this. You might work with her and see she's tapped out on talent."

"True. Okay, thanks. Talk to you later."

We both hang up, and I pocket my phone and walk to the top of the stairs to head down for dinner. Hearing the laughter from Phoenix and Maverick in the kitchen makes me smile. Even if she did come here for the wrong reasons, I can't deny how good she is for Maverick.

When I reach the kitchen, she slides a plate my way from where she stands on the other side of the island. "Hopefully, it's good."

"I'm sure it is." I side-glance Maverick, who's halfway done with his dinner. "So tell us about this Founder's Day Parade."

Her cheeks redden, but she slides a stool over, her own plate in front of her. "Well, my family owns Bailey Timber Corp, and they do a big Founder's Day party every year."

Her words are simple, but there's something that doesn't seem so simple in her eyes.

"Do the floats pass out candy? Dad took me to the Rose Parade one time, and it was like Halloween!"

I smile at Maverick, happy he remembers that day so well.

"Yeah. In fact, my grandma just made it official that my family float will be throwing candy."

Maverick's eyes widen and he looks my way. Who knew the kid would get this excited over a Tootsie Pop?

"The parade isn't anything much. But it's sentimental to me," she says with a shrug.

"You said this morning the parade was boring," I say.

She smiles and forks a carrot into her mouth. Maybe she wasn't lying to me. Maybe she doesn't want to be discovered. If she didn't want us to go to the parade, she didn't want me to find out she could sing. That shouldn't make me want to ask her to stay up late and work on a few things, but it does.

When I met Cammie, she thought she was nothing more than a singer who could sing a song for her sister's wedding day. Fate had me at that wedding. I've always believed that. But things were different with Cammie. I wasn't already Griffin Thorne. I was Griffin, college friend of her new brother-in-law who happened to move to LA to try a career in music production. We were both young and had nothing to lose. But that situation ended badly, and I don't want another repeat.

The stakes for Phoenix feel greater. She's my nanny, my buddy's sister, and if she has no interest in pursuing singing as a profession maybe I should leave it alone.

"It's very much about my family and I tend to be embarrassed when it comes to them. There's a float as a tribute to my parents' wedding song too."

"That's nice." I slide my potato around the gravy. "Do they sit on that float?" I shove the forkful in my mouth.

She tilts her head and eyes Maverick. "Denver's never told you?"

For some reason, it's difficult to swallow my mouthful. I'm obviously missing something. "Told me?"

"Our parents died when we were young."

"Fuck."

"Dad!" Maverick puts his hand out for the money I owe him for swearing.

I push it down because now's not the time. "I'm sorry, Phoenix. I had no idea."

She takes her plate and dumps her barely touched dinner into the trash before turning back to us. "Thank you. It was a long time ago."

"How long?" Maverick asks.

I shake my head at him.

"Fourteen years ago." Her shoulders slump. "I can't believe it's been that long."

I abandon my meal and put my hand on her shoulder. "I'm sorry."

She nods and slides a smile onto her face. "Sometimes it just sneaks up on you. But anyway." She turns and my hand falls off her shoulder. She directs all her attention to Maverick. "They show a picture of my parents on their wedding day and play 'Sea of Love' by The Honeydrippers the entire float ride."

"Great song," I say.

She smiles. "Yeah."

"Can I hear it?" Maverick asks.

"Only if you'll dance with me."

"Never mind," he mumbles.

She grabs his hand and pulls him off the stool. "Come on. No one is around except your dad. Has anyone taught you how to dance?" Phoenix's devilish smile finds me over her shoulder. "Will you find the song?"

I grab my phone from the counter and hook it up to the Bluetooth speaker. The song begins, and Phoenix holds her hands out for Maverick. He begrudgingly clasps his hand around hers. She positions his hand on the lower part of her back and they sway.

"See how easy this is?" she says.

Maverick looks at me like 'please make her stop,' but I lean my hip on the counter, watching them and admiring the connection she's made with him already. If I'd asked him to do this, he'd have shot me down without question.

Then she starts to sing the song, and I'm not even sure she's aware she's doing it. She sways, the lyrics falling out of her mouth easily, her eyes closed like she's lost somewhere in her mind.

Mid-song, Maverick pulls away from her. "That's enough for me." He runs upstairs, presumably to his room.

Phoenix turns to me and laughs, shaking her head. "Lasted longer than I thought." She picks up his dish and takes it over to the garbage.

My hand falls to hers to stop her, taking the plate and placing it on the counter. I grab her other hand and lead her to the open area where she was dancing with Maverick. She sucks in a breath when I draw her close and tuck our hands between our bodies. I lead her around, and I'm rewarded by her singing quietly in my ear.

When the melody of the song slows and comes to an end, I hold her for a few seconds longer than I should. She draws back, and even though my brain is telling me not to do it, I can't help myself.

"Let me work with you on the song?"

"Okay," she says easily.

THIRTEEN

Phoenix

Griffin's playing the guitar that's been on a stand in the great room since they moved in. He's sitting on a chair, strumming the chords to the Brantley Gilbert and Lindsay Ell song.

"Can you send me the recording?" he asks, never looking up from his fingers.

I retrieve my phone from the pouch of my sweatshirt and send him the recording I took with Kingston. The screen on his phone lights up and he stops playing, taps his phone a few times, then my voice starts over the speaker. I cringe.

"You lack control," he says matter-of-factly. "You need to be careful when you're changing pitch. And it's like you're not feeling the lyrics, you're thinking about the next note you have to hit."

I sit on the couch.

"And your brother needs to find the timbre to pull this

off since you two are flipping parts. You can hear that he feels the words though."

"Okay," I say.

He looks up and puts down the guitar. "Sorry. I can get excited and forget that you're new to this."

I shake my head. "I've heard criticism before."

He stops the song from playing. "I'm not a sugarcoat-it kind of producer. But you never asked for me to help you and here I am just telling you exactly what I think." He stands, setting the guitar on the chair, and runs his hands through his hair. "Have I overstepped?"

"No. I just didn't know we were gonna start right away."

He comes over and sits next to me on the couch, his fresh scent wrapping around me like a vise-grip. I hate to admit it, but I'm worried about working so closely with him. Half the time, my libido says to be the naughty nanny—especially at night when we don't have Maverick as a buffer between us. It makes him hard to resist.

"That's my fault. I can be obsessive when I get my mind set on something." He glances around the room. "When I decided to leave LA, I hired an architect and had the plans for this place drawn up in four weeks. So if this is too fast, I understand."

"No." I shake my head. "We only have a week before the parade, so it's not like we have a lot of time."

"If you want to stop at any time, just say so, okay?"

His hand falls to my thigh, and I stare at it, unsure of whether I should be happy I put on my comfy shorts after dinner or not. My body warms under his calloused fingertips. Did he get those from playing the guitar or working with the knobs on soundboards most of his career? Not that I care. All I need to worry about right now is how scorching hot they are on my bare skin.

"Okay, I will." I shift in my seat. He retracts his hand, and I force a smile. "You said I need more control?"

Standing, he heads toward his guitar, but instead he grabs his phone and the remote.

"Let's deal with the lyrics first." Sliding onto the couch next to me, he extends his legs out on the chaise part of the sectional and points the remote at the television. "Okay, this song is all about living in a small town. Surely it resonates with you?"

He finds the video on YouTube on the TV.

"I've never had a serious relationship," I admit, feeling the age gap between us more than I ever have.

"Never?" he asks, his thumb pausing mid click.

"No." I shake my head.

"You're young, I suppose, but I'm surprised."

"Why?"

He stares at me for a good minute, seeming to wrestle with something. Maybe I shouldn't have asked.

"It's not for me to notice, but you're a beautiful young woman. And you get along with kids. And you can sing."

A nervous laugh escapes and I bump my shoulder to his. "I'm not sure 'gets along with kids' and 'vocal talent' are on many guys' checklists for girlfriends."

"They're on mine," he says, and my laughter stops. His eyes widen as though he didn't mean to say that, and he backtracks. "I mean if I was looking. Which I'm not. And I pay you to be my son's nanny, so that wouldn't be on the up and up, not to mention your brother."

"You can stop listing all the cons now."

He shakes his head. "Man, I am zero for two tonight. First I insult you with my critique and now I'm..." He shifts and faces me, lips pressed together. "I shouldn't say this...

but I can't deny that I'm attracted to you. But the fact remains—"

"We can't. I know." I play with my fingers in my lap. "I'm attracted to you too, for what it's worth."

I glance up and I swear it looks as though my statement has knocked the wind out of him. He takes a second to recover.

"So we're in agreement that we'll ignore whatever this is and pretend it's not there?"

"I guess so."

He nods and clicks on the video. Brantley Gilbert fills the screen.

I know we're doing the right thing, but I so desperately want to straddle him right now and feel those calloused fingers graze under my sweatshirt and over my nipples.

After clearing his throat, he says, "Let's watch the video."

The video depicts every classic small-town love story.

"This is kinda like my brother's story."

The video ends and Griffin stops the next video before it autoplays. "How so?"

I shrug, not about to talk about another case of forbidden love. Not that the feelings I have for Griffin are love. They're lust. A helluva lot of lust that has had me pulling out toys I'd long forgotten about with the hopes I'll find one to fill his imaginary void. "I think he's still in love with the one who ran away."

He nods. "Love is powerful. That's why ballads sell—people feel the truth in the vocalist's voice and the words. Take Adele's 'Rolling in the Deep.' She's amazing, but the lyrics resonate with everyone who has been scorned. Tell me about a song you connected with recently?"

I'm probably about to out myself, but I trust Griffin knows what he's doing. "'Fight Song' by Rachel Platten."

"Why?" He leaves me on the couch and ventures into the kitchen, then comes back with two beers.

"Because I'm not getting what I want out of life."

"How so?" He twists the caps off using the edge of his shirt, giving me a glimpse of his treasure trail. That does nothing to dampen my arousal for him, but it works to dampen my panties.

He passes me a beer and I nod my thanks. "Sometimes I feel like I'm lost, and that song gives me this hope that others who have been in my position before have won. That I just need to fight harder if what I think I want means that much to me."

"And what do you want?" He sips his beer and I watch his Adam's apple bob. How is that sexy?

"I want to sing." I speak the truth, worried he'll see through me. See that I went around the truth last night.

He smiles. "For?"

"For the world."

His smile grows and the anxiety living inside me calms. "Then let's get to work." He sets his beer on the table and presses his phone on. "I'll be right back."

He disappears to his office and returns moments later with a printed piece of paper. He hands it to me and sits next to me with a pen twirling through his fingers. "These are the lyrics. Since it's not love you can connect to, we need to find something else for you in this song. If we had more time, I'd suggest writing a song specific to you."

"Do you write songs?" That's something I don't know about him.

"A little, but I have a lot of friends who help, and if that fails, I know people to buy them off of."

"I didn't know that."

He laughs and taps his pen to the paper. "It doesn't matter anyway. This is the song, and we need to make sure when you and your brother get on that float, everyone is talking about it afterward."

"It's just Lake Starlight," I say with a shrug.

"And High Aces Record Label." He raises his eyebrows.

I drop the paper. "Oh no. I can't do that."

He laughs. Where is the man who said he was out of the business? "Why not? You said you want to sing, right?"

He's right, but now that the opportunity might be here, I'm afraid. Afraid it'll end up like it did when I was in LA—failure.

"Yeah, but—"

"I'll have you ready. I promise."

"Have me ready?"

"Yeah, you need some tweaks, but I can get you good enough for Van and Trey."

"Good enough?" Ugh, so I *am* a shitty singer. "Why are you doing this?"

He slides closer to where I've slid into the corner of the couch. "I see something in you."

"You just said 'good enough.'"

He shrugs one shoulder. "You have some things to work on, but you have a rawness I think they'll love."

I bury my head in my hands.

"I thought this is what you wanted?"

I spring to my feet. "I did. I mean, I do, but you can't just stroll into town and make promises like a huge record label coming to see me sing on a float. This is all happening too fast. It feels too easy."

He leans back on the couch and brings the beer bottle to his lips. "It might seem easy, but you haven't gotten anything yet. You're getting ahead of yourself. Just because I work with you and tweak what needs to be tweaked doesn't mean anything will happen."

"Everything you've touched has hit platinum," I deadpan.

"Not true. I've had failures too. I've watched dreams shatter and then sour." He pats the seat cushion next to him. "Listen, we'll take it slow. If you really don't want Van and Trey to hear you, then I'll keep them away from the parade."

I sit down, my back straight, my legs pressed together. "I still don't understand. Why are you helping me?"

He takes another pull of his beer. "I don't have an answer for you. I thought coming to Lake Starlight would be a fresh start. Get me out of music. But then I heard you sing, and I couldn't stop thinking about all the ways I could help you. I was excited to see what we could do together. That's only happened a handful of times in my career. To put it as simply as I can, I enjoy being driven to work on a project."

"Does that mean you're giving up on the sink?" I grin.

He looks behind us at the kitchen as though the sink is an actual person. "Oh no. The sink and I are not even close to being finished yet."

We both laugh, and it eases the tension and anxiety between us.

"So read the lyrics and find a reason this song can mean something to you. Find something to connect to." He hands me the paper and pen. "We'll start tomorrow after you take Maverick to school. Can your brother meet us at some point?"

"Um." I stare at the piece of paper. "He's a firefighter in Anchorage. I'll talk to him."

"Perfect."

"You just dive right in, don't you?"

His grin is wide and contagious. "When I see something I want, I'm rarely detoured."

I should only be thinking about my singing career, but I can't help but wonder if that extends to personal relationships as well. Shaking my head, I grab the paper. "I'll be in my room."

"Goodnight." He clicks on the television and scrolls through the channels as if we didn't have a life-changing conversation just now.

It's then I realize, it's only life-changing for me. To Griffin, this is like getting a coffee.

He's about to hand me the opportunity to make myself a success. But I'm worried because I have a habit of destroying most things that fall into my lap before anything good can come from them. The lie by omission that I told Griffin about only being his nanny for the money lights up where I stored it in the back of my brain, a silent reminder.

This didn't fall into your lap—you forced it to happen.

FOURTEEN

Griffin

After Phoenix leaves to take Maverick to school, I head to my office and boot up my laptop. All night I debated whether I should look into Phoenix's past. To google her and see if I can find out anything more about her.

The cursor blinks in the empty box on the Google search engine, and I lean back in my chair. It blinks and blinks like a metronome keeping time while my conscience yells at me for doing this.

Straightening my back, I let my fingers land on the keyboard and tap lightly, not hard enough for a letter to pop up on the screen.

"Fuck," I mumble.

I type in Griffin Thorne instead of Phoenix Bailey.

My Wikipedia page is the first result, but I don't need to read about how I was brought up by a carpenter and a school guidance counselor. Nor do I need a reminder that I was married to Maggie Cooperton and share a son, Maverick, with her. All of that, I'm well aware of. But what I notice are the headlines of "Cammie Sanchez leaves Griffin Thorne after two hit albums," "Tyler Vaughn's newest single a disappointment," and of course my favorite, "Griffin Thorne, music's biggest sellout." Then comes the article discussing me relocating my son.

I slam the lid of the laptop and my chair rolls out as I abruptly stand. Pacing the length of my office, I end up pushing open the doors to the small patio that overlooks the mountains and I admire what brought me to Alaska to begin with.

A fresh start and a better life for my son.

Maybe my wish is being granted differently than I'd planned. Perhaps Phoenix is my fresh start.

I should've never admitted last night that I'm attracted to her. I've felt guilty ever since. Denver would probably wanna kick my ass if he knew. But part of me wanted to know where her head was before we started working together. There's a transference theory when you work so closely with someone on something creatively. I don't want her transferring her feelings toward the process onto me, though it seems I'm not alone in my attraction.

"After Cammie…" I shake my head.

"I'm back!" Phoenix yells into the house.

In the last week, she's really become more comfortable around me, and I like the uninhibited version of her.

I need to quit it with this bullshit. She's eleven years my junior, my employee, and my buddy's kid sister. I wish I'd installed the music studio before I moved in. This would be easier if we were separated by glass.

I leave my office and make my way to the couch in the great room, grabbing my guitar. She pours herself a coffee and opens the fridge, grabs the milk, and adds a dash to her cup.

"Are you purposely delaying?" I ask, strumming a few chords of the song.

"No. I'm getting coffee. It's just after eight am. I need it." She walks over, sipping from the cup as though she didn't already have a to-go mug of it when she left.

"Did you think about what I said regarding the song last night?" This is where I'll get my answers as to what she's about. Not with a Google search.

"I suppose you're used to working so closely with someone?" she asks. Unsure of what she means, I'm silent, trying to process, when she adds, "I mean, all of this is making me feel vulnerable. I don't do well with vulnerable."

I place the guitar on the cushion beside me. "I've noticed you shut down a few times."

Her gaze rolls to the side, but I don't say anything. She crosses her legs and my eyes track the movement too closely because when my gaze slides up to her face, she's smirking.

I clear my throat. "What is it?"

"It'll sound stupid."

"Nothing is stupid."

"I don't really believe in that whole notion," she says. "Nor do I believe that there are no stupid questions—there are."

I chuckle. "Okay then, I promise not to laugh if it is stupid. That better?"

"I think it's this town that makes me feel vulnerable and that's what the song is about, so..." She inhales deeply. "After high school, I tried to run away from the memories."

"What memories?"

A grin appears, and she shakes her head. "Are you a therapist? I feel like I should be lying down and you should be scribbling notes on a pad of paper."

"Would that make it easier for you?"

"You having to be a little vulnerable in return would." Her eyes lock with mine.

I'm pretty sure she's not joking. Some women are open books, but I think Phoenix is out of her element here, and I don't think it's her age. I think she usually holds everything very close to the vest. But I also think that if I can dig down far enough, I can discover her biggest fear and help her tap into it when she's performing. That would only make her a bigger star.

"Okay, I'll share something about myself that no one knows if it'll make you feel better." I take the guitar and put it back on the stand. "You first though."

She seems to think it over and surprises me with her next question. "Can I take you somewhere?"

"Like where?"

"You like the outdoors, right? I thought we could go hiking."

"Hiking?"

"It's only a day trip. We'll be back in time to get Maverick. Unless you have something else to do."

I motion to her. "You're the only thing on my to-do list today."

A beautiful blush fills her cheeks.

"Sorry. I meant—"

She giggles and stands. "I know what you meant." She walks over to the stairs and I follow.

"Good. I swear you're going to have some good stories to sell whenever you leave here. Though I guess that NDA helps, right?" A dark chuckle escapes my throat.

She stops at the bottom of the stairs, blocking me from going up to change. "I'd never do that. I realize you barely know me, but you can trust me. Whatever you tell me, I won't tell anyone. I know for someone in your position…" Her words trail off.

I smile at her, tucking the one strand of hair that fell out of her ponytail behind her ear. "You're a rare creature, Phoenix."

"People have been telling me that my whole life." She walks up the stairs, leaving me with the perfect view of her ass in those leggings.

Do I have time to beat off before we go hiking?

FORTY-FIVE MINUTES LATER, we're halfway up a hiking path that will take us toward a glacier.

"This is something I love about Alaska." She extends her arms and lets the sun sparkle against the small amount of makeup on her face. "Any day you need to get away, there's a beautiful scenic area waiting for you to explore. You can hike, kayak, bike. This is when I'm jealous of Denver and Cleo."

"Yeah, they don't have a bad gig at all."

Watching the chip fall off Phoenix's shoulder only makes her more appealing.

She circles around to face me. "But life in Lake Starlight comes with the good and bad."

We fall into step beside each other. Since it's a weekday, there aren't many people around. We've only passed a couple of people on the trail.

"Give me a bad."

She inhales deeply. "My parents' deaths, obviously. The stories that circulated afterward. The way this town thinks they need to make up for them dying so young."

We continue on the path that's becoming steeper by the

step. Thank God I work out regularly. "Why is it bad that the people in town care?"

She shakes her head like of course I don't understand. "Because sometimes the people who act like they care are the same ones talking behind your back."

"That's anywhere. Big town or small. When Maggie and I divorced, rumors were all over the place about affairs, money problems. That I wasn't comfortable with her making so much money and taking all the fame. And then they brought Maverick into it."

She touches my arm. "I know. I've read them."

I nod because of course she has. "You getting upset over a few thousand people doesn't compare to the whole world. They're in my business, and the tabloids lie constantly."

She leans closer and lowers her voice. "If we're going to compare, you weren't eight years old."

"True enough." I picture the girl in front of me going through the loss of her parents while the same age as my son and my heart sinks.

We come to the edge of a rock and I signal for us to sit down.

She sits and pulls out her water, downing a bit before she speaks again. "Each of us has our own wounds from losing them so young. My twin, Sedona, seems to have all her shit together. I'm the fuckup. The one who doesn't fit into the puzzle no matter how many ways you try to jam me in."

"Have you considered that maybe it's your family and not this town that makes you feel vulnerable?"

She pulls her legs up to her chest and rests her chin on her knees. Admiring the view in front of us, she speaks low. "My family is a whole other can I'm not ready to open."

I examine Phoenix looking so childlike, as though her

legs can protect her from all her turmoil washing out of her like waves to the shore.

"My dad thought I was going to take over his company," I say.

She leans her cheek on her legs and looks at me. "Really?"

Now I divert my gaze to the glorious scene in front of us. "Yeah. Imagine his disappointment when I said I was moving to LA to pursue a career in music. I always felt like he was rooting for me to fail so I'd have to come back home with my head down. But over the years, he's come around. But in the small town I'm from, everyone just assumes you're sticking around and if you go to college, you come home afterward."

"The pressure of expectations."

"Exactly. Did you go to college?"

"No."

Okay, it's clear from her voice that college is a touchy subject. Time to get back on track and the real reason we're discussing all of this in the first place. "So the song... your love-hate relationship with Lake Starlight. There are things you love about living in a small town. Tell me about those."

Her lips tip up in a smile. "I love my family. This is where my parents grew up. When I'm in the gazebo, that's where my parents once sat. Downtown is where they walked us in strollers. Where their own dreams were born and fulfilled. But there's another side that I never knew existed until they died. Maybe it's different for my other siblings, because they were older, but rumors were all over the place when they died. How did they die? Were they drunk on that snowmobile? Rumors about my dad having an affair. Why would people say stuff like that when their nine children were now orphans?" She shakes her head. A tear trickles down her cheek, but she wipes it away. "It was so long ago. I have no idea why it still bothers me." She stands and heads up the trail without another word.

"Do you think there's truth to the rumors?"

She whips around, the dark eyes I usually find calming shooting lasers at me. "My mom was my dad's whole life. My dad's blood alcohol level came back showing he'd had a drink, but he was *not* drunk. My mom was..." She shakes her head. "Just no. I'm not upset because they're speaking the truth. Jesus, Griffin, I thought you of all people would get it."

She turns her back to me and walks steadily up the incline. I follow her, feeling like a dick for asking. Because she's right. I know exactly what it's like when people speak untruths. We reach the top of a hill that overlooks the glacier and a large lake.

"Hey." I grab her arm, but she yanks it out of my grip. "I didn't mean it like that. I was just asking." Then I look at her face. Her red-rimmed eyes make my heart squeeze painfully. I'm a shithead. Pulling her into my body, I wrap my arms around her shaking torso. "I'm sorry. I didn't mean to upset you."

It only lasts ten seconds before she draws out of my arms and wipes her tears. "This little experiment is over. I'll sing the song how I want. Thank you for the offer, but I'm done."

Without taking in the view, she heads down the pathway, leaving me behind.

FIFTEEN

Phoenix

I hear him behind me the entire walk back to the parking lot. He's yet to approach me though.

"Phoenix, I'm sorry."

My footsteps slow, and he catches up to me. "Obviously you've figured out what to bring up to make me mad."

He chuckles once. "I shouldn't have overstepped. I get it. I mean, LA isn't a small town, and I was an adult when people started spreading shit about me, but it hurts and makes you not trust anyone easily. But I want to be someone you trust."

We stop at his truck and he unlocks it with the fob, the headlights blinking twice. "It's my fault. I said I had a love-hate relationship with this town. The hate seems larger at this point because when I think about what I hate, it's linked to my parents. Founder's Day always brings them front and center in my mind, and I feel cheated by life. You know? That splinters out to what my family expects from me now, and then you get Phoenix the bomb blowing up in front of your eyes."

He steps closer to me, his hand sliding along the hood of his truck. I don't move. "I'm wondering if I know the real Phoenix. First you were so amenable I thought you were a robot. Then you started laughing, joking, and making a few smartass comments. Now the blowup. Tell me, who is Phoenix Bailey?" I open my mouth, but he places his finger on my lips. "And I don't want to know who she is in someone else's eyes. I want to know what you see in the mirror every day."

When is his psychoanalyzing going to end? A small part of me likes that he's trying to figure me out, because maybe that means he cares. I'm reluctant to tell him who I really am, but I might as well see if he can handle it.

"I'm passionate, and I protect myself fiercely. I don't like bullshit, and I hate two-faced people. I say what I want without worrying too much about repercussions. If I want something, rarely does anything stop me, but lately a heavy dose of self-doubt has stopped me from being the fighter I always believed I was. Are we being completely honest?"

He nods.

"And we still have the one-for-one agreement?"

He rolls his eyes but nods with a smirk.

"I also have the hots for my boss. Your turn," I say in a soft voice.

His hand moves away from me a bit. He glances around then locks eyes with me. "I'm also passionate about my work. Most of the time too passionate, which means long hours. I'm obsessive. So much so that I just made a woman cry because I had to keep digging. I love discovering new talent, so I'm not surprised that after only a month here and hearing you sing, I'm ready to dive in. My son is the most important thing in the world to me." He stops briefly and licks his lips as though he's nervous. "And I'm the cliché dad bad movies are made about, because I want to nail the nanny."

I draw back, but he steps forward.

"What do you suppose we do about that?" I ask.

"Well, we could sleep together."

"And what happens when it doesn't work out?"

"I should also mention that I'm a very optimistic person."

I step closer until we're almost chest to chest. "By optimistic, you mean..."

"I'd like to think we're adults. Either it's out of our systems or we enjoy sleeping together and maybe do it more than once."

I pretend to think about it. "Hmm... and what if it's not out of our systems and we continue to sleep together? Are you suggesting a secret relationship?"

His fingers graze my cheek as he moves a loose strand blowing in the breeze behind my ear. "We take it slow. No need for labels. Maybe I don't satisfy you?" He laughs. "Nope. I guarantee I'll satisfy you."

I know he would. My gaze dips to his crotch.

"I see you're considering my suggestion."

"And Maverick?" I ask, thinking surely mentioning his son will cool him off and bring in a dose of reality.

"He goes to school. We'd have all day to play naughty nanny. Maybe mix it up with messy maid, kinky cook."

I grin. "I can't say the offer doesn't appeal to me, but I don't even know how you kiss. How do I know I want to take things further?"

He leans forward, and I wet my lips in anticipation that I'll finally feel the mouth I've stared at for weeks. The closer he draws, the worse this idea sounds. What am I expecting from Griffin? That if I sleep with him, he'll help me more? He's already doing that, but what if after he gets me in bed, he doesn't think he needs to help me?

I push away all my negative thoughts. I've done far stupider things than sleep with my boss, so I meet him halfway and our lips brush once. The electricity that's always present between us ignites. I'm ready for more—until his phone vibrates on my leg.

He tears his lips off mine and shoves his hand into his pocket. "You've got to be kidding me." Looking down, he sighs and swipes his thumb across the screen. "Griffin Thorne." His eyes widen then close tightly. He nods as he says, "Uh huh."

He ushers me inside the truck, but he's already hung up before he climbs into the driver's side.

"Maverick got into a fight at school," he says.

I cringe then bite my lip. Shit. Maybe I won't have to worry about any of this because I may be unemployed soon.

GRIFFIN IS quiet on the way to the school, but it's clear he's brooding. I really hope Maverick isn't at fault. I told him that eventually he'd have to end what's happening with Chad Billings. I should probably tell Griffin now, before we arrive at the school, about the money Maverick was giving Chad, but I know he'll be pissed.

Before I'm able to decide, we're at the school.

Damn.

We get buzzed through the entrance and walk to the office.

"Phoenix Bailey," Betty Lansing, the office assistant, says.

She's *still* here?

"Hi, Mrs. Lansing. How are you?"

She holds up her finger. "Give me one moment with this gentleman and we'll catch up."

Griffin looks at me over his shoulder then turns to Betty. "I'm Griffin Thorne. I received a call about my son, Maverick."

Betty's smile drops and her expression says Maverick probably isn't the innocent one in this situation. I'm familiar with the judgmental look on her face. "Let me call Principal Nutters." She picks up her phone.

I somehow manage to suppress a smirk at the principal's last name.

After a brief conversation with Betty, Principal Nutters comes out of his office, Maverick by his side. Thankfully, he doesn't know me because I was out of here before he moved into town.

"Mr. Thorne, please come in. Maverick, go have a seat."

Griffin nonverbally asks me to keep an eye on him, and I nod.

Maverick exchanges a look with Griffin as he leaves the principal's office and the door shuts behind him.

"What happened?" I lead Maverick over to the chairs along the window, not interested in catching up with Mrs. Lansing.

"Chad said he wanted ten dollars a day."

I run my hand down my face. Damn Billings. "So what happened?"

"I told him no. And he said I'd be sorry. You were right. I had to end it."

I lean in and whisper, "Meaning?"

"I hit him, and blood squirted out his nose." He examines his hands as though there should be some evidence of his act.

I cringe. "Yikes."

"What? You told me to do that!" he whines. "The principal said I might be suspended."

I glance at Betty, who's trying to act as though she's stapling, but she's listening. Just like she did when Austin had to pick me up after I kneed Jackson Irving in the balls. She told everyone at her church meeting. One person told another and another until Grandma Dori was at our door by seven o'clock telling Austin he wasn't handling me well.

"Did you tell Principal Nutters what Chad Billings was doing to you?"

"I tried, but he said that I hit Chad, so I'm the one at fault. Does suspended mean I'm kicked out of school?"

I'm surprised he appears scared. I put my hand on his leg. "Don't you worry. You're not getting suspended."

As I say the words, Griffin comes out of the principal's office—and his expression says Maverick's been suspended. But I wait for him to round the desk and meet us by the chairs.

Griffin runs his hand through his long hair. "He'll be at home for two days."

"Oh no." I stand.

Griffin takes my arm and leans in. "Just let it go. I spoke my piece."

"I need to speak mine."

I free myself, which doesn't take much effort. Griffin only sighs.

"Phoenix, you can't go in there," Betty says.

I put up my hand. I'm twenty-two now, not eight. "I'll only be a moment."

I open the door to the principal's office, but Betty stands and tries to stop me. Sadly, my defiance toward authority has only grown through the years, and unfortunately for her I'm faster. I shut the door in her face and turn around. Principal Nutters is in mid-bite of a carrot, looking up from his Scholastic book flyer.

"Hi," I say.

"Hello." He looks out the window of his door to Betty as if she'll give him an explanation as to why I'm standing in his office.

"I'm Phoenix Bailey, Maverick's nanny."

He places his nub of a carrot on a napkin, next to his sandwich—which is cut in triangles—and an open bag of plain potato chips. I guess he's young at heart too, because all he's missing is a juice box. Did his mommy pack his lunch?

"Nice to meet you," he says.

"May I sit?" I point at the chair in front of him, but I don't wait for permission.

The door opens a second later.

"Sorry, Principal Nutters." Griffin's rough voice fills the room. "I'll escort her out."

Escort me out? If Griffin Thorne wants to know who I really am, he should pull up a chair because I'm about to show him.

I put up my hand to stop him. "Principal Nutters, I know you're new to this town, so I don't expect you to know about the Billings, but my assumption is that Chad Billings —much like his relatives—have been through this principal's office more than a time or two. Chad tore Maverick's shirt then proceeded to blackmail him for five dollars every day in order not to do so again. Now, I told Maverick that Chad would one day come looking for more, and it seems that day was today. He decided he wanted ten dollars a day." I cross my legs. "Aren't there lunch aides outside during recess? Who's watching the kids? I'm surprised this hasn't been observed before."

"Why didn't Maverick mention this?" Principal Nutters asks.

Griffin groans behind me. I'm surprised he's allowing me to take the lead.

"Because he's the new kid," I say. "He was probably scared and doesn't want to make enemies or be a tattletale. Don't you remember what it was like to be eight years old?"

Based on his lunch, I'd have thought it'd be really easy for him to relate.

"I can see that."

"So don't you think Chad Billings should be called in and asked to explain? I'm sure you'll use discretion where Maverick is concerned."

He nods and picks up his phone. "Betty, can you please call Chad Billings to the office?" He hangs up the phone. "Okay, I'll send Maverick back to class, and you two can go home. I'll call once I get to the bottom of this."

I stand and catch Griffin's smirk. "Thank you for investigating this further, Principal Nutters."

"Can I give you some advice, Miss Bailey?" Principal Nutters says when I reach the door, and I turn around to face him. "You should probably inform the school when Maverick comes home and tells you something like that."

"With all due respect, Principal Nutters, in my experience, the tattletale always loses."

He says nothing—probably because he knows I'm correct.

"Have a good day." I walk by Griffin and out the door.

Maverick waves to me and I give him a thumbs-up. Let's

just hope the punch in the face taught Chad Billings to pick on someone else.

"Let's go," Griffin mumbles, opening the door for me.

"Bye, Phoenix, give my best to your grandmother," Betty says.

I wave bye to Betty and make my way to Griffin's truck.

"I think we need to talk," he says once we're pulling away from the curb.

I am so fired.

SIXTEEN

Griffin

I can't even decipher my mood as we pull away from the curb of the elementary school. I want to kick an eight-year-old's ass while at the same time I'm hurt that Maverick trusted Phoenix over me. And why the hell didn't she tell me my son was being bullied for money?

"Before you say anything, I think it's safe to say we're even now," Phoenix says.

I glance in her direction before turning out of the parking lot. "Even?"

"Yeah, for what you did on the hike and for me hiding the fact Maverick was paying his bully."

I chuckle. "I'm not sure I see it quite the same."

"You hurt me in an effort to try to make me feel the words of a song. I hurt you by not telling you Maverick was stealing money out of your loose change jar to pay Chad Billings. We're even."

"He took the money from me?" I ask, bypassing downtown to head to our house.

She swivels in her seat to face me. "How else did you think he'd get the money?"

"I figured you gave it to him."

"Oh, no."

"Listen. I want you to tell me this stuff, but at the same time, I understand why you didn't. I would've gone to the school immediately and Maverick would have probably been picked on the rest of his life here."

I glance over and see her smiling. "Are you saying you agree that I did the right thing?"

We stop at a light and I take the opportunity to really look at her. "In hindsight, maybe. On the upside, I guess it means my nanny isn't stealing from me."

Her smile drops. "You thought I was stealing from you?"

"I'm kidding." I raise my eyebrows and accelerate when the light changes.

"I would never."

I grab her leg. "I'm kidding. And yes, we're even. If you accept my apology, I accept your—oh, that's right. You haven't apologized."

She's quiet until we pull into my garage and I take the keys from the ignition.

She unbuckles herself. "I'm sorry."

She opens her door and climbs down.

"That wasn't very heartfelt." I meet her at the driver's side before she can go into the house.

"There's something you should know about me." She stops, and I circle the keys around my forefinger. "I do things without thinking. I know Maverick is your son and I should've told you what was happening, but I usually think I know best."

I can't stop the laugh that erupts out of me. I knew that

about her already. It's half the reason for what happened on our hike.

"You don't say?" She pushes my chest when she sees my smirk, and I wrap my arm around her waist. "I think we were still negotiating when the call from the school came in?"

The two of us is a horrible idea, but I'm done being the only one who thinks of the repercussions. For once, I want to be the one who takes what he wants.

Adam didn't give a shit about the repercussions when he was fucking my ex-wife. And Maggie didn't give me a second thought while she entertained men inside her on-set trailer.

My attraction for Phoenix only grew when I watched her in the principal's office. She was on Team Maverick and I loved every second of it.

Her hands splay on my chest. "I think that call happened at exactly the right time."

I nod, staring at the hollow of her neck while my thumb runs along her waistline. I love having her in my arms. "I know we shouldn't, but you did something I'm not sure I can get out of my head."

"Which is what?" she asks, and I notice her voice has a breathy quality.

I walk her back until her ass presses against my truck, and I lock her there with my hips. "You stuck up for my kid. You went into that principal's office and got Maverick what he deserved. He puts on a tough exterior but being suspended would've bothered the shit out of him. You saw that, and you didn't care what I or the principal had to say about it."

"Yeah, that goes with the whole me thinking *after* I act thing of mine."

I shake my head and lower it. "I really want to kiss you."

Her eyes and her nostrils flare. "I want you to kiss me, but there's a line we shouldn't cross."

"It's just me and you here. We're the only ones who need to know what we're about to do. I've held off on doing what I want for way too long." I dip my head lower and her hands push a little harder against my chest. "Just say no and I'll walk through that door and we can forget this ever happened. Are you able to tell me you don't want this as much as I do?"

She looks into my eyes and her hands slide up my torso, her fingers delving into my hair. She arches her neck, and I lower my lips to the spot I've wanted my mouth on since the first time she had her hair in a ponytail.

"I can't say that," she practically whispers.

"Then stop fighting this thing between us." My tongue slides up the arc of her neck.

Her fingers dig deeper into my hair, and my hands move around to her back, resting just slightly lower than appropriate.

"This might be the worst decision I've ever made," she says softly, but her body responds to my touch. She arches into me, and I cast small kisses along her jaw before claiming her lips.

The world around us fades as I slide my tongue into her mouth. Her tongue meets mine right away, as though she was waiting for me this entire time. I pull her into my chest, needing her as close as possible. As I assumed she would, she meets me match for match. Swipe for swipe. Touch for touch.

I worried she'd be a hard one to forget if I took us over this line, and now I know that's true. But my new philosophy is to take what I want. And I want Phoenix Bailey.

The crunch of gravel on my driveway stops us all too soon. I rest my forehead on hers, and she's yet to disentangle herself from my hold.

"Who the hell is that?" I grumble.

We're shielded enough that we can see the car, but the people in the car can't see us.

"My grandma," she says with disappointment and shakes her head, sliding out of my hold. "I forgot that I told Kingston to come by so we could practice. I have no idea what she's doing here."

We walk to the garage opening and watch as her grandma steps out of her giant Cadillac, along with an auburn-haired woman and a large man with the same dark hair as Phoenix. I guess they're making this visit a family affair?

"Juno. Kingston."

That's Kingston? I didn't think a guy who looks as rough as him would have that much sentimental longing in his tone when he sings.

"The house is beautiful, Griffin." The grandmother I met at the bakery approaches us while the other two stare at the house in awe. This is nothing compared to my house in LA.

"Thank you. They did a great job."

"Griffin, you remember my grandma, Dori," Phoenix introduces us.

I glance down to make sure I've calmed down. Thankfully, the appearance of a grandma tends to do that. "Pleasure to see you again."

I put out my hand, but Dori waves it away and hugs me. My arms loosely hang off her body and I kiss her cheek as I would my own grandma.

"And this is my sister Juno and my brother Kingston."

I extend my hand to each of them and they shake it.

"Great voice," I say to Kingston, and a red tint colors his cheeks.

"I prefer to be part of the group, but Grandma Dori had other ideas." He side-glances her and sighs.

"Well, you'll do a great job. I'm not worried," Dori says.

"Phoenix said you wanted to work with us on the song?" Kingston says.

I nod like I was expecting him.

"How exciting that a famous producer is going to work with you, Phoenix." Juno's hands come together in a little clap.

Phoenix looks at me.

"Where are my manners? Come in. Would you like a drink?"

"Oh, I almost forgot. Juno, get the donuts." Grandma Dori walks by me toward the narrow opening between my truck and the side of the garage.

"Sure thing." Juno rolls her eyes but heads back to the car where she retrieves a box of donuts.

Kingston looks around the ceiling and walls. "You should have sprinklers in the garage."

"You're not on duty," Phoenix says and follows her grandma into the house.

"It's in my oath." He continues to look around. "Are you sure your builder put in the right outlets in here in case you're running bigger equipment? If the load is bigger than what it's designed for, it can be a fire hazard."

"I'd have to ask Cedric," I say.

"Oh, you used Cedric?" He appears impressed. Hopefully, that means Cedric is reliable. "I'm sure you're in good hands." He claps his hand on my shoulder and smiles at me, walking into the house after Juno.

Phoenix is already making a pot of coffee. I glance to the clock to find it's only twelve-thirty. It feels like it's been forever since Maverick left for school this morning.

"Why are you driving?" Phoenix presumably asks her grandma, but when she turns around, Dori's nowhere to be found. Appearing unsurprised, Phoenix looks at Juno. "Why are you letting her drive?"

"Because the sheriff said after her cataract surgery, she could try again for her license. And guess what?"

Phoenix's mouth hangs open. "No way."

Juno thumbs toward Kingston behind her. "He prepped her."

"Kingston!"

He shrugs. "She deserves the freedom. Don't worry. We practiced."

"Where is she?" I whisper to Phoenix.

"I'll be back." She walks into the other room. "*Grandma!*"

"You two seem to be working well together," Juno says.

"It's only been a few weeks, but so far so good," I say.

"Did Phoenix tell you what I do for a living?"

I grab two coffee mugs and look over my shoulder at her. "She didn't."

"Don't do it, Juno," Kingston says.

"I'm a matchmaker."

Since the coffee is still brewing, I walk over to the island where Juno slides her card across to me. Sure as shit, it says professional matchmaker. Is that a thing in a day and age where you can swipe left or right?

"I'm always looking for bachelors. Then again, I'm looking for women mostly since Alaska has more men than women. But..." She waves mid-thought like that doesn't matter. "Anyway, want to get on my list?"

Kingston shakes his head behind her.

I shift under the weight of her gaze. "Um. I'm not really looking right now."

"Why not? I mean, if you don't mind me asking."

"Juno," Kingston says with warning in his voice and shoots me an expression to say he's sorry.

"Truth is, my sole focus is on my son at the moment. I wouldn't be able to give one hundred percent to a relationship."

"Then I suggest you stop locking lips with my little sister."

Huh. I guess we weren't as hidden as I thought.

SEVENTEEN

Phoenix

"Grandma, you cannot be in his bedroom," I whisper, finding her looking through Griffin's closet.

"I just wanted to snap a picture of his Grammy. We don't know anyone else with one of those. The most Ethel's son has done is buy a used Tesla."

"Why must you continue to be in competition with your best friend?" I ask, weaving my arm through hers. "You could've just asked. He has them downstairs."

"Them? Oh, I can't wait to show Ethel that my grand-daughter is working for a multiple Grammy winner." She allows me to lead her out of Griffin's room, but not before his scent surrounds me. My knees weaken with the thought that I was *this* close to lying down with him on that bed.

Damn family.

"Tell me again why you compete with Ethel?"

"Because what else do we have to do? Hello? We're old and live in a retirement facility. It keeps our minds fresh." She taps her temple as I hold her hand going down the open wooden staircase. "Why isn't there any carpeting in this house? It's going to be cold in the winter."

"Let Griffin worry about that."

We reach the downstairs and I notice that Griffin's hair is now pulled back and the flush that was on his face is gone. Kingston eyes me with a look that says sorry. Ugh. What has Juno done?

"Griffin, do you mind if I show my grandma your Grammys?"

He hands two cups of coffee to my siblings and comes our way. "Let me show you."

"I want to see too." Kingston leaves the kitchen and Juno's gaze remains on me.

"Nailing the boss isn't going to get you a record deal," she whispers then sips her coffee as though she's not trying to get up in my business.

"I'm not nailing the boss," I whisper-shout. I walk over to the coffeemaker and pour Grandma Dori a cup, then I grab the milk out of the fridge to add to her coffee.

"Is that only because we showed up?" She leans over the island. "Do not sleep with him to get ahead."

"I'm not sleeping with him to get ahead." I shake my head at my sister. Of course she thinks I'd do that. My family always thinks the worst of me.

She looks down her nose at me. "Then why are you kissing him in the garage?"

I don't know whether it's that she picked matchmaker as her career or the fact that she's Grandma Dori's new side-kick now that Savannah is with Liam and I'm busy, but Juno's the worst person who could've seen that kiss.

Actually, I take that back. Denver would be the worst.

"Don't say anything to Denver," I say.

Her face distorts as though that's the last thing I should be worried about.

"I'm serious," I whisper-shout.

"Be careful," Griffin says from the other room.

My gaze shoots to the family room where Kingston grabs the Grammy from Grandma Dori.

"Heavier than I thought," she says, appearing even more impressed. "Kingston, take a picture of me and Griffin."

Kingston hands Griffin the Grammy, and Griffin puts it back in the case next to his others.

Juno snapping her fingers in front of my face pulls my attention away. "Stop staring at him."

"I'm twenty-two. I can handle this myself."

"Really? Does he know you were in LA two years ago? Or how you schemed to get this job?"

I lower my hands to get her to shut up. "What does that have to do with anything?"

"Because if you're kissing him and it's not to get ahead, it's either because you haven't thought it through and you're going on what you want physically, which is destined to blow up, *or* you're entering into a real relationship. And if it was a real relationship, he'd know all about what I just mentioned."

Damn Juno. I hate the way she's so insightful about everyone's life but her own.

"How's Colton?" I sneer.

"What?"

"Colton. The man you should be entering into a serious relationship with."

She rolls her eyes and blows out a breath like she used to do when she was sixteen and I was her annoying little sister. "If you must know, he went out on a date the other night."

My eyes widen. "And how do you feel about that?"

"Fine. Why would I care?"

"Gee, I have no idea why that might bother you." I roll my eyes.

"This whole family is so annoying sometimes. Men and women can be friends. Not that you and Griffin are a great example of that. It's been a month and you're already sucking face in the garage."

"Sucking face? How old are you?"

Both of us look into the other room. Griffin has his guitar out, and Kingston is sitting next to him. Grandma Dori is smiling from the chair, phone out.

"Oh Jesus." I leave Juno and her need to give every family member advice when she should be worried about losing the man she's been meant to marry since preschool. In the family room, I ask, "What's going on?"

Griffin smiles at me. Kingston groans and shoots me a look to say, "This is why I fight fires, to keep me from doing shit like this."

"Griffin said I could observe him work with you and Kingston." Grandma Dori crosses her arms over her flowered purse and crosses her ankles, leaning back into the chair, getting comfortable.

Griffin pats the spot next to him. "Come on over."

Shivers run up my spine, though I'd rather him do that same thing when three members of my family aren't present.

I sit on the couch, and Griffin strums the guitar. "Okay, Phoenix is going to sing the first part." He pulls out the song sheets he must've printed earlier.

Kingston looks at his and puts it on the table. He's not even nervous, but then again, what does he have to worry about? This isn't his dream.

"I need to stand." I get up, step over Griffin's legs, and shake out my arms, trying to dispel some of the nerves that are suddenly bearing down on me.

Juno takes a seat on the chaise part of the couch with her arms crossed.

I try to channel everything Griffin and I spoke about this morning on the hike. The fact that I ran from this town. How freeing it felt to be in LA, where no one knew me. All the shit I've had to hear people say over the years. Rumors that don't hold a hint of truth.

When I open my mouth, my voice cracks.

Griffin stops. "Water?"

I shake my head and clear my throat. I've been lax on my vocal exercises since I moved in here. "Let me just run through a quick vocal warm-up." I take a few minutes to warm up my voice while everyone watches on. "Okay." I signal for him to start over.

Griffin plays the song on his guitar, and I tap the beat on my fingers against my thighs.

"I can't go for a ride..." I continue singing, hardly having to go off the sheet music.

Kingston comes in with his deep rasp that blends perfectly with mine. I allow the images of my past to float to the surface. The pain, the good, the indifferent. My parents, my siblings, my friends. The good and the bad weave together while the lyrics belt out of me. When there's an instrumental break, I soak in the room and see Grandma Dori's wide smile. She's never showed much interest in my singing, so I take it as a good sign.

The song draws to a close and Griffin smiles at me, taking out a pen and scribbling a note on both of our sheets.

"Try this." He points at the section in question. "You need to be louder here, Phoenix. Drown him out. And here." He touches his pen to paper again. "Kingston, you need more control. Let it come and don't waver. I can give you a few exercises to help with that."

We go through the song three more times, each time Griffin tweaking us to be the perfect blend of opposites.

When we take a break, I head to the kitchen and make myself a cup of tea.

"The lyrics resonate with you," Griffin says to Kingston.

He looks up from his phone and shrugs.

"Seriously?" Juno shakes her head. "It's like the song was written for him and his high school crush."

"It is not. It's totally Liam and Savannah," Kingston grumbles.

"How is Stella?" Grandma Dori asks, mentioning she-who-shall-not-be-named. She's never one to beat around the bush. "I heard she was thinking about returning home but decided not to at the last minute."

"I don't talk to her anymore." Kingston's fingers fly on the screen of his phone.

"It's good that you feel the words," Griffin says. "A song with meaning will get people more emotionally drawn in. I've been trying with your sister—"

I cut my finger across my throat at Griffin when I enter the family room.

"Phoenix doesn't have a lot of emotions," Kingston says.

I slap his head as I walk by. "That's rich coming from the guy who runs away."

"So do you," Kingston counters.

I instinctively glance at Griffin, who only seems to enjoy our banter.

"Okay, we should go." Grandma Dori stands.

"Kingston, how about you come over tomorrow night?" Griffin asks.

Kingston looks at me. "Sure. I start shift in a couple hours, so I can come here before I crash for the night."

"Perfect."

I set down my tea, and Griffin stands to walk them to the front door. After hugs and kisses on the cheek, Grandma Dori backs out of the driveway. We watch her retreat and don't miss her taking out Griffin's mailbox.

"Sorry," I say as she drives away without even knowing she did it. Either that or she's ignoring it.

He laughs. "It's okay. That can be my next project after the sink." He shuts the front door and cages me against it. "We have a bit before you have to pick up Maverick. What should we do with our time?"

I bite my lip, doing my best to push Juno's words out of my mind. It's not as if Griffin has confessed his love to me or divulged all his deepest dark secrets. He hasn't told me anything about his ex-wife or whether the rumors are true about her and his partner.

Why does it feel as though I'd be betraying him if I sleep with him?

I put my hand on his chest. "We can't." I duck under his arm and free myself, heading to the kitchen. "Not until you know something."

My stomach twists because I could be ruining everything by telling him the whole truth. Where is this conscience coming from? It's highly inconvenient.

"You do know this isn't a 'let's start a relationship' thing, right? You don't have to tell me anything other than if you're on the pill and if you've been tested." He follows me into the kitchen.

Damn Juno. Why did she have to show up and give me her little speech?

"I know, but..."

He laughs and climbs onto the breakfast stool. "We're adults. You don't need anyone's permission."

I wonder if he noticed Juno's and my somewhat heated conversation.

Is it kind of sad that I thought more of Griffin Thorne? That maybe he wasn't a douche who slept with people to get them out of his system? Am I going to be forgotten tomorrow or replaced by someone else he'd like to sleep with? I thought I knew the man, but maybe I was wrong.

"You should know that I went to LA after I graduated high school. I tried to make it for two years and returned home when I couldn't. I knew who you were when we met, and I knew you were looking for a nanny. Those kids in the bakery are my nieces and nephew. I've never been a nanny before, and I lied to you that night. I did hope that you would discover me."

The flirtatious gleam that was sparkling in his eyes fades, and his gaze turns cold as though he's been doused by an ice bucket. He stands. Somehow, I didn't realize until right now the height difference between us.

When he heads over to me, I have no idea if he's going to tell me to get out or kiss me. I have to grip the countertop when he leans into me.

"Pack up your stuff and leave." Then he walks out of the room. A door slams shut seconds later.

Damn it, I knew not to listen to Juno.

EIGHTEEN

Griffin

On my way to pick up Maverick, I retrace how things went from normal to awesome to shitty, back to awesome and eventually landed in the shitter. I can't believe she lied to me. After I asked her point-blank. You'd think she was from LA to be able to look me in the eye like that and lie.

Now I have to tell Maverick that Phoenix is no longer his nanny.

I park in the pick-up line and spot Principal Nutters walking down the sidewalk with Maverick at his side. You've got to be fucking kidding me.

Maverick opens the back door.

I roll down the window on the passenger side. "What now?"

"I thought it would be Phoenix picking him up." Principal Nutters peers into the truck as though she's hiding and ready to pop out and surprise him.

"Not today."

"Well, I just wanted to tell her she was right. I talked with a few other kids who were also paying Chad Billings. No worries about Maverick taking the fall. Chad has been suspended for five days. The teacher and lunch aides are now aware of what was going on and will keep a close eye on the situation when he returns to school."

"Thank you, Principal—"

"Kevin, please."

"Thank you, Kevin." I reach my hand out and lean across to the passenger side, and we shake hands.

"Thank Phoenix for me. If she hadn't told me, I'm not sure how long Chad would have gotten away with this."

"Sure thing." No need for the principal to know that Phoenix is no longer involved in our lives.

"See you tomorrow, Maverick." He smiles into the back seat, and Maverick tightly smiles back at him but thankfully doesn't say anything. Principal Nutters looks through the window. "Looks like the line is moving."

I follow his vision. "I better go before I get honked at."

He backs away from the truck, and I roll up the window while driving around the circular drive.

"Where's Phoenix?" Maverick asks.

I figure this is a conversation best had over ice cream. I look at him through the rearview mirror. "How about we go get a snack?"

"Sure. Will Phoenix be there?"

"We'll talk about that after we get a snack."

"Why? You're not mad because she went and told Principal Nutters, are you? Or because she kept my secret?" His nervousness of the unknown shines through.

I haven't seen this side of him since Maggie and I split. The repercussions of having divorced parents. Phoenix was a part of his life, and now she's abruptly left

—just like Maggie did. I'm a shitty father for not realizing this.

"No. I'm not mad at her for that."

"Then where is she?"

I pull alongside the road and park the truck, turning to look at him. "She's not going to be your nanny anymore."

"Why?" His eyes widen and he crosses his arms.

"We had a disagreement, and I think it's better this way."

He stares out the window. "I liked her. She stuck up for me today! She made things fun. We had dance parties after school. And she was going to take me to the park today."

The park? I didn't even know he enjoyed the park still.

"I'll take you to the park," I say.

"And what? You'll just sit there."

"Watch it. I know you're upset, but I'm still your father."

"You take everything good away from me! What kind of father does that? You took me from LA. My school. My friends. My mom. Phoenix is all I had here. And now you took her from me too!" He looks out the window.

It's clear that he's closed himself off for now, so I face forward and put the truck in gear. I'd tell him the truth, but I'm not sure he'd care. She didn't lie to him. She lied to me, and I was too blind to see through the lie.

What kind of woman with talent like Phoenix wants to live in a small town, working as a nanny? I was the dumbass from the beginning.

WE PULL into our driveway after Maverick refused to get out of the truck to get ice cream. I tried the park and he wouldn't do that either. The truck is barely in park before Maverick opens the door, gets out, then slams it shut before running into the house.

I remain in the driver's seat, unsure what my next move will be, until a loud engine causes me to glance in my rearview mirror. Denver's truck is roaring up the driveway.

I squeeze my eyes shut for a second. *Fuck.* Somehow, the thought that Denver might find out about all this slipped my mind. I told him I'd stay away from his sister. That he could trust me. But at some point, my dick took over and I pushed away all thoughts of my promise. There's no way he knows that though. He's probably here because I fired her. I guess I have to decide now whether I want to tell him all the rest.

I climb out of my truck and Denver leaves his. We stand silent for a moment, staring each other down. I've never seen Denver pissed off, but it's clear he is right now.

"What the hell, Griffin?"

I walk out of my garage. "I'm sorry."

"Are you fucking my sister?"

"No. No." Shit, I thought for sure he was here because I fired her. How does he know I even entertained thoughts of having his sister? She doesn't strike me as the kind of person who would tell him, but then again, I fired her.

"Juno told me she saw you guys kissing." His hands fist at his sides.

I sit on the rear bumper of my truck. "I know you don't owe me anything, but can you keep it down? Maverick is home."

"Explain." He lowers his voice, which I hope means he doesn't want this to be the demise of our friendship.

"There's no explanation. I shouldn't have kissed her. I

shouldn't have touched her. I never thought... I never meant to..."

"Struggling for words?" He crosses his arms and widens his stance. Denver's probably used to intimidating people.

"All I can say is I'm sorry. I really am. But you don't have to worry about anything else happening because I let her go this afternoon." I concentrate on my hands instead of on Denver because I feel like a total asshole at the moment.

"Let me get this straight. You kissed her... and then you fired her? Please don't tell me it's because she wouldn't sleep with you."

My head flies up. "What? Are you insane? Do you not know me at all?"

I know Denver and I haven't known each other our whole lives and we haven't shared a ton of shit, but I like to think we know enough of what to expect of one another.

"Well, you told me you wouldn't touch my sister, and you did."

Okay, he's got me there. Shit. Maybe I should just move back to LA where it takes more than only a few hours before everyone knows your business.

"I know and I'm sorry." I run my hand through my hair. "I wasn't thinking."

"You were thinking, just with the wrong head." Denver makes his way to the front porch and takes a seat in one of the Adirondack chairs. I follow his lead and take the other chair. "Truth is, I worried this would happen. Phoenix is..."

I wait for him to fill the quiet space. I never understood why Denver didn't want Phoenix to be my nanny. Why, if she was so qualified, he didn't suggest her to me himself. Now that Phoenix has confessed her lie to me, I realize that it was because he knew the truth.

"She's persistent. She's headstrong. When she gets something in that head of hers…"

"You knew why she wanted to be Maverick's nanny." It's not a question, it's a statement.

He looks at me, sorrow in his eyes. With one solid nod, he looks away. "I told her not to, but she's been begging me for years to introduce you two. She found out you needed a nanny, and I'm not sure what she expected to accomplish, but she would've done just about anything to have you hear her sing."

He stands and paces in front of me. I see that day we had the conversation about Phoenix being Maverick's nanny in a new light. How pissed he was. It wasn't at me or even that he worried I might have sex with her. It was because he knew she wasn't qualified to watch Maverick. He knew she was doing it for all the wrong reasons.

I want to be pissed off, but he had to choose between his loyalty to me and his sister. How could he choose? I'm not sure I would've done anything differently than he did.

"Why me? She's got the voice to make it. Surely she could try to go on one of those reality television shows and be heard?"

"I'm not sure. It wasn't easy for her to convince our brother to allow her to abandon college to pursue a career in singing. It took a lot for her to come back from LA. I think she's hesitant to put herself out there now. As shitty as this will sound to you, as much as I wanted to keep her away from you, I also hoped you'd get her connected to the right people. She pisses me off, but she's my sister and I want her to be happy. It always felt like a double-edged sword."

"And being a star would make her happy?"

He huffs. "My dad used to say she was meant for the spotlight. If you ever met Sedona, you'd see how opposite identical twins can be. She's the extrovert and Sedona the introvert."

The mention of his parents brings to mind what I learned from Phoenix about their past. "I'm sorry about your parents. You never said anything."

He shrugs. "Not much to tell. They died. It sucks."

I'm not going to dive into that conversation right now, since he clearly doesn't want to.

"So you fired her after you found out she had her sights set on you?" he asks.

I lean farther back into the chair. "Basically."

He blows out a long breath. "If it means anything, when I confronted her, she told me she respected that you were out of the music industry, but she couldn't pass up the opportunity for the money you were going to pay her. She planned to turn in her notice after the summer and use the money to go back to LA." He crosses his leg and rests his ankle on his knee. "It doesn't mean much, but she's not a bad person. She's just persistent as hell. Phoenix doesn't mean to hurt people, but she can have tunnel vision when she has a goal in mind." His phone dings in his pocket, and he pulls it out.

While he's dealing with whoever is on the phone, I contemplate the past few weeks. Phoenix was good to Maverick and good to me. I have no doubt that if Denver had thought Phoenix couldn't handle an eight-year-old, he would have told me the truth. And it was purely coincidence that I heard her sing, and I'm the one who pushed to work with her.

Denver says she's going back to LA to pursue a singing career no matter what. I have the connections to help her avoid all the sleazy people who would take advantage of her. My own path toward success travels through my mind.

I don't want that for Phoenix, even if she did piss me off. I remember what it was like to be that desperate. Can I really fault her? If I was twenty-two again, and in her position, wouldn't I have done the same thing?

Shit. Did I overreact?

If I can do anything for Denver as a repayment for kissing his sister when I said I wouldn't, I can do this. Van and Trey could be huge for Phoenix.

"No, I'm not doing it," Denver says into the phone, then he's quiet for a second. "Because I can't fucking sing! When is he gonna be back?" He pulls the phone away from his face for a second. "Kingston got called out to a wildfire."

There are only two days left before the Founder's Day Parade.

I pull out my phone and text Phoenix.

Me: *Can we talk?*

Denver hangs up and pockets his phone. "Hopefully, he's back in time. That would suck."

"Listen, man, I'm sorry. Truth is, I'm really attracted to your sister, but I'll table that. I have two industry friends coming to town this weekend, and I'll make sure they hear Phoenix sing. I'll help her in any way I can, because she's got the voice, she just needs the connections to get her where she should be."

He stares at me for so long, I dodge his gaze.

"Do you only want to sleep with her? Be straight with me."

I didn't really think about what I wanted when it was all happening—other than her under me—which wasn't fair to either of us. I thought we were on the same page, but maybe we weren't. It's easy to forget that I have eleven years on

Phoenix. Hearing everything Denver has said, I feel like the slimeball who took advantage of her.

"In the moment, I did, but I think maybe there's something more there. I just didn't realize it. But it doesn't matter. My rule will be in place if I'm working with her. I don't sleep with the artists. Makes shit complicated."

He nods. "You're a good guy. My sister is young, but she's an adult—as hard as that is for me to see sometimes. Maybe I'm sentimental because of Cleo, but I don't want to be the reason two people aren't together, so if there's something more, you don't need my permission. Just remember that if you fuck her over, you can expect a late-night visit from me for an ass-kicking."

I laugh. "Noted."

"Then it's settled. I gotta go tell Cleo I'm not being arrested for assault and battery." He chuckles and stands, then puts out his hand.

I rise up from the chair and shake his hand. "Thanks for understanding."

He turns around and stalks back to his truck. "I'm the king of fuckups, Grif, so I get it. If you're looking for her, she's at Juno's."

A smirk is splashed on his face as he starts his truck and backs out of my driveway.

Once he's gone, I pull out my phone. Nothing from Phoenix yet.

Maybe that's good, because it gives me time to process my feelings toward her. Was it really only her looks that made me want to sleep with her, or was it something more? I should have an answer to that before we move on. I need to be sure, because if it's the latter, nothing can happen between us. But if it's the former, then you bet your ass I'm gonna make sure something happens.

NINETEEN

Phoenix

"Kingston," I plead.

"Sorry, Phoenix. I might have to fly into the bush today or tomorrow. I hate to miss Founder's Day, but I think the people of Granger would prefer me doing everything I can to save their town rather than singing in a parade."

"I have to stand out there on the float by myself now."

"I'll let you know if it changes, but you'll need a miracle for me to be there."

I sigh and pace Juno's apartment. She's in the kitchen, pouring the Pringles container upside down to get out the last of the chips.

"Stay safe, Kingston. That's what's most important."

"Hey, it's me. I always do." He laughs and says hello to some guy in the background. "Try not to sleep with the music producer."

"How did you hear about that?"

"You know there are eyes everywhere in that town."

Kingston speaks the truth, and he's learned from personal experience. This town torments him as much as me, but for different reasons. I'm surprised he hasn't moved away. If the reason he hasn't is what I think it is, it's romantic as hell and so very non-Kingston. Which means I'm probably completely wrong.

"You know that Griffin hasn't made it into Buzz Wheel once since he got to town?" I say. "Isn't that odd?"

"Not odd." Juno joins me on the couch. "If someone reports him here and news gets out, it could bring people into the town and who wants that?"

"Yeah, but he was in it before. Like, a long time ago," I say.

"Yeah, but now he lives here. It's different," she says.

I study Juno for a second. "Are you the Buzz Wheel author?"

"Yeah, between trying to fix people up, I spread our family gossip."

"She sounds guilty. Go give her the third degree. I gotta go," Kingston says with a chuckle. "Love you, sis. Sorry about the singing thing."

"Love you. Don't worry about it, just be safe."

We hang up, and Juno stretches her legs out onto the table. "Let's go eat."

"You just ate Pringles."

"Crumbs. There were crumbs. Come on, let's go binge-eat to overshadow our heartbreak." She stands and puts her purse crosswise over her body.

"What do you mean *our*? Do you have heartbreak?"

She guffaws. "I mean your."

"Oh that's right, Colton was going on a date last we spoke." I get up from the couch and grab my purse.

"It's not me. It's you. I don't care if Colton is going on a date. It's about time. He fills all my nights on the weekends."

I roll my eyes, but I could definitely use some junk food to get me through this. I wonder how Maverick took the news when Griffin picked him up? I promised him we'd go to the park today after school. There was one part of today when I thought Griffin and I could take him together. I had visions of the two of us sitting on the park bench, his fingers secretly brushing up against mine.

"I'm stupid, right?" I ask, meeting her at the door.

"You're a woman. We all need a little wooing even if it's not serious and woo isn't asking if you're on the pill."

"I never pegged him like that, you know?" I stand at the top of the stairs of her apartment.

Juno and Kingston's apartment is in the heart of Lake Starlight's small downtown and over Juno's matchmaking office.

"Men are just wolves in sheep's clothing." She leads us out the door and onto Main Street. Two minutes later, we walk into Lard Have Mercy. Juno slides into the far booth. "Hey, Karen."

I slide in on the other side.

Karen, our sister-in-law Holly's mom, comes over and holds up two menus. "Do you girls need 'em?"

Juno looks at me, and I answer for us both. "Nope. Fries, cheeseburgers, and shakes."

Juno raises her hand. "Strawberry."

"Chocolate." I raise my hand.

Karen laughs and tucks the menus under her arm. "What sorrows are we drowning today?"

"How do you know we're drowning our sorrows?" I ask.

"A mother's hunch." She shrugs.

Juno's smile falls and she leans over the table, lowering her voice. "How are things going?"

Karen's smile dims and I wonder what I'm missing. Is something wrong with Karen? Or my uncle Brian? Did they break up? Have I really been stuck in a Griffin Thorne bubble that long?

Karen puts her hand on Juno's and squeezes. "I pray every night. But she was in here earlier, drowning her sorrows with turtle pie."

Juno leans back and shakes her head. "I'll stop by this week and try to cheer her up."

"She'd love that. Let me get your orders going."

Karen leaves and I say through clenched teeth, "What's going on? Who's drowning in turtle pie?"

"Holly." Juno looks around, and since we're in the back, there's no one in the booth behind me. "She and Austin have upped their efforts at trying to get pregnant."

"Like fertility treatments?" I whisper.

She nods. "Austin is giving her shots now. They're pretty private about the whole thing."

"How come no one told me?"

"You haven't come to the girl whine and dine nights in a while."

She's right. All they talk about is marriage and my brothers and sex. And who wants to imagine their siblings having sex? I had to stop going when Cleo explained how Denver's appetite was never quenched. I heard enough living with them. I didn't need explicit details so I could envision what was going on behind the bedroom door.

"I've been busy," I say in my defense.

I feel shitty for not knowing about Austin and Holly. I gave her so much shit when I was seventeen and they were getting together. She's always been nothing but great to me.

No one ever said so, but I'm sure she had something to do with Austin letting me go to California after high school. And how do I thank her? By having no idea what she's going through.

"And Harley still feels guilty because Rome blinks at her and she's popping out another Bailey."

"She's pregnant again?"

Juno laughs and shakes her head. "No, but you figure Phoebe is what, seven months now? It could be any time." She sobers. "Not that I'm making light of the situation. I feel horrible, and there's no explanation for the infertility. The doctor told them to go on vacation and see if the relaxation helps. Rekindle their love."

"They're not having problems, are they?"

"You really need to get to the whine and dine nights."

"I'll be at the next one, promise."

She nods with her lips pressed together, clearly not believing me. I wouldn't either. "Let's talk about you."

"There's nothing much to say. I told him the truth."

"And he kicked you out." Her gaze focuses on the window behind me for a moment then lands back on me.

"Yep. End of story. But it's fine. I'm going to sing at the Founder's Day Parade, then I'll come up with Plan B. He's not going to stop me."

"I'm not worried about you becoming a singer. I'm worried about how you fell for your boss." She glances behind me again.

"That's being a tad dramatic."

"Come on, Phoenix. You have so many people fooled in this town, but I'm your sister. You don't sleep with men just to sleep with them. That's not you."

"What? You have no idea what you're talking about." I glance over at Karen, who's helping a customer at the counter. We need our food stat so Juno will shut her mouth and curb her line of thinking.

"I do know what I'm talking about, and that's why you're looking for the food."

"I'm starving." She kicks me under the table. "Ouch."

"It's me. Juno. You can trust me. Come on."

I stare across the booth. I'm not up for reliving the past right now. As sad as it is, Juno is partially correct. I lost my virginity in LA to a douche who was a struggling artist like me.

"You like Griffin?" she asks when I don't say anything.

I'm quiet for a minute before I answer. "I did."

"For what he could do for you?"

"No. At first that's what it was about, but I knew before I took the job that he'd quit the music business. Then after I started working for him, I figured out how sweet he is." Finally the truth slides out. I need someone to confide in, and Sedona isn't back until late tonight when her flight comes in. "He's almost unsure of himself, and I wanted to know why. Like, why is a man with so much success hell-bent on installing a sink himself?"

She shrugs. "You mentioned that article. Sometimes other people's opinions change someone. I know they never change you, but for others, it's important they're liked."

She's got that part of me all wrong. Ever since I returned from LA, I've doubted myself more than I ever have. In high school, I thought I would be Lake Starlight's star. The one who came back to town and they had a parade for. Oh, how naive I was. Instead, I sneaked into town in an Uber and hid out at my childhood home, imposing on my brother and his soon-to-be wife.

"I think you should talk to him," Juno says.

I think back to the texts Griffin has sent me. "No. It

would do no good. He had a chance to hear me out, but he wouldn't. Moved from wanting in my pants to kicking me out the door in sixty seconds flat."

Karen comes over and slides the milkshakes in front of us. Neither of us wait before sucking the thick, cold deliciousness through the straw.

"So good," we say in unison and smile over our straws.

Juno's gaze detours to the window once more, and I turn to see what has her so distracted.

Colton is there, talking to a woman. They're close enough that it looks like they might kiss.

"Um... Juno?"

She tears her gaze away. "Did I tell you that Owen came to me to fix him up?"

I let go of the fact that she's jealous and maybe nursing heartache. "No, you didn't."

Her fake bravado shines through as she dramatically tells me about how Kingston's frenemy came in and said he had to date someone to get Stella off his mind. I let her forget her problems because she's letting me forget mine for now.

TWENTY

Griffin

The morning of the Founder's Day Parade, I park the truck on a side street downtown, and we all file out. Van teases Maverick about whether or not he has a girlfriend while Trey tries to get Van to lay off. Both guys arrived last night, and Van, having a huge-ass mouth, told Trey about Phoenix. So after Maverick went to bed, a whole pile of questions landed in my lap, most of which I didn't have any good answers for.

Maverick is still giving me the silent treatment and giving it well. He gets that from my ex-wife. My texts to Phoenix are still unanswered. Apparently, she does the silent treatment well too.

"This place is crazy," Trey says when we round the corner of Main Street to find wall-to-wall people standing on each side of the road.

There are kids on parents' shoulders, others sitting eagerly on the curb while the parents talk to one another. We end up finding a place closer to the beginning of the parade route since it seems like most people prefer the end.

Van looks around. "This is quaint. Not."

"Founder's Day tends to bring out everyone in Lake Starlight and a few surrounding towns. Plus, it's finally spring and everyone has to get outside before they murder their loved ones," the woman with the dark bob next to us says with a smile. "I'm Francie, and this is my husband, Jack. He owns Hammer Time Hardware." She points at where it's located behind us.

"She likes to pimp me out," the man by her side, who I assume must be Jack, says.

"Be careful where you say that. Where we come from, that has a very different meaning." Trey sticks out his hand. "Trey, good to meet you."

"You're Maverick, right?" the little girl at Francie's side asks.

"Yeah. You're Kayla, right?"

She nods.

"Oh, this is my niece. You're in the third grade too?" Francie asks Maverick.

"Yeah."

Jack pushes back and forth a double stroller with what I think are two toddlers inside. Francie keeps Kayla and Maverick occupied with questions about teachers and favorite classes and Principal Nutters.

"Nutters?" Van asks.

"No way," Trey chimes in.

"Yep." I'm still bummed Phoenix and I never got to joke about that.

"You're in for a special treat. I heard that the Bailey float is passing out candy this year," Francie says with enthusiasm to the kids.

"I heard that too." Maverick points at himself.

"I have the intel because this guy is Austin Bailey's best friend. How did you find out?" Francie asks in a joking manner that has Kayla laughing and Maverick eager to tell her how he's in the know.

"Phoenix is my nanny." I can't help but notice how he puffs out his chest when he says it.

Francie's eyes shoot up to me. She's definitely got the intel because she casts her gaze over me. Not in a 'I want to strip you down' way, more in a 'oh, so you're the one' way. Great.

She recovers quickly. "Phoenix? Why didn't you say so? I've known her since she was younger than you. I love her."

"We are talking about Phoenix Bailey, right?" Jack pipes in, but his smile says he's joking. "I'm kidding." His eyes lock with mine. "She's like my little sister."

I nod. God, could I feel any more awkward right now? How much do they know?

Van and Trey crack up next to me.

"You're not making a very good reputation in this town," Van says so just I can hear him.

"Her brother Kingston was supposed to sing with her today, but he fights fires in the bush and got called away. She has to sing all by herself up there on the float." Francie's speaking to the kids, but all us adults know she's really speaking to me. "That's scary, huh?"

Maverick looks at Kayla. "Yeah."

Van and Trey look at me. "Yeah," they say in unison.

Then Trey adds, "Someone should really help her out."

My head falls back. "What can I do?"

"She won't answer your calls, right?" Van asks.

"No."

"You've got a voice, don't pretend you don't," Trey says.

"I can't *sing* sing."

"You can do backup, don't give us that excuse." Van pats me on the back. "We've got Maverick." He winks.

I shake my head, and my gaze lands on Francie, who's taking in our conversation. She raises her eyebrows. Damn, why did I move to a small town?

"Maverick, you stay with Uncle Van and Uncle Trey, okay?" I look around the crowd.

"They set up on Acorn," Francie says, pointing down the road.

"Corner of Acorn and Maple," Jack adds.

"Thanks."

"You'll have to hurry though."

I wave to Francie. She can stop pushing now. Message received loud and clear. I've been an ass and I'm going to have to pay for my sins with public embarrassment.

I jog past the mass of people to side streets littered with floats. Weaving through a group of six drummers and dodging five color guard flags, I finally catch a glimpse of Phoenix with her back to me, talking to some guy. Since I'm able to keep an eye on her, I slow down to a walk to get some much-needed oxygen.

"Hi, Griffin," Ethel, I believe, says and waves from the float beside me. She's dressed as a witch, and I read the sign on the float for the library—Professor Minerva McGonagall from *Harry Potter*. She tips her huge black, wide-brimmed hat.

"Perfect fit." I wink, and she smiles, a slight blush appearing on her cheeks. Looking at the float, I see a little Harry Potter and Hermione eating the candy from a bowl.

Turning my vision back down the street to Phoenix, my stomach drops when the spot she was in is vacant. I scour the area, but what I find only makes my stomach drop farther. She's pressed to a brick wall with some guy caging her in. They're in a heated conversation and his lips are only millimeters from hers.

My jaw hangs open as I try to wrap my thoughts around the visual. I mean, we weren't a couple, so I can't be upset that she's with another guy, can I? She was insulted by my approach to a casual fling. And now she's with some other guy? I think I have reason enough to storm over there and yank him away from my girl.

Shit. I run a hand through my long hair. She's not *my* girl. Hot energy zaps through my body while my hands twitch with the urge to beat the shit out of the guy who's now kissing her neck. She giggles and—yeah, this is not a normal reaction if you don't care about the person. Is this jealousy?

Two large hands clasp my shoulders and swivel me around in the other direction.

"That's Sedona and her boyfriend, Jamison," Denver says. He moves me to the side. "This is the girl you're looking for."

As if she knows, Phoenix looks up from the papers in her hand to find me staring at her. She quickly diverts her attention back to the papers.

"Just so you know, you would have a better chance if it was Sedona you wanted forgiveness from." Denver laughs.

Cleo comes over to him, sliding her hands around his waist. "Hey Griffin."

"Cleo." I nod hello.

"I'm going to head to the street to watch."

He gives her a chaste kiss on the lips. "Soon you'll be on that float with us."

She shakes her head. "Don't go marrying me just to secure my spot on the float."

"That wouldn't be why, and you know it," he says.

She looks at him adoringly. "Throw me a Tootsie Roll?"

"You can have my Tootsie Roll when we get home tonight," he says with a grin.

She giggles and rolls her eyes. "You're so cheesy."

"You love it." Denver kisses her again—with tongue this time, so I make my exit.

I walk toward the girl I'm going to apologize to for being a sleaze bag. She turns around as I approach, and I can see she's not going to make this easy for me.

"Phoenix, we need to talk."

She circles around and splashes on a fake smile. One I'm not sure I've ever been on the receiving end of. "Can't. I have to practice this song. Kingston got called away, so I'm on my own."

"I heard." I move one step closer, but she takes a step back. "Listen, I don't trust people easily."

She drops the papers onto the float that's set up with two microphones. I guess someone didn't get the memo that Kingston wouldn't be here. "Listen, no hard feelings, but I really need to focus on this song right now."

She seems nervous and I have no idea why. She has killer vocals and I know she's going to blow this crowd away.

My attention is drawn to the huge float behind this one where Rome is trying to wrestle Calista. It's then that I realize I don't even know her family. I mean, I thought Calista was Holly's, based on our interaction at the bakery.

"Excuse me," I say, walking away from her.

I approach Holly's husband first, because if I'm correct, he's Austin, the oldest and the kind-of dad figure to the rest of them.

"Austin?" I ask.

He swivels around. When Holly spots me, she appears

embarrassed. I want to call her out on it, but I give her cool points for helping Phoenix that day in the bakery.

"Yeah, Griffin?" He holds out his hand, and I shake it.

"I just wanted to introduce myself since Phoenix was watching my son. I'll be taking Kingston's place on her float today."

He nods and looks over my shoulder to where I imagine Phoenix is staring at us. "Nice to meet you and... thanks. This is my wife—"

"Hi, Holly." I put out my hand.

She bites her lip, staring at Austin while she shakes it.

"You two already know one another?" he asks.

Holly laughs. "We ran into one another at the bakery."

Austin protectively secures his arm around Holly's waist and nods.

No worries from me. I suddenly became exclusive to a specific brunette only moments ago when I wanted to rip someone limb by limb.

"What are you doing?" Phoenix says behind me through gritted teeth.

I circle around, hearing Austin asking Holly about the bakery. "I never met your family. Now that everything is out in the open, I figured I should."

She grabs my hand and tugs me away from everyone until we're secluded in the vestibule of a store entrance. "This isn't a game. My family already knows I'm a fuckup, so if your idea is to tell them what I did, don't bother. They probably all know already, and they won't be surprised."

"That wasn't what I was doing. Listen, I acted like an asshole and I wanted to apologize, but you wouldn't take my calls, so I had to track you down here. And to make it up to you, I'm going to embarrass myself on that float today and sing with you."

"Why would you do that? I'm not going to sleep with you no matter how guilty I feel about lying."

I inhale deeply. "I overreacted, but if you would've let me explain a few minutes ago, I would've told you that I used to trust easily before I moved to LA. My wife cheated on me numerous times, artists backstabbed me more than I care to admit, and almost everyone in my life was after something from me. Add on the pressure of the media and the microscope every little decision I ever made was under, and it all ruined my ability to trust. So when you told me you lied, I didn't think, I just reacted."

"I'm sorry. I really am. You have every right to be upset with me. I shouldn't have done that to you and Maverick."

I shove my hands into my pockets to stop myself from touching her. "Now that I've had some time to think about it, I get it. I did some crazy shit when I got to LA. I should've remembered that before firing you."

I step closer, but she steps back so that her back hits the glass door. She puts up her hand. "I probably gave you the wrong impression, but I'm not a casual fling type of girl."

"I was callous in my approach to the whole thing, and then after you told me the truth, I snapped. I shouldn't have treated you like that."

She looks out at the crowd where it seems as though everyone is taking their places. "I have to get going and do my vocal exercises before it starts. You don't have to sing in the parade. I can handle myself." Leaving the vestibule, she walks toward the float.

"I want to help."

She turns right before she's about to step on and smiles at me. "Thanks for the offer, but I'm good."

I watch her step onto the float and position the microphone to her height. She doesn't bother to look at me again while she runs through her vocal exercises. Glancing back at her family on the other float, I see them all talking and laughing and arguing about who's going to stand where. Grandma Dori sits higher than the rest of them on a chair, like a queen presiding over her subjects.

Screw this. Phoenix's not going to be by herself. I jump up on the float.

"What are you doing?" she asks.

"I'm on your side now. This is where I need to be." I position the second microphone in front of my mouth.

"Griffin," she says.

"I'm not getting off the float without you."

A small smile creases her lips. "Okay."

Then the float jolts forward and I almost fall on my ass, but the music plays. Time to do what I can to show Phoenix that I meant it when I said I was on her side.

TWENTY-ONE

Phoenix

I did not need another reason to like Griffin Thorne. I needed him to be the asshole he was at his house. To stay in that box and not pop out with apologies and eyes so genuine I think I actually believe him.

Truth is, I was really nervous about being up here by myself today, so Griffin's presence is welcome. Before LA, it wouldn't have even fazed me. But it's hard to feel like a winner and like I'm fulfilling my life's calling after falling flat on my face.

The music starts and the usual butterflies fill my stomach.

"Remember, put yourself in the song. Connect to the lyrics," Griffin whispers. "And please cover up my awful voice."

I chuckle as the float rounds the corner onto Main Street. My eyes scour the crowd to find what Griffin's talking about. My love-hate relationship isn't going to be what gets me through this song. It's the memories I've made with my sisters and brothers and their growing families. Along with the few I've made with Maverick and Griffin. I don't dare examine why those are even on my radar.

My hand falls to my stomach and I inhale before the first line leaves my mouth, sounding a little scratchy. Griffin smiles at me without an ounce of worry that I'm about to fail. He nods at me to continue, and I allow myself to look at the road. People are lined up on either side of the street. People who know me. People who knew my parents. People who have cheered with us and grieved with us.

To my left, Maverick stands on the curb with Kayla Gregory, and watching them triggers memories of Kingston and Stella before Owen entered the picture. Their whole relationship flashes through my mind. With him only one year older than me, I witnessed all their good and bad. Channeling why Kingston picked this song, why the words mean so much to him, why he chose to take a job that keeps him out of this town for half the year, I find the heart of the song in me.

As though I need any other triggers to keep me in his frame of mind, Stella appears on my right, next to her mom, Selene. The two frantically wave with hands full of kettle corn.

Griffin holds his own with his vocals. I had no idea he had the voice he does. He should have the lead, not me. We gravitate together, moving closer as our voices grow louder, more comfortable and more confident that we're pulling this off.

Watching him, I realize that this song might ring true for *me* in a couple months. Griffin has the capability to do to me what Stella did to Kingston—to block out the good with a shit-ton of bad memories.

Finally, after I have no idea how many times of singing

the same song over and over, we round Main Street and the music stops at the same time the float does.

Griffin wraps his arm around my waist and pulls me to him before I can escape. "You did awesome. Where did all that come from?"

I shrug. "I kind of channeled my brother and why he wanted this song."

He smiles so big you'd think... well, that we didn't have a huge fight only days ago. "You were so damn good."

"Thanks."

"Come back. Be Maverick's nanny. Let me help you, get you ready for the big leagues. I won't touch you. I won't overstep. But let me help you get to where you wanna be."

His conviction slams into me, and I can only ask the one question that's on my mind. "Why?"

"Because I see something in you. I get what it's like to want to get somewhere but feel like you're tied to a chair no one will free you from. And to be honest, I selfishly want to. You're the first artist I've wanted to work with in a long time. You're giving me a high I haven't had in a while."

"No sleeping together?" I ask.

He inhales but shakes his head. "Agreed..." He shakes his head again as though convincing himself.

I step back and his hands fall from my body. Hopping off the float, I dodge my family who are leaving their own float and congregating on the sidewalk. Instead, I head out of town.

"Are you going to answer me?" he asks, catching up to walk beside me.

I'm silent for a couple blocks while I think it over. "Okay."

"Okay to what?" His brown eyes light up.

"Let's work together."

His tongue slides out of his mouth and runs along his bottom lip.

"*Dad! Phoenix!*" Maverick's shouts pull us from our conversation. He's running toward us with... you've got to be kidding me. How did I forget that Van Brewton and Trey Galger were going to be here?

"Oh my God." My face heats with embarrassment or nerves or I don't know what.

Griffin slides his hand across my lower back. "Let me introduce you."

I swallow past the dryness that has taken over my mouth as Maverick walks up with a brown bag.

"The parade was cool. I got all this candy." He holds up the brown bag.

Props to Griffin for being organized enough to bring a bag.

"Thankfully, that Francie woman had an extra bag. We were putting it all in my hat," Trey Galger says, laughing.

I stand there dumbfounded that I'm in a circle with music producer Griffin Thorne, who just asked me to work with him on my career, and the two men who own one of the biggest record labels in the country.

"I'm Van. Phoenix, right?" His V-neck T-shirt and leather jacket echo every magazine picture or television interview I've seen him do. He and Trey are opposites in their outward appearances.

"Yeah. Phoenix Bailey." I shake his hand and he smiles widely. It seems genuine.

"Trey Galger." The other man takes his hand out of his sweatshirt. He looks as if he just came from the skate park.

I shift my hand into his. His gaze roams my body once, and Griffin clears his throat.

"Can we go to the carnival?" Maverick asks.

"Yeah, you know Uncle Van loves the Ferris wheel, right?" Griffin says with a grin.

Trey punches Van in the shoulder. "Wimp."

Van looks at me. "I'm afraid of heights and these"—his eyes fall to Maverick, looking at him with rapt interest—"jerks like to make jokes."

"I don't like heights either," Maverick says.

Van picks him up, circling him around until he's on Van's back. "Let's go play some games and win stuff for girls."

Maverick looks at me. "I'll win something for Phoenix."

My heart warms, and Griffin's hand lands on the small of my back again. "I need to talk to my family, but I'll catch up to you guys."

Trey follows Van and Maverick, but Griffin stays back. "Are you really going to meet us?"

I nod. "I'm a Bailey. I have to show my face the entire day." I force my biggest smile. It's not really true—I usually leave midway through, no matter what Grandma Dori says.

"Okay. Are you going to move back in tonight?" There's that hopeful gleam in his dark eyes again.

"I'll wait until your friends leave. Monday morning, I'll come pick up Maverick for school then move my few boxes back in."

He nods and stuffs his hands into his pockets. "So we'll see you over there?" He signals with his head toward the carnival area.

"Yeah."

His expression says he has a million other things he wants to say, but he turns around and heads down the street. I watch until he's swallowed up by the crowd.

"So?" Sedona practically skips over to me she's so giddy, which I know has to do with Jamison.

"Where's Jamison?" I ask. It's nice to have her to myself though.

"He's with his host family at the carnival." She puts her arm through mine. "What happened? You two looked good from where I could see on the float."

Juno tears away from Holly and Austin and joins us. "What did she say?"

"She's being tight-lipped so far," Sedona says.

"What are you two talking about?" I ask.

"Since we didn't have to sing this year, we spent the float ride dissecting what was happening between you and Griffin in front of us," Sedona fills me in. "Come on. I'm dying for a crab rangoon from Wok For U."

The three of us walk down the street that's now thinning out of people since the parade is over and the carnival is in full swing. Grandma Dori walks with Austin and Holly to the library, a tradition that started five years ago when they started dating.

"How are things going?" I leave my question vague, and since they're my sisters, they know what I'm asking.

"Nothing more to report other than they're trying in vitro now." Juno tightens her arm around mine, and my gaze shoots to Harley and Rome. Calista and Dion are being pulled in a wagon by Rome and swapping candy while Phoebe is in her wrap on Harley's chest. "I have a good feeling this time."

"I hope so," Sedona and I say in unison.

"Where's Colton?" I ask once we reach the library parking lot where the rides are all set up.

"He's manning Dr. Murray's booth, handing out pizza cutters with their logo on it like everyone with a pet in Lake Starlight doesn't already go to them." Juno rolls her eyes.

"You should've opened a booth," Sedona says. "There's got to be a lot of single people looking on a day like today."

"I do the farmer's markets, but Founder's Day is for us to remember our family."

Juno's always been the most sentimental one of us.

"Stop dodging our interrogation. Now what's going on?" Juno asks, tugging on my arm.

"He hired me back, and he wants to produce a demo for me."

Their feet stop, which means I have to stop unless I want to fall flat on my face.

"You said yes, right?" Sedona asks.

"I did, though I'm not so sure. What if something almost happens between us again? It could screw everything up." Just the thought of spending time with him where I'm his sole focus makes my stomach flip.

"Don't overthink it," Juno says.

I look up and find Griffin standing with Van and Trey while Maverick is on a ride. Our eyes lock and he smiles at me. I can't deny there's something between us.

"Hey." Sedona turns me toward her. "Don't be afraid to have everything, okay? I know you've been going through a shit-time these last few years, but if he's willing to help you, do what Phoenix does best."

I wrinkle my forehead. "What's that?"

"Go full throttle without a care. That's you. You're the girl who moved to LA all on your own. You didn't know anyone. You were just on a mission. Find that girl and make her go after what's hers."

I bite my lip, looking across the parking lot again. Griffin has Maverick on his back now and they're smiling. My body yearns to head over to them. "I just—"

Sedona covers my mouth with her hand. "Wrong

answer." She takes her hand from my mouth. "Now... go!" She pushes me forward. "Juno, take me to get crab rangoon."

I head toward Griffin, knowing my sister is right. I need to be the girl who takes life by the balls and lives it to its fullest. When did I stop being her?

TWENTY-TWO

Griffin

Maverick rides the spinning ride with the Kayla girl, and I'm amazed by how he seems younger than we first moved here. He was excited about collecting candy from a float. He didn't bring his phone today. Dare I say he's becoming more childlike? I love it.

"So we wanna sign her." Van slaps my shoulder as he and Trey come to stand on either side of me.

"What?" My head whips in his direction then Trey's.

"Phoenix," Trey says, shoving his hands into his sweat-shirt. "It's seriously so cold up here. Isn't it spring?"

I ignore his question. The state name Alaska should tell him to layer up. "You can't be serious. You heard her sing one song."

"Over and over again. She got better each time she sang it." Van looks around as if someone's about to overhear him and pluck her away from his grasp. "We followed the float down Main Street for a bit." He shrugs.

I blow out a breath. "She's raw. I understand why you

like her. She's got that magic someone is either born with or not, but she's not ready to be signed yet."

Van crosses his arms and gives me a look that suggests I'm being deliberately difficult. The same look he gave me with Cammie, but what happened with Cammie isn't going to happen with Phoenix. I'll never allow it.

"What?" I ask.

"I think you want to make sure she stays here," he says.

Trey attempts and fails to bite back his laughter.

"I just told her I'd work with her. I'm willing to give you first listen once we're finished, but I'm telling you she's not ready. You sign her now and she'll fail."

Van huffs.

Trey diverts eye contact.

This is the way they do the business. Van is the hard-ass, Trey is the... well, Trey avoids confrontation. But what Trey lacks in aggression he makes up for in talent. Everyone knows Van is the businessman behind Aces High Records, while Trey is the visionary and the creative genius.

"She's new and fresh and I can make her a star." Van leans in closer. "Stop with your perfectionism."

I refrain from arguing since we're in the middle of a carnival where everyone is having fun—or supposed to be anyway. "That's my job."

"Technically you quit your job."

Van's cocky smirk only makes me want to wrap my arms around Phoenix and protect her even more. I thought Van wanted to have long-standing career musicians, not one-hit wonders.

"Phoenix just agreed to work with me. If you decide to go to her directly, I'll sign her on a contract with me beforehand."

"You have no say over her," Van says.

"Listen, guys, can we get coffee and put this whole pissing match aside? My balls have icicles hanging off them." Trey's attempt at lightening the mood fails.

"If you take her now, she'll have one album that'll get mediocre reviews. If you wait until I'm done, you're going to have a star. A woman who will make a name for herself, which in turn will put money in your pockets for years to come."

Van huffs once more. "You're going to give me first listen?"

"We're friends. You can trust me."

He nods. "Fine. But I'm giving you two months max. She better be perfect enough by then."

"Maybe I'll be done with her sooner."

"I have a feeling you're never going to be done with her," he grumbles.

Maverick runs off the ride toward us. "Can we play that game?" He points at the pyramid of clowns you try to knock down with a baseball.

Van pulls out a twenty and hands it to him. "Definitely."

Maverick runs over and waits in line behind a bunch of adult men razzing each other. As we get closer, I see the four guys are Denver, his two brothers, and his brother-in-law, who I met when we were staying at the resort. The four of them turn around when we approach. We go through all the introductions and Trey takes Wyatt's hand.

"You're related too?" Trey looks at Van. "It's like the damn *Brady Bunch* around here."

Denver spots Maverick waiting. "Hey, Mav, you want a turn?"

"Maverick," he corrects.

I chuckle to myself that he won't allow them to shorten his name.

Denver rustles his hair. "That's right. Come on. I bet you can take my brothers."

Rome and Austin glance over. Austin has a baseball in his hand and is winding his arm around in a circle as if you get more than a stuffed animal for winning. My guess is bragging rights is really what they're after.

"My team was state champs," Rome says. "And this guy was recruited for college ball right out of high school." He thumbs toward Austin.

From what I know, Austin is a biology teacher and the coach of the high school baseball team. I wonder how he ended up back here?

Their intimidation tactic doesn't change Maverick's mind though, and he grabs the baseball out of Denver's hand. He throws the ball, and it lands short, never hitting a clown.

"Here." Austin hands his baseball to his brother and comes up behind Maverick. Denver puts another baseball in Maverick's hand, and Austin shows him how to bring his hand back and throw it straight. "Push off the foot and end with your arm—"

"You're not teaching how to pitch for the majors," Rome says, throwing his ball. All but one clown falls down. "Seriously? This is rigged."

"Arguing about a carnival game, babe?" Harley comes over, pushing a stroller with Calista and Dion holding on to each side. She has impressive mom skills, being able to get them to behave so well at a carnival where there are a thousand and one distractions.

"I just wanted to win you a stuffed animal." He bends over the stroller and kisses his wife.

"You've given me enough but thank you." She smiles sweetly.

Rome laughs, picking up Dion. "Never too early to learn, buddy."

"What about me?" Calista abandons the stroller and runs over to her dad.

Rome turns around, and Harley's eyebrows are high with the implication that he picked Dion because he's a boy.

"Definitely." Handing the woman money, Rome gives both of his kids a ball, showing Calista how to throw while Dion's ball hits the ground.

Denver runs over and grabs Dion.

"Man, how many of them are there?" Trey whispers next to me.

"I lost count."

"Kinda cool how they all do things for each other. I just had my ma growing up."

I see the envy in Trey's eyes, and any regret I had for moving Maverick up here vanishes in the mountain air because he's right. These guys barely know me or my son, and look at Austin kneeling on the ground, really showing Maverick how to throw a baseball. Something a boy should do with his dad.

"You're a natural. Ever think about playing Little League?" Austin gives Maverick a high five when he gets four of the clowns down.

"I don't like sports." Maverick gives his usual answer.

For the first time, I realize I might be the one to blame for that. I never encouraged any extracurriculars. Maverick has spent majority of his life with a nanny, in a recording studio, or in a trailer on set with his mom. We raised him in an environment where people are out for themselves. But that's not the case in Lake Starlight.

"Way to go, Maverick!" Phoenix exclaims, walking past. She raises her hand, and Maverick's smile grows wider as he hits her hand.

"Thanks." He grins wide at me and looks like he might want to hug me for a second, but then he looks around at everyone and takes a step back.

"I just told him he should play Little League this summer," Austin tells her.

All the Bailey women come over, inundating the area.

"Shit, look at all of them," Trey says next to me. "Any of them single?"

"Um, I think only Phoenix and Juno."

Trey leaves my side and heads to Juno after I point her out.

Van slides into Trey's spot next to me. "You should've said they're all taken. You know as well as I do Trey isn't looking to live in Mayberry like you."

"Someone might've said the same thing about me not that long ago."

Van nods and he pulls his vibrating phone out of his pocket. "I gotta get this. I'll catch up."

"Okay."

I watch him disappear into the crowd with his phone pressed to his ear. I'm still a little pissed about him trying to take Phoenix before she's ready. Meaning he only really has concern for himself, not Phoenix. Has he always been that way? Then again, he's in the business to make money.

"You've never ridden a Ferris wheel?" Phoenix's screech brings me back to the Bailey clan in front of me.

Sedona looks at Phoenix, and they nod in unison. Must be a twin thing.

"We're taking him on a ride on the Ferris wheel. Is that okay?" Phoenix asks me.

"Sure."

"I wanna go," Calista whines.

Rome picks her up. "What my princess wants..."

"Princess?" Harley asks.

"She can be my princess *and* throw a killer curveball." Rome stalks away.

Harley laughs, catching up to me. "It's fun to give him hell."

Denver runs by me, holding Dion up like an airplane, Cleo not far behind.

"I have no idea how you do it with three. I barely survived with one."

Harley peeks through the stroller window and smiles at her baby girl. "We're fortunate to have a lot of family who love our kids just as much as we do."

As she says that, Wyatt's wife comes over and takes the stroller. "Phoebe's time with Auntie Brooklyn."

Harley smiles at me. "See what I mean? I barely have them." She laughs harder so that I understand that's not really true. She sobers after a few seconds. "Truth be told, I didn't have a lot of family growing up, and at first, they scared the crap out of me. I wasn't used to people caring without a hidden agenda, you know?"

I nod. Do I ever.

"But they're genuine. Sure, they fight with each other, but the love is deep, and it's fierce." She puts her arm through mine. "Come on. Let's go get a funnel cake."

Phoenix and Sedona are talking to Maverick as they wait in line for the Ferris wheel.

The two of us go to a food truck that's still in view of the ride. Harley orders two funnel cakes. She digs money out of her back pocket and hands it over.

"She really is great. Phoenix, I mean."

"Oh yeah." Please tell me this wasn't her whole reason for approaching me. To convince me to like Phoenix. I like her so much it's going to be a problem. "I know she is."

She grabs a stack of paper napkins and stuffs them into her jacket pocket. "I know you know, but speaking as someone who isn't her family, I wanted to tell you that she's still finding herself. She's young and insecure, though you'd never guess it. She appears confident, but..."

She continues talking as I search out Phoenix, finding her and Sedona on either side of Maverick, now in a cart on the Ferris wheel. The two of them are laughing, and Maverick is forcing a smile. Phoenix puts her hand over Maverick's on the bar and squeezes as they rise for another cart to load.

"But I like you, Griffin. I think you're a good fit for her. I know I'm only a Bailey by marriage, but if you hurt her, I will be the first in line to junk-punch you."

My head circles her way, and she's smiling. I reflexively squeeze my legs together.

"Funnel cake?" she asks as if she didn't just threaten my ability to have more kids.

"No thanks."

She shrugs. "I'll save this one for the kids to share then."

Harley sits on a bench next to Holly, but Austin comes over right away, holding his hand out for his wife.

Holly shakes her head, but Austin doesn't move his hand. "I'm not accepting no."

Harley nudges Holly. "Go."

Holly finally takes his hand, and he leads her over to the Ferris wheel. I sit on the bench, leaving a bit of space between Harley and myself.

"You just never know what life has in store for you." She stares at the couple as they get in line and Austin takes

Holly in his arms, nuzzling her face into his chest. "One minute I was a broke single mother who had no family, and now I'm a married woman with three healthy kids and an amazing husband whose family has taken me in as their own." I'm not even sure she's talking to me because her eyes are on Austin and Holly. "Be careful, Griffin. Sometimes you have no idea what your future holds, but it's the people around you who'll get you through it. Speaking as someone who never had a family of her own, the bigger the better."

We sit there, and I find Maverick on the ride. He's now raising his hands as the Ferris wheel goes down. He's only got them halfway up while Phoenix and Sedona have their arms all the way in the air, laughing. I can't deny this town and its inhabitants are having a lasting effect on not only me, but my son too.

TWENTY-THREE

Phoenix

I t's only been a week since I moved back in, and things are back to normal. The first few nights I spent up in my room and not downstairs with Griffin. But by the third night, he asked if I wanted to work on some stuff with him. I reminded myself that the entire reason I was here, other than Maverick, was so Griffin could help me.

As I sit here trying to help Maverick with his diorama project for school, I find my mind wandering to Griffin's and my interaction last night. He wants me to have an original song before going into a recording studio, which he's footing the bill for, in a month. Of course he wants my input on the lyrics to make them meaningful to me. But it's hard to communicate without admitting I like him. Not just as the father of the child I nanny. Not just as a music producer who's taken me on. But in the way a woman likes a man.

"Fuck!" Griffin's rough voice interrupts my thoughts. A wrench clatters to the floor a moment later.

"Swear jar," Maverick says.

I smile, noticing Maverick's staring at two fingers that won't come apart because he's glued them together.

"I know. I know." Griffin's head pops up over the counter. "I am not this stupid."

"We could call a plumber."

Griffin glares daggers at me.

I put my hands up in front of me. "Or not."

"The sink is mine."

Cedric is finished with the house now and asked Griffin no fewer than ten times if he could install the sink. Griffin politely refused each time, saying he had it under control.

"We have a bigger problem," I say.

"What?" He finally notices what I do—his son watching his fingers not separating.

"I have to head to the store to get nail polish remover."

Griffin shakes his head. "I'm done with filling pots of water up from the bathroom sink." He grabs his keys and wallet off the counter. "Come on. We're going to eat."

"Okay, then make sure you get the nail polish remover with acetone and some Q-Tips. Wet the tip of the Q-Tip— do you want to write this down?"

He stares at me as if I teleported in from space. "Why would I need to write it down?"

"So you know what to do."

"You're coming with us."

Maverick stands from the table. "Yay!"

"Oh, I don't have to—"

"I'm taking all three of us to dinner. Get in the truck."

I nibble my lip to stop my smile from growing too wide as I go to the closet and grab our jackets. After putting Maverick's over his shoulders and putting mine on, I meet Griffin by the back door, and we climb into his truck.

After stopping at the pharmacy, we sit in the gazebo in the town square so I can unglue Maverick's fingers.

Griffin stands beside the bench, looking out at Main Street. "Where do you want to go to dinner?"

"We could go to the diner. Or we could go to Rome's restaurant. Or Grandma Dori's retirement center."

Griffin gives me the same look he did back at his house. "I don't want instant mashed potatoes."

I chuckle. "We can go out of town if you want."

"Perfect. You tell me where to go."

As I work the Q-Tip, Maverick's fingers pull apart. They're still sticky but separate when he pulls them apart.

"Here, I'll do a little more on each finger," I say.

"Thanks." Maverick's eyes swim with gratitude and it brings a warm feeling to my chest. Sometimes I can't believe he's the same kid I met not that long ago. Are kids really this resilient?

As I'm gathering our garbage and tossing it in the trash can, Juno walks toward us.

"What are you guys doing here?" she asks.

"Maverick got his fingers stuck together with superglue, so I just separated them for him. Now we're going to dinner."

"Where are you guys going?" she asks.

"I might take them to Greywall or Sunrise Bay."

Juno looks... unhappy. Which isn't like her at all. Usually she's my peppy sister. The one who always sees the positive in everything.

"You okay?" I ask.

She nods.

"We can leave you two if you'd prefer?" Griffin suggests.

If my sister needs me, I'm there for her. But I kind of

hope she doesn't need me because I really want to spend time with Griffin and Maverick. We're finally getting our groove back after the fight.

"No. You guys go. I'm good." Juno waves us off. "Have a good night."

I watch her for a moment, and Griffin comes so close to me all I smell is him. He's never asked me to pick up body wash when I go to the grocery store, but I kind of wish he would so I could know what he uses to smell so delicious.

"If you'd rather go with your sister, feel free," he says.

As I'm contemplating skipping the pseudo-family dinner and running toward Juno, Colton comes around the corner. They both stop, looking alarmed for a second. After a few words between them that I can't make out but wish I could, Colton joins Juno and they walk over to her apartment.

"She's in good hands," I say.

"Who's that?"

"Colton. Her best friend. I thought she had feelings for him, but with the way she was at the carnival with Trey, I'm not so sure."

Griffin and I walk as Maverick runs ahead to the truck. "I wanted to apologize for that. Trey is... opportunistic. He means well, but sometimes he acts before he thinks."

I side-glance him. "My sister's grown. She makes her own decisions. No worries."

Visible tension rolls off his shoulders. "After what happened with us, I didn't want you to think... I mean—"

I rest my hand on his forearm, and we stop. He watches Maverick climb into the truck and shut the door.

"That's behind us now," I say. "I don't want this to be awkward between us."

"Me either," he rushes to say, holding my gaze.

My breath hitches with the way he's looking at me—as though he's doing everything in his power not to cross the line with me. "Griffin..."

"Yeah?" He steps forward, and I feel the heat from his body through my coat.

The words are on the tip of my tongue—to tell him that I can't stop thinking of him, that I lie in bed at night, wondering what he's doing, what he's thinking. Is he thinking of me like I think of him? But it'd be unrealistic to think that he'd look at a woman eleven years younger than him as anything more than a hookup. He agreed to help me achieve my dream, and I can't look a gift horse in the mouth and want more.

"Nothing." I shake my head.

Before I can get away, he grabs my arm and circles me around. "Phoenix, talk to me. It's just us right now. Set aside the outside noise. Tell me what's on your mind."

I look into his chocolate eyes, and the butterflies inside flap their wings. "I don't want to ruin anything. I mean, it'd be stupid if we... we can't... what if..." For the first time in my life, I'm hesitant to take something I want. Maybe because my dream is bigger than one man. But people get both all the time. My siblings are examples of that.

"Is that really what you want?" he asks.

"Yes, you're Griffin Thorne. I can't."

He runs a hand through his hair. "I hate when you say my first and last name."

"We should get back to Maverick." I walk toward the truck, but he doesn't allow me to go far.

"What are you scared of?"

I divert my attention toward the gazebo. Anything not to be held captive by his stare. "Because you're Griffin Thorne."

His hands ball up in fists at his side. "Please stop saying that. I'm Griffin."

"No, you're not. Don't you see that? You represent my dream. And what if I allow myself to get involved with you and you destroy me? I've done stuff before thinking it through my entire life. I shouldn't have gone to LA without a plan. I shouldn't have tried to get this nanny position. I shouldn't have... I shouldn't have... my entire life is filled with 'I shouldn't haves.'" I place my hand on his strong chest. "You're offering me something I could never obtain on my own, and I tend to screw things up. So if things got messy between us, I'd have another 'shouldn't have' in my arsenal."

His hand covers mine. "Do you think if things didn't work out, I'd just drop you?"

"I don't know, but taking that chance feels risky." I don't bother mentioning that I'd probably have to drop him if I couldn't handle the rejection after my feelings for him grew.

He squeezes my hand, and I take a second to glance around.

"I would never do that," he says. "I'm not that type of person, but you probably don't know that about me. I've been cautious since Maggie, but with you, I don't want to be cautious. I want to take what I want, and that's what I was doing that day in the kitchen. I was acting like someone I'm not. All I'm asking for is one date. We're going to the studio in three weeks. Let me get a sitter for Maverick, and we'll go up to Anchorage to record and have dinner after. Spend the night—and I'll get you a separate room if you want. But by then, everything will be off the ground. I'll give you the demo before we go on the date. That way you'll know whether we work out or not, you're covered."

I inhale a ragged breath.

He raises his hand before I can respond. "But I have one stipulation."

"What's that?"

"You have to call me Griffin. I never want my last name to leave your mouth from this point forward."

I laugh and nod. "Okay. Let's do it."

I'm still scared, but these feelings I have for him aren't going anywhere, and I know myself well enough to know that I'll likely eventually give in anyway.

"I'll make the arrangements. Let's feed Maverick, then we have to get down to work. Try to keep your hands to yourself." He winks.

"What?"

He releases my hand, tucking his into his pockets and walking down the path toward the truck. "I know I'm irresistible."

He's joking, but little does he know how many times I've walked away so I don't touch him.

"You haven't seen how irresistible I am yet," I tease.

His nostrils flare as he opens the door to his truck. "Oh, I never told you about the cameras?"

I look at him as though I'm bored, but inside I'm imagining the fun I could have if he weren't kidding.

As though he can read my mind, he smiles before he gets in and shuts the door.

I walk around to the other side and hop in.

"What took you guys so long? I'm starving!" Maverick screeches in my ear.

"We were talking about your birthday." I probably shouldn't lie. His birthday is four months away.

"Oh cool. Presents?"

I shrug. "It's a secret." I zip my lips and toss the imaginary key.

Griffin pulls the car out onto the street.

I direct Griffin to Greywall, and the awkwardness between us somehow disappears while we have a tic-tac-toe challenge on the paper napkins at the crab place. When no one wins, we move on to hangman.

To an outsider, we probably look like a family. No one looks at us as though we don't belong together, and for the first time since my feelings for Griffin moved beyond boss/employer, I let myself hope that I'm one of those people who can have everything too.

TWENTY-FOUR

Griffin

Three weeks of blue balls. Three weeks of hard-ons that I've had to rub out myself. Three weeks of seeing her ass in yoga pants. Three weeks of hearing the sweet sound of her voice grow more mature and more controlled. Three weeks of helping her find the perfection in her voice.

Her confidence is up ten times from before Founder's Day. She's trusting herself and her vocals, and the excitement I get from watching her grow as a singer can't be matched.

Denver and Cleo volunteered to watch Maverick this weekend while I take her to a rented studio in Anchorage. I've toyed with the idea of building a studio in the house, but I don't want to rush it. I mean, we haven't even slept together, I can't go building her a studio.

"You sure you're okay leaving Maverick with Denver?" she asks from the seat next to me.

"I trust him. Plus Cleo is like his conscience."

She laughs, sipping her tea. It's early and we both

needed a caffeine fix before we left town. "That's true. I never thought about it that way."

We drive to Anchorage and park outside of the small studio.

"You're ready for this."

Her gaze fixates on the sign and her chest rises and falls. "I think so. I mean, we've done a lot—"

I put my hand on her thigh. "I wasn't asking. I was telling you. You are ready for this."

Climbing out of my truck, I allow her the time she needs to get out and believe in herself the way I do. Van wanted to come up here and listen while we laid down her track, but I put my foot down.

A minute later, she comes out and I grab my guitar. We walk through the studio doors and I give my name. We're introduced to the managers and escorted to the studio I reserved for two days.

Phoenix looks around while I sit in the chair, checking over their board and inspecting everything in the booth for her. It's not top of the line, but I can make it work.

"Ready?" I ask her about fifteen minutes later when she's done with her vocal warm-ups, and I've laid down the guitar portion of the track for her to sing along to. She's chewing on her lip, ghost-white. "What's the matter?"

"This is it."

I chuckle. "Yeah."

"I'm nervous." Her hands fidget in front of her.

I hold out my hand and she accepts it, allowing me to guide her into the booth. "It's just like at home. Me and you. We can be here all day and all night if we want. There's no rush, and I will not let this not be perfect. Which might mean our date will suck because you might hate me after today."

A soft smile tilts her lips. "I'd never hate you."

I fiddle with the microphone stand and move the stool away since I know she prefers to stand. "Don't promise that until after we're done. I can piss people off with my perfectionism." She says nothing as I get her situated. "You good? Warm enough? I'll have someone bring you in some water. And just remember, me and you in my family room."

She rolls her eyes. I let her because we need to get started in case this takes a long time. It's her first time in a booth and she might need fifty takes before she feels comfortable. And it's only then that we can start experimenting and finding her sound.

I step back out of the door and roll the chair to the board.

I push the button to speak into the microphone so she can hear me in the booth. "Okay, I want to start by singing the song the entire length through a few times. You'll hear the guitar in your ear. Then we're going to concentrate on specific sections. I want to try some fun things."

She nods.

"Breathe, Phoenix." A long stream of air floats through the microphone. "There you go."

I admit, being behind the board again feels awesome. I feel at home and at ease. Starting us up, I listen as Phoenix's voice fills the booth. She's so talented, and she has no idea how fast her star is going to rise.

But right now, I can't get ahead of us. I'm going to enjoy this moment because I'm not sure how many artists I'll have a chance to coach through their first single again.

TWELVE HOURS, two meals, and countless water bottles later, we finally wrap. Phoenix sits in my truck with her head leaning on the window. I'm sure she's exhausted, but she was a real pro today—taking my notes and incorporating them, up for trying some different ideas and arrangements, and never complaining that she was tired.

"Was it at least fun?" I ask, because sometimes the hype doesn't live up to first-time artist expectations. Recording can be a long, arduous process. Once she gets signed and does an actual album, she'll have more than just me in the studio. I could even see a collaboration with another artist in her future. What happened today is just the beginning for her.

"It was. Just more exhausting than I expected."

"Go to your room, take a hot bath, and go to bed early."

She tilts her head at me. "I thought we had a date?"

"I'm not going to have you only half-conscious on our first date. I should've thought about that when I suggested it. We'll plan it for another time."

It sucks and I hate that there's no possibility that she'll end up naked next to me tonight. I had hopes that we'd seal whatever this is between us, but today took a lot out of her.

"I'm fine. I want to."

"Phoenix." I park the truck in the hotel parking lot.

"What? You said we'd have a date, and that's what I expect. I'm only twenty-two, Griffin. I have lots of energy." She shoots me a teasing smirk as she opens the door and the interior light illuminates her beautiful face.

"Energy for what?"

Her eyes soak me up, and she bites her lip. It's like a jolt of adrenaline right to my dick. "What do you think?"

She gets out of the truck and walks into the hotel while

I trail behind, staring at her behind and thinking of all the ways I could make her pay for her teasing.

We check into the hotel, and Phoenix takes her key. Our rooms are next door to one another.

"So what time are you coming to pick me up?" she asks.

I look at my watch. It's already nine o'clock at night. "I'm thinking room service. The question is, your room or mine?"

We step into the elevator and I'm thankful that no one else joins us. "Your room."

"I owe you something first." I dig the demo out of my pocket and hand it to her. "I do have copies though."

She smiles at the USB stick. "Thank you. I mean it. You have no idea how much this means to me."

I know exactly what it means, and that's why I loved doing it for her. "We don't have to have dinner, you know."

The elevator doors ding open and we follow the signs to our rooms.

"I want to."

I nod. "Okay. Let me know what you want me to order and I'll see you in about a half hour?"

"Just order whatever. I'm going to shower and then I'll be over."

We each stand at our hotel room doors with our keycards in hand, a nervous energy between us.

"Perfect. See you soon."

She smiles, swipes her keycard, and disappears into her room.

What the fuck am I doing? I'm acting like a damn thirteen-year-old kid who approached a girl at the first boy/girl dance. *Man up, Griffin.*

I order the room service, opting for things I've seen Phoenix eat. After stripping down, I turn on the water to have a quick shower. It's amazing how dirty you feel after a day in the studio. Then again, maybe it's only because of the dirty thoughts I had about Phoenix and what we could be doing in the studio besides recording.

The nerves set in once I'm showered and dressed. I probably shouldn't touch Phoenix. We should go back on the dating idea because once this demo gets to Van, she's going to LA and I won't be joining her. Then again, maybe a night or two of sex is a nice celebratory ending to what we've shared these past couple of months.

A knock sounds at the door and I pad across the carpeted floor on my bare feet.

Phoenix stands on the other side in a short black skirt and black shirt scoop next shirt. Her hair is down in waves, her makeup freshened up from earlier.

"Hey," I say.

"Hey." She steps into my space and inhales a deep breath. "What cologne do you wear?"

"Creed Aventus."

She sits in a chair by the table, crossing her bare legs. All those doubts about not wanting to do this disappear.

"It smells amazing. That's one thing I miss from LA. In Alaska, hardly any guys wear cologne. I remember walking down the streets of LA, and it'd be one smell after another."

"You liked LA?"

She shrugs. "Yeah. It took a lot of getting used to at first."

There's another knock on the door, so I head over to answer it before we get into more questions. A hotel employee rolls a cart in, another guy following right behind with a second cart.

Phoenix laughs. "How much did you order?"

"I'm usually hungry after a successful recording session."

She stands and takes lids off the dishes as I sign my name on the slip and see the men out. "I'm hungry too."

When I return, she's already got a fried green pea pod in her hand with half of it bitten off. "Sorry." She covers her mouth with her forearm. "I should've waited."

"There's no should-haves in this room tonight. Got it?"

A slow smile washes over her lips at me remembering her words, and her footsteps are soft thuds on the carpet as she makes her way over to me. "I'm not going to mislead you. I haven't had a ton of partners." Her hand slides up my chest.

She says that as if it's a bad thing.

"You don't want to eat first?" I ask.

She tosses the half-eaten pea pod on the tray and shakes her head. "I like to have dessert first." Her hand runs through my damp hair. My eyes close from the intimate contact. "I've wanted to do this since I first met you."

Her other hand runs along the other side of my scalp, and my hands slide down her torso to her hips, locking her in place.

"I've wanted to do this." My lips fall to her neck, the scent of her perfume making my dick pop up to party between our hips.

She moans, and the string I've been hanging onto for months snaps. When I lift her, she wraps her arms around my neck, and I press her back to the wall, locking my hips to hers, grinding my hard length into her center.

She's so verbal in her responses. The noises rising up her throat and escaping her lips only make me harder. My hands are more urgent. I need to have her bare skin against mine. To slide and grind and suck. I've never felt this compelled to claim a woman.

Her hands land on the hem of my T-shirt and she raises the fabric up my chest. Breaking apart our kiss, she pulls the shirt over my head before my lips land on hers again. My tongue dives in to meet hers, needing the soft moans it elicits from her. My fingers run along a patch of skin between her skirt and her blouse, but quickly lose control and slide up her back to undo the clasp of her bra.

"Take them all off," she says, pressing on my chest for distance.

I sit on the bed and pat the spot next to me. "Come over here."

She wastes no time, and our lips connect in a series of short kisses, one after the other until I swallow every 'ooh' and 'aah' escaping her. Having her in my lap with her tits about to fall out of her shirt and her bra straps hanging down to her elbows is the best view I've ever had.

Pushing back all the bullshit reasons we shouldn't be together, I claim her lips as mine. All I see, all I hear, all I feel is Phoenix. Damn the should-haves. They're not welcome here tonight.

TWENTY-FIVE

Phoenix

Griffin continues to kiss me, his tongue diving deeper. His hands roam and grip and mold while mine seem to be stuck running through his long hair, holding his head in places that I don't want him to venture away from. I didn't know anyone could elicit this kind of arousal from me.

Was my first partner that shitty or is Griffin gifted? Regardless, I push my ex out of my head to be clear and present, because if this doesn't happen again, I need to remember tonight.

My hands finally leave his hair and travel down his muscled torso. He spreads my legs, one hanging off of his and the other one behind him. When he skims his fingers up my inner thigh, I clench with the expectation of what's to come, but even as I prepare myself, I jolt from the contact when his fingers lightly run the length of my soaked silk panties.

"Relax. I've got you," he whispers. His tongue does

crazy things to my earlobe that ignites a trail of goose bumps up my spine. His other hand squeezes my breast.

Griffin surrounds me—his hands, his lips, his scent. I want to stay in this room for the rest of my life and discover him over and over again.

His fingers continue stroking between my legs, and when my orgasm builds to a near explosion, Griffin removes his hand and slides both hands up under my blouse until it's over my head. My bra slides down my arms and I'm bare from the waist up. He pulls away, his eyes saturated with lust. His hands mold to my breasts and he watches himself manipulate them, teasing my nipples, gripping the flesh as though they're clay and he's the sculptor.

"You're so fucking beautiful." His head dips and captures my nipple in his hot mouth, his tongue twirling the already peaked pebble. "So talented." He tugs on my nipple with his teeth. "So incredible."

My fingernails scrape his back, holding him to me so that he can't move away. "Griffin," I say just above a whisper, clinging to his body and writhing under his touch.

His hand slides down from my breast, pushes my panties to the side, and teases my center again. A low, deep groan erupts out of him and he tears his mouth off my breast. "Shit. You're soaked and I'm losing control."

He slides me to the side and stands. My legs hang off the bed as he manipulates the snap and zipper on his jeans before sliding them down his legs, leaving him in a pair of black boxer briefs. With his tanned skin, long hair, and hard length stretching the confines of his cotton briefs, he's model material.

He holds out his hand for me and I accept, getting to my feet. I'm on my feet for less than a second before his fingers dive into my skirt and push it past my hips. I step out of it, but Griffin already has my panties following suit, and he falls to his knees.

With a light push, he has me falling back onto the mattress. He grabs my legs, pushing to spread me open. His lips travel the path up my inner thigh, and the anticipation has my orgasm hanging like ripe fruit dangling from a tree branch.

The first swipe of his tongue makes my head fall back against the mattress as my hands grip the sheets next to my hips. Sliding me closer to him, he swings one leg over his shoulder and all I feel is him.

A hot puff of air hits my clit, and I look down to see his eyes are fixated on my core. The sight of his tongue emerging from his mouth has my insides clenching. I watch intently as the tip of his tongue connects with my clit, and my head once again falls back down to the mattress. Taking his time, he circles my clit with his tongue. His movements are painfully slow and a torment of the best kind. He groans, his tongue sliding down and back up before concentrating on my clit once more.

I clench my lower half to keep my orgasm away because I don't want him to stop. His exploration of my pussy continues, and all I can do is grip the sheets tighter and try not to buck against his face. When his finger joins the party, rimming my entrance, I lose control. His other hand grabs my breast, squeezing the way I love because apparently, he's a quick learner.

The slow and meticulous stroking of his tongue builds my orgasm as though it's a whole tree of ripe fruit ready to fall with only a shake of the trunk. His finger pushes into me and arches up while he sucks lightly on my clit. My orgasm rips through me and I buck with abandon against his face, crying out. The speed of his tongue increases, and his hands grab my ass. He allows me to ride his tongue until white dots are all I see.

My pelvis finally falls to the mattress and his fingers loosen their grip, easing my legs off his shoulders.

"Whoa," I say, still trying to catch my breath.

Griffin has more plans though. He rises up, kissing a path from navel to breast. He takes a pit stop on each breast and sucks hard on my sensitive nipples. Will I ever be finished with Griffin? If he fucks like he just ate, I'm going with a hard no.

He widens my legs with the nudge of his knee and settles over me. I use my hands to push his hair from his face, and his lips capture mine in a slow and bottomless kiss that makes my naked body warm from head to toe. His lips explore while his hard cock is pressed into my center, grinding and teasing.

A carnal urge to have him deep inside me has my hands gliding down his chest. Understanding where I'm going and where my goal resides, Griffin raises his hips. I pull down his boxer briefs, stroking his steel length with my palm.

His lips stop kissing me, and he rests his forehead on mine. "Damn, Phoenix." His eyes close briefly, only making me grip him harder. He grinds into my palm and I take my time to perfect the way he likes to be stroked. "Are you on anything?"

"I have an IUD but..."

"You're right." He gets up off me and my body goes cold, watching him walk over to his bag. "You make me lose all common sense." He pulls off his boxers, rips the foil packet, and runs the latex down his length.

"Come here."

When we're in the same position we were in moments

ago, I guide him to my entrance, and he sinks into me inch by inch until he's fully inside and I'm stretched around him.

"Fuck," he growls and circles his hips once. Sliding his hand down my leg, he brings it to rest over his hip and drives into me deeper.

It takes me a minute to get used to his size, but I meet him with each rock, our hips moving as one. Our mouths find refuge with one another and the world outside becomes a blur. My arms grasp to keep his body to mine, needing him as close as I can get him. His tongue slides and glides into my mouth until his lips travel down my jaw to my ear where his heavy breathing rings in my eardrums.

I bring my other leg over his hip. His breath is warm and his moans soft while he cups my ass with each dive into my depths.

I keep pushing away the impending orgasm because I never want the weight of his body off of me. I don't want to wake up from what feels like a dream. My hands slide into his hair, and I pull his lips to mine.

I can't hold back any longer. The fruit is ripe, heavy, and ready to be plucked. I fall apart around him, pulsing against his length while bliss travels through my nerve endings and I'm moaning his name.

His pace increases, and he rises up on his palms, staring at me as he drills in and out of me. His eyes darken in a way I've never seen from him before, and it only adds another layer to my arousal.

His chest heaves, and after a few uncoordinated thrusts, he stills inside me. I reach my hand up his sweaty chest and bring his lips down to mine once more. We kiss for what feels like hours.

Eventually he withdraws and disappears to the bathroom, returning after a minute. He pulls the sheets back for us to get under, then he slides one of the trays over to his side of the bed.

"I bet you're hungry now." He lifts the plate of fried green pea pods and sets it on my lap.

I dip one in the ranch dip and bite off a piece. He grabs a plate of fries with parmesan and aioli sauce on the side. I steal one, and he grabs a pea pod.

"Can I ask you a question?"

"That's scary. Right after we have sex?" I say.

He chuckles and his hand slides under the covers to my bare thigh, which he squeezes. "When you said you hadn't had many partners, you meant what exactly?"

Heat rushes to my cheeks. "That noticeable, huh?"

"No, you're amazing. The way you have sex is so you."

"Meaning?"

He shrugs and grabs another pea pod. "You looked to me the entire time to make sure what you were doing was making me feel good."

Now I laugh. "Um, that's not me outside of the bedroom."

He presses his lips to my bare shoulder. "It is when it comes to me and Maverick."

I choose to ignore the warm feeling in my chest his words conjure up. "That's probably because my experience at being a nanny is the same as sex. I've only done both with one other person until now."

"Really?" He chokes on his pea but grabs a glass of water before I have to save him.

"Okay, so far, the post-climatic bliss isn't very blissful."

He picks up our plates and puts both on the tray next to him. Sliding under the sheet, he leans over me. "I was curious, that's all. But it changes nothing. You're amazing in bed. I was barely able to hold out for as long as I did and..."

He peers down under the sheet. "Now I'm ready for round two."

I palm his steel length. He's hard and ready. All those fears and worries fade away, and he buries us under the sheet, his lips falling to my neck.

"I hope those fries and pea pods filled you up, because we're not coming up for air for a long time."

I giggle and slither down, never growing tired of the weight of his body over mine. Yeah, I'm in trouble. This only made me want Griffin more—not less.

TWENTY-SIX

Griffin

As sad as it is, I've never felt this way before. Sure, there's always that feeling at the start of a new relationship, when you can't keep your hands off each other. I went through that with Maggie. But as I lie in bed with Phoenix sprawled on my chest and my hand running the length of her back, I know this is different somehow.

Maybe with Maggie, it was our busy schedules from the start. But when we went through the new relationship "sex all the time" part of our relationship, it was quickies then on to the next thing. When I was feeling romantic after she got pregnant, I booked us a bungalow over the water in Tahiti— only for her to complain about the internet not being strong enough so she could call her agent. I was writing a song. We spent the majority of our time apart, since I was up late at night, working to the sound of the waves.

"Parents?" Phoenix asks.

We've been going back and forth, asking questions of

one another. Usually I'd be hesitant to share anything personal, but I want Phoenix to know everything about me.

"Dan and Deena Thorne. Dan owns Dan the Man Carpentry and Deena guides the youth of Oberlin High School."

"Dan the Man?" She props her chin on my chest.

I look down into her gorgeous brown eyes. "Yeah. I better get the sink in before they come to visit."

"It's not like your dad's a plumber."

"No, but to my dad, you do jobs like that yourself. And if you don't know how, you learn. He might be the first dad to be disappointed his son is a successful music producer."

She slaps my stomach playfully. "I doubt that."

"Wait until you meet him."

She says nothing and lays her cheek back on my chest, her finger twirling in my chest hair.

After a few moments of content quiet, I ask, "When did you first realize you wanted to sing?"

"That sounds like my music producer asking, not the man I just slept with."

"I'm curious." I bring my free hand down to move her chin up to look me in the eyes.

"I was young. My sister and I were obsessed with *The Parent Trap* movie. Not the Lindsay Lohan one, but the original with Hayley Mills. My parents had gotten into a fight. I don't remember about what, but Sedona and I planned this entire night and sang that song, 'Let's Get Together.'"

I nod, knowing what she's talking about.

"Sedona can sing too. My sister can hold a note, but my dad picked me up and swung me around. He said he couldn't tell the difference between Hayley Mills and me.

That someday I'd have a spotlight over me, and the world would love me."

"That would do it." I smile at her, picturing a young version of the woman in front of me.

"After they died, singing felt more important and took over my life. I felt like I had to do it, you know. For him."

I feel the corners of my lips go down. "I'm sorry."

She buries her head in my chest, and I sit up straighter to make sure I didn't make her cry. When she picks up her head because I shift, she wipes her eyes.

"You okay?" I ask.

She nods. "You have this way about you. Why are you always making me cry?"

I chuckle and pull her into my arms. "Sorry. Ask me anything. Make me cry."

She laughs, which sounds even better when she's naked and in my arms. Though I think I might prefer the low moan she makes right as I take her nipple into my mouth.

"Are you sure you're ready to be in the hot seat?" she asks.

"Take your best shot, lady."

"Where's Maggie?"

I cover my throat and my head hits the headboard. "Man, right for the jugular, huh?"

"I've wondered is all. You never mention her." She shrugs.

"She's off filming."

"This entire time?"

I nod, taking her hands. I slide my fingers through hers, tightening our grip then doing it all over again. "She likes to work."

"I know, but other than a few phone calls I've heard Maverick answer..."

"Yeah, but honestly, I can't fault her. We're the same in a lot of ways. Maverick hasn't really had either of us present throughout his childhood so far. He might be closer to me, but only because I don't travel for work. Maggie's gone. She tried to take Maverick with her once, but it was too much work, even with a nanny. Plus, once Maverick got to school age, I told her I wanted him to attend school, not just be sitting in a set trailer with a tutor."

"He's a great kid."

I squeeze her hand. "Thanks. That means a lot."

"How come you and Maggie didn't work out?"

I chuckle. "Because of everything I just told you. She'll film movie after movie away from home. Maverick was... a surprise." I hate the word mistake and I refuse to use it in reference to my son. "He wasn't on our radar yet, since we'd just started dating not too long before. I'm not even sure I'd use the term dating. More like hooking up exclusively."

She's quiet, so I continue. "We married because we were young and into each other and when you have that much success, you rarely think bad things can happen to you. Anyway, I'm not sure I was happy throughout the entire marriage. Her either. Obviously. You've read the tabloids, right?" I quirk my eyebrow.

Her lips form a thin line, but she nods.

"I finally had to stop caring how many people she cheated on me with."

Her hand runs down my chest. "I can't imagine why anyone would cheat on you."

I capture her hand. "I'm a lot different than I was then. I'd obsess over clients and spend weekends at the studio. When I built one in our house, I thought it would help, but it turned into me working all the time. I'd go down, telling myself I just wanted to listen to a recording one more time to adjust something or tell a client one more hour, and it always turned into four. I had my priorities backward."

"Still. She didn't have to cheat."

I hear the judgment in her tone. I've forgiven Maggie for everything except sleeping with my business partner Adam. There was no reason for either of them to do that. I might as well just get everything out while we're talking about this.

"It was over between us, but it screwed with my head when I caught her and Adam. Maybe because he was my sounding board during the divorce. Did you know Adam was engaged? They screwed over that girl too." I shake my head, remembering how badly it sucked.

She swings her leg over my waist and her long hair falls to one side of us. "There's one upside to your marriage not working out."

My hands run down the length of her torso, my eyes eating up her bare tits with the Hershey kiss nipples ready for devouring. "What would that be?"

"I'm in your bed tonight, not her."

I flip her over and she squeals. "You'll be in my bed for more than tonight."

Her hand lands on my chest. "Should we talk about this? Whatever's going on between us?"

I kiss her forehead. "Let's take it as it comes. Not put a label on it and see where it goes."

She smiles and rubs her hand on my beard.

I don't have the heart to tell her that she's going places and we're not headed in the same direction. But that's okay, because when it's time to say goodbye, she'll be living her dream and barely miss me. I'll be the one left behind.

"Okay, good idea. I guess that's why you're the older and wiser one between us."

I tickle her ribcage and she squirms under me. "I'm not that much older than you."

She stops laughing and looks at me with a serious expression. "Does my age bother you?"

I hem and haw for a minute. "At first I felt a little pervy, but to be honest, no, not really. Maybe it's a byproduct of living in LA for so long, where there are all kinds of older men with younger women on their arms, but I think it has more to do with the connection between us. As long as you don't call me old man, I'm good."

"Kiss me," she says, and I gladly lower my lips to hers.

She might've been named after the city of Phoenix, but she represents the symbolism of her name well. She'll always resurrect herself and rise. I just hope I don't suffocate in her ashes when she soars to heights only few in this world ever reach.

TWENTY-SEVEN

Phoenix

I never realized how fast things would move once I had connections and a demo. Griffin sent Van and Trey my demo first—with the warning that he was sending it to other people as well.

"I thought you trusted Van and Trey?" I ask him, sitting on the counter while he tries once again to install the sink.

Maverick's at school. The best part of that, other than I get to have Griffin all to myself, is that he's making some friends and looks forward to going to school now.

"I do trust them." His breath is labored. "But I'm not doing my job if I don't give them some competition. Believe me, they aren't the only ones who are going to want you. What we want is a bidding war. If my friends win, then great, but I won't let you end up in the hands of the wrong label." He slides out from under the sink and looks at me. "You know how distracting you are while I'm trying to do this?"

I hop down from the counter and straddle his middle, running my hands under his T-shirt. "How distracting?"

He groans and I rock my pelvis. "Very." His hands tighten on my hips to keep me in place.

"Have I told you I love track pants?" I slide off him.

His hands reach for me. "Why is that?"

I pull down the front of his track pants and his cock springs up. That I can get this reaction from him so quickly feels addictive. I rub up and down his shaft, my thumb teasing the tip.

"What are you doing?" He groans and the wrench falls from his hands onto the wood cabinet.

"Just a little payback for last night."

I lick up his length with my eyes locked on him. He takes the ponytail holder out of my hair, and the dark strands cascade down either side of my face. "You never have to pay me back. Having my face between your legs is always a pleasure."

For me too. I can still feel the scratch of his beard between my thighs.

Holding his dick by the base, I lick the tip. "Okay then, let's just say that I'd love to suck your cock." His hips jut up and we both laugh. His chuckle turns into a moan when I stroke him. "I think someone likes when I talk dirty."

His fingers thread through my hair, pushing it away from my face. "I fucking love it when you talk about my cock, period. Especially when you have it in your hands."

"Mmm." I lick my lips before wrapping my mouth over the head. His fingers tighten on my strands, and I run the tip of him along the roof of my mouth.

"Shit, Phoenix."

We've been having a lot of sex over the past week. After Maverick goes to bed, while he's at school, but this is the first blow job I've given Griffin and I really want to make a lasting impression. I'm hoping I achieve a spot in his brain that no other woman will ever meet.

Continuing to stroke him, I suck him and twirl my tongue around the crown while he grows stiffer in my mouth. When his hips pump as if he can't get far enough down my throat, I speed up my pace.

The only sounds in the kitchen are his pants and moans and the sound of me working his hard length.

"I'm gonna come," he says.

I glance up to see his back is still on the floor and he's no longer staring at me while I work him over. A string of warm liquid hits the back of my throat, and his hips jut up into my mouth a few times. After I swallow and lick him clean, I tuck him back into his track pants and stand.

"Where are you going?" He slides all the way out from under the sink.

"Back to where I was." I hop up on the counter.

He stands and his hands slide to the back of my neck, pulling me into a kiss. "Thank you. Just another thing you're amazing at."

I giggle, happy to hear the compliment.

His large palms slide up my inner thighs, spreading my legs apart for him. "But did you really think I'd just go back to working on the sink?"

"You do have to finish it. What round are we on now?"

He presses a kiss to the hollow of my neck. "I'd rather count our rounds." Picking me up, he swings me over his shoulder. "I've got two hours to ravage your body. What position haven't we tried yet?"

He carries me upstairs and tosses me onto his bed, then pulls off his track pants and tears his T-shirt over his head.

"Strip, girl."

"How about a please?"

He crawls up the bed and my heart rate speeds up the closer he gets. "Please, baby, let me see your gorgeous body. I promise to touch you in all the right places."

"How can a woman deny that request?" I tear off my shirt and hook my hands into my yoga pants. Griffin helps with my undergarments, throwing them across the room.

For the next two hours, he keeps his promise, leaving me spent. After we get out of the shower—so I don't smell like sex when I pick up Maverick—my legs are wobbly. I sit on the bed to watch him pull on a pair of jeans.

Oh, how nice it would be if he was really mine for the long term. I mentally chastise myself, knowing that's not likely how our story will end. We agreed to take things as they came and that's what I'll do. I don't even know how that thought ever got in my head.

GRANDMA DORI WANTS to see us, so after we pick up Maverick, we head to Northern Lights Retirement Center.

"What does she want?" Maverick asks from the back seat.

I shrug and look back at him. "I'll apologize now if she oversteps. She doesn't have a filter."

Griffin laughs and his hand moves to grab my thigh but diverts back to the steering wheel at the last second.

That's the only thing we have no idea how to handle. Do we tell Maverick or not? Griffin said he'll have to talk to Maggie first because they have an agreement that any new boyfriends or girlfriends will be discussed before introducing them to Maverick, but I'm not even sure we're classified as boyfriend/girlfriend.

"It's fine. If it wasn't for her, I might've bypassed you as Maverick's nanny. I owe her one." Griffin parks the truck, and Maverick opens up the back door and hops out. We stare at one another as his hand slides to my thigh and squeezes. "I'm calling Maggie tonight. We'll tell Maverick tomorrow evening."

I smile, liking the sound of being able to be public, but unsure of what it means in the long run for us.

We walk into the retirement center, and before we can get to Grandma Dori's hallway, we're flagged down by Ethel, who's watching TV in the common area. There are about ten elderly people crowded around watching *Temptation Island*.

"You guys watch this?" I ask.

Maverick sits down, but Griffin covers his eyes when a girl and guy are in a bed, making out.

"Dad!" he whines, wiggling to get out of his dad's hold, but Griffin is strong.

"It's a great show," some guy on the couch chirps.

"Grandma in her apartment?" I ask.

Ethel nods. "Yeah. She's in her room."

I chat with Ethel for a minute then leave them to their show, and the three of us head down the hall. When I reach Grandma Dori's apartment, I knock once, and she yells for us to come in. Maverick steps inside first.

"Brave man," Griffin jokes and I laugh.

Grandma Dori is sitting on her couch with her phone in her hands. "There you are. Help, Mav, I'm stuck."

"It's Maverick," he says with an eye roll reminiscent of a tween.

Griffin tugs on my shirt, and we share a quizzical look.

"Stuck on what?" I ask.

Maverick sits next to Grandma Dori. "Oh yeah, you need to get more accessories."

"I already have…"

The two of them talk a language I'm not familiar with, and the fact that Griffin looks as lost as me says he doesn't understand either.

"Is this what you called us over for?" I sit in the chair.

Grandma looks up briefly before her thumbs move on the screen again. "My arthritis slows me down."

"Here." Maverick holds out his hands, and Grandma passes him her phone.

"Why don't you two go to dinner? Maverick is going to teach me all about this RPG game."

"You're using the lingo now?" I raise an eyebrow.

"Come on, Phoenix, everyone knows RPG." She leans across to watch what Maverick is doing with her phone.

"You okay, Maverick?" Griffin asks and Maverick ignores him.

"We'll order pizza. You pick the toppings." Grandma nudges him, and Maverick tears his eyes away from his phone.

"I'm good," he says, then hands Grandma Dori back her phone, pulling his own from his pocket. "We can play against one another."

I stand from the chair and Griffin discreetly touches my fingers.

"Okay, we're going then," I say.

They don't look up as we step back.

"We won't be long. He has school in the morning," I say. Still nothing.

"Just go. They don't care about us," Griffin says.

We walk out of Grandma's apartment and shut the door.

"So?" I ask Griffin, who slides his hand in mine and walks us down the hall and out of the retirement center.

"I'm finally taking you on a date."

He opens his truck door and I climb in, waiting for him to round the hood and join me.

"You didn't plan this, did you?" I ask.

He winks. "Please. I never would imagine Maverick's playmate would be your grandma. Who could predict that?" He starts the truck and we drive out of the parking lot.

I'm not convinced he didn't have something to do with it, but like we agreed, I decide to take it as it comes for as long as I can.

TWENTY-EIGHT

Griffin

I press Maggie's name in my phone, and I calculate the time difference in my head. It's eight o'clock at night there and she's been saying how she's had late call times because they're shooting some night scenes, so she should be in the trailer by now.

"Griffin." She says my name as if I harass her or something.

"Hey, Maggie. How's shooting going?"

"Let's not do the small talk. Why are you calling me? I talked to Maverick last week. For some reason, he sounds happy in that no-man's-land you took him to. Did something happen?"

I inhale the deep breath I'll need to get through this conversation without an argument. She won't make it easy on me. I've never talked to her about anyone special. She hasn't either, and since we don't ask permission to sleep with someone, she doesn't need to call me once a day to fill me in. She has the libido of a sixteen-year-old. Sadly though, not when she was with me. I think monogamy kills her sex drive.

"He's still happy. When are you returning again?"

"Another three weeks. Are you gonna fly him down to LA?"

"Why don't you come up here? You can see his new life. I'm sure he wants to show you around. There's this donut place—"

She huffs. "Why are you calling me?"

There are voices in the background, and I know I'll only have her attention for so long, so I'd better spit it out. "I'm seeing someone, and I'll be informing Maverick tomorrow about the relationship. I'm only telling you because we agreed we would."

"Seeing someone?"

Suddenly all the voices in the background grow quiet. She's silenced them.

"Yeah."

"Who?" she asks. "One of Santa's helpers?"

"Yes, because we live at the North Pole."

I can picture her rolling her eyes, but her question was ridiculous.

"Who's the lucky woman?"

"That's not part of the stipulation, but just so there are no surprises, she's the woman I hired as Maverick's nanny."

Her manic laughter is like nails on a chalkboard. I have no idea how I stayed married to her as long as I did. Love for my son and drowning myself in work are my excuses.

"Seriously? I thought you decided to leave the LA life-style behind?" She laughs some more. "And you're telling me this why?"

"Because we said if anyone serious came into our lives, we'd tell each other before telling Maverick. I'm holding up my end of the bargain." I pace the bedroom, unable to stay seated. I knew she'd have something to say about the fact that Phoenix is Maverick's nanny.

"This is temporary, and you know it. Do you really think you're gonna marry the nanny?"

My fist clenches. It's tormenting to hate the woman who gave life to the person you love the most. "I like her, and I plan on pursuing a relationship with her."

"There's the romantic I know. The man who actually believes all the lyrics in a love song. I've told you how many times that love songs are for giving people false hope. They aren't reality."

"Maybe for some people. And having faith that you're meant for someone isn't such an absurd thought." Why am I even bothering to debate with her? Like I give a shit what she thinks.

"I give it a month."

"I don't give a flying fuck what you give it. It's none of your business. You've been told. Let me know when you actually want to see your son." I pull the phone from my ear and press the red button.

The phone vibrates in my hand. As quickly as her assistant can dial me up, I'm sure.

"What?"

"I'm sorry. Jeez, you're protective," Maggie says.

I was protective of us once upon a time, when my mom stared at me in the kitchen and asked what I was doing with a woman like Maggie Cooperton. At first, I'd thought she meant how did I get a movie star to fall in love with me, but it was clear from my mom's sour look that she meant it differently. I stuck up for us. I stuck up for her.

Years later, if my mom was less than spectacular, she

could've said I told you so. Instead she came out to help me for two months after the split. Moms are the best, and that's why I hate that Maverick's mom breezes in and out of his life.

"Why did you call back?" I ask, squeezing the bridge of my nose.

"I don't want things to be weird. Tell me about her."

"Don't you need to get on set?"

"I always have time for my family."

Ugh. Let me throw up my dinner now. "She's Maverick's nanny. She's from this town, and I like her. That's all you really need to know."

"What does she do?"

"I just told you, she's a nanny."

"Yes, but what will she do after you start a relationship with her?"

Frustration swims through my body until all my muscles are as tense as a stretched elastic band. "It's really none of your business."

She laughs again. Her fake one. I'm not sure I've heard her genuine laugh since Maverick was a baby and peed on me while I was changing his diaper. "Fine. Well, enjoy her for however long you can stay interested."

"You were the one who couldn't stay interested."

She huffs. "Just because I strayed doesn't mean I was the one who lost interest first. See you in a few weeks."

The line dies and I throw my phone on the bed.

Pressing my palms to my eyelids, I sit on the edge of the mattress. I didn't want Phoenix and me to be a secret. Mostly because once we step foot in LA, pictures will be taken and it'll all be out anyway. Tabloids will report. Word will get back to Maggie. Her ex-husband showing up with someone more than a decade younger than her? She'll be compared to Phoenix. It's just another part of the industry I hate.

Eventually I'll have to tell Phoenix that a future with me won't look like what she expects. She naively thinks she can have it all right now. Me *and* her stardom. But what she'll find out is that it's never that easy. Maybe her star will rocket to the top as soon as her first single hits the radio, or maybe it'll be a slower climb that builds and builds until the inevitable happens. Either way, she's going to be a star and out of my reach at some point. I plan on enjoying whatever time we can have together until I have to let her go to pursue her dream.

A soft knock lands on my door, interrupting my line of thinking.

"Come in," I say.

Phoenix slides in and shuts the door. She's wearing a pair of boxer shorts and a tight white tank top. Like a fucking wet dream. Even her long dark hair is pulled high in a ponytail, revealing one of my favorite parts of her body—her neck. Definitely the spot I love to kiss. I open my arms and she tiptoes across the floor.

"He's been asleep for two hours. I think you're good," I say with a smile.

"I heard you on the phone," she whispers, finding her spot between my legs.

I place my hands on her thighs, running my palms up and down the smooth skin. When I lower my head to rest on her stomach, she runs her hands through my hair.

"How did we get here?" I ask, because I feel as though we've gone from zero to sixty in the blink of an eye. One day she was my nanny, then I fired her, and now I want her with me all the damn time.

"Um... how do you want me to answer that?"

I shrug, pulling her closer. Needing her close to not allow the questions and doubts to fill my mind. Resting my chin on her stomach, I stare up at her. "She gives us a month."

Phoenix raises her eyebrows. "And you think she's right?"

"No." I cling to her harder.

Maggie is cynical, much like most of LA. Relationships only work for so long, and if Phoenix's dream was to stay in Lake Starlight, I'd say screw Maggie, she doesn't know. But it's not. Phoenix has to be in LA in order to fulfill her dream.

"Then who cares what she thinks?" Her fingers thread through my hair, scratching my scalp in the best possible way.

"You're right."

The only one whose opinion matters is Maverick and I'm not telling him. Not because I don't want to but because I've arranged for a long weekend in LA for Phoenix to meet with some record labels, and my gut tells me she'll be leaving us soon after.

She sits on my leg and wraps her arms around my neck. "I better get to bed." She kisses my cheek and stands to leave.

"Where do you think you're going? Get in my bed." I pull her back down and slide my thigh between her legs.

"Such a caveman. I like this side of you."

I swallow her laughter with a kiss, pushing all the bullshit out of my head.

TWENTY-NINE

Phoenix

We land in LA, and right away I pick up on the fact that this is a different Griffin than I'm used to. All of his actions and words toward Maverick and I feel cold and calculated. So Maverick and I stick together, walking behind Griffin as if I actually am just his nanny.

A car waits for us once the luggage is taken off the private plane, and Griffin ushers us inside as if we're Kardashians.

Maverick's been on his phone the entire time, his thumbs moving a mile a minute, and he seems unfazed by all this. Griffin has said nothing to him about it, and because I'm still in that weird zone between nanny and daddy's girlfriend, disciplining Maverick when Griffin is around feels odd, so I let it slide.

"Maverick, you're going on a playdate with Harrison," Griffin says once the car is driving away from the airport.

"Harrison? Why him?"

"Phoenix and I have a few appointments this morning. Harrison's mom agreed to watch you."

"Why didn't I just stay in Lake Starlight?" He peeks up from his phone.

"Because I didn't think you'd want to stay there for four days without me and it'd be nice for you to see your old friends." Griffin shuffles through paperwork in his lap and pulls out his phone.

"I could've stayed with Denver or someone."

I side-glance at Griffin, who appears as shocked as me that Maverick would rather be in Lake Starlight than in LA.

"Well, it's only for today." Griffin turns his attention back to his papers, and Maverick buries his head back in his phone.

A half hour later, we pull up to a gated house and Griffin presses the button for security, tells them who's here, and the iron gates open. Uncomfortableness sets in when I realize I'm going to be around these uber-rich people.

As the car pulls around the circular drive, Griffin's hand lands on my thigh. "We'll be right back."

I let out a quick sigh of relief. Okay then, I don't have to worry about meeting anyone and feeling inadequate.

"Bye, Maverick," I say.

He smiles and climbs out without even saying goodbye. I watch through the tinted window as Griffin rings the doorbell. A woman opens the door, but based on the uniform she's wearing, she's a housekeeper or staff member. They step inside, and the door shuts.

Pulling out my phone, I text Sedona.

Me: *This is like another world.*

Three dots appear right away.

Sedona: *You lived in LA. For two years.*

Me: *Griffin's LA is VERY different than my LA.*
Sedona: *:P Welcome to the big time sis.*

My stomach coils with tension. Is it nerves about what this could mean for my career or is this about Griffin?

Me: *Griffin's acting weird.*
Sedona: *Well he did run away from that place.*

God, I'm so selfish for not even considering what it's taking for him to come here and help me.

Sedona: *And before you ask, the answer is yes. You need to talk to him about it.*
Me: *I hate you.*
Sedona: *You hate that I always know what you're thinking.*
Me: *True enough.*

The door opens and I hammer out another text to Sedona.

Me: *Gotta go. I'll text later.*
Sedona: *Love you.*

Griffin slides into the back seat and I lean into him, finally comfortable enough to show affection now that Maverick is gone. He smiles at me and kisses my temple.

"Hey," I say, taking his phone out of his hands and putting it on the other side of me.

"Hey," he mimics, and his eyes focus on the phone at my side.

Directing his chin with my finger, I drag his attention to me. "Are you okay being here?"

He presses a light kiss to my forehead. "Yes. I'm just trying to make sure you get what you deserve. It's not as easy as you think to get you the best deal."

"That's not your job. Should I get an agent or a manager or something?"

"Eventually yeah, but I can get you this far. My assumption is Van and Trey will come in the highest. They love you and trust me. But we have to show them there's competition."

I sit up straighter since he doesn't seem interested in making out in the back seat. "But they're your friends. I'm cool with signing with them. I just want to get out there."

He smirks and shakes his head, tapping his finger on my nose as if I'm some naive little kid. "They might be my friends, but if you don't make demands now and show them you have options, they'll walk all over you. We're going to get you a deal that'll give you everything you've dreamed of. There's more than money to think about. You have to consider subsidiary rights, writing credit, who owns the tracks once they're recorded, who gets final say on what makes it onto the album and gets released by radio."

I sit rigidly in my seat, feeling overwhelmed.

Griffin reaches over me, picking up his phone. "I'm sorry though. I've grown to hate this city, and it's put me in a sour mood."

I put my hand on his thigh. "Thank you for doing this for me."

"You're welcome," he says while looking at his phone.

Though I'm more grateful than I could ever express, I don't like this Griffin at all.

WHEN WE REACH the first record company, Griffin walks in ahead of me, his posture straight, chin up, almost as if he's preparing for battle. It's strange to see him almost put on a mask before we walk through the door. He refrains from holding my hand or showing any affection—which I guess I shouldn't be surprised by, but that doesn't mean I have to like it.

The receptionist greets him with a huge smile. We're not in the waiting area for longer than a few minutes before a guy comes out, giving Griffin a boisterous hello.

He puts his hand out in front of me. "Ben Jennings."

"Phoenix Bailey," I say and shake his hand.

"Let's go have a chat." He motions toward the hallway he came down.

Griffin lets me walk in front of him, and when we arrive at the conference room, I'm surprised to find two more men waiting in sharp suits, coffees with their order scribbled on the side beside them.

"Phoenix, this is Ashton Cash and Teddy Newton."

I shake the two men's hands, but they only grant me their attention for a moment before smiling at the man behind me.

"Griffin," Ashton says. "Glad to see you around again."

"Last I heard, you were fighting mountain lions," Teddy chimes in.

Griffin laughs and shakes their hands.

"But I guess there's some talent up there in Alaska." Ben pulls out a chair for me and I sit. "We're impressed, Phoenix."

Griffin sits next to me, and Ben joins Ashton and Teddy

on the other side, creating an imaginary dividing line down the middle of the table.

"Thanks," I say.

"This should be easy, and we'll make it quick," Ben says. "We know you have meetings with Aces High and Conner Label, so we're going to give you our figure upfront." He slides a contract across the table toward Griffin.

I'm feeling as if I'm some little girl who can't negotiate for herself. Then again, I would've just gone with Van and Trey. They were nice when they were in Lake Starlight.

Griffin sits back in his chair and glances through the paperwork, then pushes the paper away from him. "I know you're kidding. She's worth a lot more than that. That's an original song, and if you release it as a single, you'll make a killing."

The three men exchange glances.

"She's a newbie. We might think she has something special, but we don't know for sure. The consumers make that decision." Ashton leans back in his chair, his fingers steepled in front of him. "Though I will say her body will help sell the image. She's a hottie, which ups her earning potential."

Somehow, I manage to keep my mouth from dropping open. Listening to someone describe me as if I'm an asset and not an actual person is upsetting and feels icky. It's not as if I didn't know that appearance matters in this industry, but I didn't think they'd be so blatant about it.

Griffin's hand slips from the table onto my bouncing knee and squeezes. "We want a clause in there that says the single releases first. If it's successful, then she gets a bonus when the album is released."

Ben sits up straighter. "Which we were wondering about, Grif. Would you be the one to produce her album?"

"Yes," I answer, seeming to throw off the men that I can actually speak for myself.

"No." Griffin squeezes my knee again and removes his hand. "But I'll find her the right person."

Ashton leans back in his chair with a smug smile. "So you're really out of the game? We thought maybe this was a comeback move."

So did I. I mean, we hadn't discussed it or anything, but I'd assumed he'd want to produce my album if I were to make one.

"No. Phoenix is..." He looks at me for a second, but with that mask on, I can't tell what he's thinking. "She's someone special and has an incredible voice. I wanted to work with her and get her where she needs to be, but my life is in Alaska with my son now."

Reality hits me like a swift fist to the chest. I spring up out of my chair, it slides out behind me, and everyone's attention shifts to me. "Excuse me. I need to use the bathroom."

Ashton stands. "It's down the hall on your right." He directs me with his finger.

I barely follow where he's pointing. Pushing the conference room door open, I steadily walk until I see the women's restroom sign. Once inside, I bend over to catch my breath.

"Are you okay?" A woman rushes to my side and runs her hand up and down my back before leading me to the bench in the fancy sitting area outside of the stalls.

I glance up and freeze, staring at a woman I've admired the majority of my life.

"Do you need a wet cloth?" Cammie Sanchez stands in front of me in a cute mini skirt and oversized sweatshirt.

I really am on another planet.

THIRTY

Griffin

I'm still in heavy negotiation with Ashton, since he's the bulldog of the group, when I realize Phoenix has been gone for a while.

"Why are you keeping yourself out of the game? You have a hidden talent under your wing," Ben says.

Teddy is quiet. He always lets his brothers—and by brothers, I mean frat brothers—talk for him.

"I made my decision when I left. Finding Phoenix doesn't change that."

"And you're sleeping with her?" Ashton asks with a cocky smirk, almost challenging me as if he wants to steal her from me in that way too.

I give a curt nod. "I am."

"But it's not serious enough to shake up your life, huh? Still a bachelor."

Ashton's one to talk. He can't keep his dick in his pants. He's the only record label owner who's regularly in the tabloids with different actresses, singers, and YouTube stars.

"My arrangement with Phoenix isn't part of the contract," I say through gritted teeth. "You'll have to come up with something better if you want to sign Phoenix."

It's chancy—because they're offering her a helluva deal financially and if it was anyone else, I'd probably advise them to take it—but Phoenix deserves the best. If I'm going to leave her, then I want her to be in the best position she can be and have control over her career.

Ashton laughs. "You forget how easy it was to steal one budding artist from you. I'm sure we can take another."

A hot burst of anger shoots through my veins. Maybe Phoenix was right. Maybe I should've gone with Van and Trey right away. This company, and Ashton especially, are willing to play dirty. They did with Cammie and no doubt they will with Phoenix.

I slide my chair out from the table. "This was a bad idea."

Ashton stands and the other two follow suit. "Afraid we'll take another girl from your bed?"

I shake my head. He has no idea what he's talking about, and though I'd love to knock that smug look off his face, I'd love it more to stay out of the tabloids. "Thanks for your time."

I turn to exit the conference room, but my feet feel as if they're in cement when I see Phoenix walking in with Cammie Sanchez right behind her. My past collides with my present and all I can think about is what Cammie could have told her?

"Griffin," Cammie says, her gaze sliding down my body as if she owns me. "It's been too long." She throws herself into my body, leaving me no option other than to hug her.

"Yeah." My eyes land on Phoenix, and I notice she's biting that lower lip of hers and wearing a fake smile.

"I thought you were out of the business, but then Phoenix just told me that you discovered her—in Alaska, of all places." Cammie and her passive-aggressive tone can fuck right off. This is exactly why I got out of the city. "We just swapped Griffin Thorne stories in the restroom. They're oddly similar."

"Not at all similar." I try to lock eyes with Phoenix, but she's too busy staring at Cammie to notice.

"When you found me, I was a nobody," Cammie purrs.

"Phoenix has never been a nobody," I say with conviction.

Finally Phoenix looks at me.

"Oh, protective of your new little star, huh?" Cammie locks arms with Phoenix.

Phoenix looks at me with one question after another in her eyes. There's so much I should've warned Phoenix about before we landed on California soil. How was I so foolish to think none of this bullshit would surface when I brought her here?

"I'm protective of my *girlfriend*." I hold my hand out for Phoenix. A wave of relief hits me when she accepts it and comes to stand at my side.

"Oh, you're willing to label it with *her*. It must be serious." Cammie crosses her arms and cocks out a hip.

"You and I both know there was nothing between us." I squeeze Phoenix's hand, willing her to believe me.

Cammie laughs, uncrosses her arms, and looks Phoenix up and down. "Funny. I always thought you were an ass man, but..." She tilts her head as if she's judging Phoenix. "I guess not."

She probably thought she shared something real with Cammie in the restroom, but she's a woman with two faces. The sweetness of a sleeping cat with the bite of a tiger.

"I'm not doing this," I say.

I push open the door of the conference room. Stopping to let Phoenix go first, I release her hand, an apology on my lips, but Cammie pipes up before any more words leave my mouth.

"I hope he isn't leading you on like he did to me—taking what he wants before tossing you aside."

She's gotta be kidding me.

"Come on." I tug on Phoenix's hand.

Finally I'm successful in getting Phoenix out of the office.

Once we're in the elevators, she releases my hand and crosses her arms. "Time for you to start talking."

"Let's go get lunch... and talk."

WE SIT down at a restaurant around the corner from the Aces High Record Label. They're supposed to be our last meeting, but after the shit show that just went down, I'm thinking it'd be best for Phoenix to work with guys I trust.

After she orders a salad and I order a sandwich, Phoenix leans back in her chair. "So? Talk."

I nod, knowing I can't put off this discussion any longer. "Like most people in LA, I had a therapist for a while, and she told me the situation with Cammie is called transference. Sometimes when you work closely with someone, you start to see things that aren't there. Cammie thought I was hitting on her. She shared deep things about her life with me as we grew closer."

"Like I did?"

I hear it in her tone. She's doubting what we have, wondering if she's doing the same thing. I can't say it's not something I'm scared of—that her feelings for me aren't genuine and could just be because I'm the one helping to get her where she wants to be.

"Truthfully, yeah."

A loud clatter sounds from a waiter dropping a dish and she jumps in her seat.

I reach across the table for her hand. "I never had a relationship with Cammie. I'm not sure what she told you, but we never even kissed. I never slept with her. She imagined something was there, and when I turned her down, she got angry. She signed with those guys and got another producer."

She releases a big breath and her shoulders relax a bit. "She said you used her to further your career."

I shrug. "Sounds like how she'd spin it."

"So you never had a relationship with her?"

I shake my head and squeeze her hand. "No."

"Okay."

"You're different, Phoenix. You know that, right?"

She nods, taking her hand out of mine and picking up her water goblet. She doesn't believe me though. Her tough front back at the office was just Phoenix being Phoenix and erecting her wall so she can't be hurt. I want her to have the self-confidence to make it in this town.

"Why aren't you going to work on the album with me?" She places her water glass down and locks eyes with me.

"Because—"

"You're worried about transference?"

I shake my head. "You do know that I won't be moving back to LA, right?"

She nibbles on her bottom lip. "I wondered about that."

Sliding my chair closer to her, I put a hand on her cheek. This is something we should've talked about before coming here. "There's a reason I got out of LA. And I can't uproot Maverick again. He likes Lake Starlight."

"But I can be in Lake Starlight. We can work on the album up there. Maybe build a recording studio. I could fly back and forth."

I smile at her naivety. It'll never work. She'll be gone more than she's there and I want more than that from my partner—for me and my son. And I care too much about her not to see her achieve her lifelong dream. "You want stardom. You want the spotlight. You want the celebrity and the fame. All that comes with a price. Eventually you'll have concert tours and press and album launches. You should go out there and claim what's yours. I want that for you. I truly do."

"Then why are you doing all this? The meetings with the labels, helping me with a single. I thought you missed music and wanted to get back into it?"

A sad sort of chuckle leaves my lips. "I enjoyed it. I did. I loved every second of working with you. It is something I love, and if I could stay in my bubble in Lake Starlight and help artists from afar, I would, but I don't think that'll work."

She stares at me for a second. "After I sign... you're done? Is that it?"

"Do you really think a long-distance relationship would work?"

Her face drops and she tears her gaze away from me. "You knew this whole time that you were going to break up with me?"

I look around to make sure no one is staring at us. "No. I mean, yes. I mean... I knew it wasn't feasible for us to continue seeing one another once your career was off the ground, but I selfishly wanted you for as long as I could have you." I tuck a strand of hair behind her ear.

"Here I thought we might have a future, and you knew our expiration date all along." A tear slips down her cheek and my chest squeezes.

"Phoenix, listen to me—"

She stands abruptly, her chair screeching across the floor.

If I was hoping there wasn't going to be a scene, there is now.

She beelines it for the exit, and once I've thrown some cash on the table, I race after her.

She's halfway down the road before I catch up to her. "Phoenix."

"You set me up for heartbreak!" Tears track down her face and I feel like the biggest douche alive.

"No, I didn't."

"You did! Is this some sick trick to pull a heartbreaking song out of me? To make me feel or whatever that bullshit philosophy of yours is?"

I pull her into the side of a retaining wall, locking her body to it with my hips. "No."

I cup her face and stare into her dark eyes. They're full of heartbreak and it cracks my chest as wide open as if a gorilla was tearing out the beating organ with its bare hands. I don't *want* to hurt her. I *want* to take her in my arms, return her to Lake Starlight, and convince her she doesn't need this in her life.

But that's not fair to her. If I told her right now how much I love her, I'd only be holding her back from moving on from me.

"You have to see that I'm right," I whisper, wiping away her tears with my thumbs.

She straightens and pushes against my chest. "You know how I see it? You're a coward." She shrugs out of my hold and stomps down the street before whipping around. "Don't follow me! Don't help me anymore! We're over! Business and relationship. Thank you for what you've done for me so far, but I've got it from here."

My head falls back for a moment. "Phoenix..."

But she flags down a cab and hops in.

I sink down against the wall and bury my head in my hands. This is the right decision. We can't be together if one of us is down here and the other one is four thousand miles away. She'll see one day that I'm right and thank me. Maybe it'll even be from the podium when she's accepting a Grammy.

THIRTY-ONE

Phoenix

Griffin sends me a text. A fucking text after I left him on the side of a road in the middle of Los Angeles.

Griffin: *You have an appointment with Aces High at three o'clock. Sign with them. They'll take good care of you.*
Griffin: *Chateau Marmont – reservation #C128736*
Griffin: *The hotel is paid up for as long as you need.*

Ugh. I throw my phone into my purse and sit on a park bench. I don't need his charity. I have the money he's paid me for watching Maverick. Not as much as I thought I would have, but the last person I need help from now is Griffin Thorne.

My phone rings in my purse and I pull it out, hoping it's Griffin saying how stupid he was, that of course we'll make this work because we're worth it. But as I pick it up and stare at the screen, I see Sedona's name.

"Hi."

"What happened?" she asks. "I got a text from Denver that said to call you ASAP. Did you get a deal?"

She's so excited that it takes me a minute before I figure out the channel of communication that got Sedona to call me. Griffin called Denver who called Sedona.

The tears come hot and fast when the finality that he's not changing his mind hits me. He's not going to appear from behind a corner and pull me into his arms, telling me he can't live without me. Maybe I was only someone to get him off temporarily. To prove that he still has it. That he can take a girl from Small Town, Alaska, and perfect her voice so that three record labels fight over her. Maybe it was all to boost his ego.

"Phoenix. Talk to me. What happened?"

"We... broke... up."

After a long silence, she says, "I'm sorry."

There's no surprise in her voice. No "he's an idiot." No "how does he throw away the best thing to happen to him?" Just two simple words that someone who doesn't even know me would say. This is my twin. She's supposed to feel for me.

"Did you know he was going to do this?" I ask.

She releases a breath. "No, but Griffin left LA for Lake Starlight. You're looking to leave Lake Starlight for LA. Your lives are going in two different directions. Of course I didn't know, but I suspected it wouldn't work." She's using her soft tone, her velvet-gloved voice, so I don't react.

"Am I selfish for thinking we could?"

She giggles and stops abruptly when I don't join her. "You're Phoenix. The world should revolve around you."

"That's not true. But I think we could make it work."

"It would be hard. You'd have to sacrifice so much. He has an eight-year-old son. How did you not think about any of this?"

Now Sedona is gonna be judgmental with me? "I gotta go."

"What? Phoenix, just wait—"

But I hang up. I don't need another "told you so" or "you don't think" or "should have." What I feel for Griffin is more than just physical and now I'm getting the 'I release you so you can fly away' line. Well, this little birdie isn't flying back.

I stand and swipe my face free of tears. When my phone rings again, I power it off and shove it into my purse. They can all go to hell. Griffin might've gotten me here with his connections, but I'll make my own destiny. He can sit on his couch in Lake Starlight and watch me do interviews and perform at award shows and regret his decision to let me go.

But first, I need a milkshake. A double chocolate milkshake. Then I'll be good as new.

I WALK into Aces High Record Label and find Trey talking to the receptionist. He's in a T-shirt and jeans, his hair askew, looking nothing like one of the most powerful men in the music business.

"Phoenix." He pushes off the receptionist's desk, and she looks disappointed that she's lost his attention. Meeting me halfway, he hugs me. "How are you?"

"Great."

"Great?" He looks down at my milkshake.

"Yep."

I'm not stupid. He knows what transpired. Griffin would've called his friends to say "yeah, I ditched the girl, so be nice." I'm pissed at him, but I also know he's too nice not to do that. The pity in Griffin's eyes when he explained how naive I was to think we might be able to make it work tells me he never wanted to break my heart. I'll give him that much at least.

"Okay then. Let's get upstairs and talk to the man." Trey nods toward the bank of elevators and I step forward first.

Once we're in an elevator by ourselves, I ask, "Aren't you the man too?"

"Van likes the business end. I like the creative. If you sign today, I have a few ideas about image we should discuss."

"Image?"

He laughs as if I'm so out of my element. "We have to put together an image of who you are and what you represent. Your single will depict some of that, but with an album, we have some room to tweak where we need to."

I sip my milkshake. "Will I have any say in any of this?"

He laughs and shakes his head. "More or less. But we'll advise you on the route we think you should go with."

My milkshake finishes with a slurp right as the elevator doors open.

Trey laughs again, putting out his arm for me to go first. "Sorry about your sister, you know? She was fun and all, but my life is down here."

Jeez, I'm a shit sister. I haven't even talked to Juno about her time with Trey because I was too concerned with the man who tore out my heart and stomped on it in the middle of Los Angeles. "Yeah, those geographical reasons are holding a lot of weight on relationships these days."

He stops before opening the office doors.

Yeah, he knows.

"Van was worried I fucked it up for us signing you. I felt like an apology was necessary." Trey opens the door and dramatically bends at the waist as if I'm royalty.

It's the least he can do without a heartfelt apology for what I assume was screwing over my sister.

"I guess you didn't make too big of an impression because she hasn't said anything to me." I pat him on the back and give him a saccharine smile.

His eyes go wide.

Yes, two can play that game, Trey Galger.

"You're dangerous." He laughs. He reminds me a little of Denver, except Trey seems to lack true emotion.

Trey leads me to a small office. I'm thankful we're not meeting in a conference room. Maybe they don't have one. This entire office is smaller than the frat boys' one. I ditched the second meeting because Griffin never sent me the information. I hope he canceled though, so I'm not blackballed by them in the future.

Van stands up from behind his desk and puts out a cigarette.

"Isn't it illegal to smoke inside a building?" I ask.

He shrugs. "I pay the rent here." Van comes around the desk and hugs me as if we're old friends. "So good to see you again." Drawing back, he signals to a chair. "Have a seat."

Trey sits on a window ledge with a foot propped up on the arm of a chair.

"We're thrilled Griffin finally released you. He's such a perfectionist. It can be annoying at times," Van says, retaking his seat behind his desk.

Finally released me?

"But the single proves his worth and why, with his help, so many artists have resulted in Grammys." Trey smiles.

I nod. "He definitely knows what he's doing."

"This is the contract. Have someone look over it and let us know if you have any concerns." Van hands me a packet of papers. "It's a fair offer. Griffin went to bat for you, and I think it has everything in there that will make you happy."

I grab a pen out of the holder and sign before pushing the papers across the desk.

"Phoenix," Van says, picking up the packet.

"You can't do that." Trey pushes off the ledge and sits in the chair next to me. Taking the contract from Van, he hands it back to me. "You have to read it, understand it, and feel good about it." He looks at Van, who blows out a breath and comes over to sit on the edge of his desk in front of me.

"We're sorry to hear about what happened. Griffin is a hard one to figure out. He's..." Van looks over my shoulder and I follow his line of sight, hoping Griffin returned, but the door is shut. "Well, Trey is right. You have to protect yourself." Van pulls a Post-it note off his desk with a name and number scribbled on it. "I want you to call this woman, and if you like her, hire her. She's a great agent, and I want you to take the contract, have her read it over, *then* decide if you want to sign."

Tears well in my eyes, and despite me doing my best to stop them, they cascade down my cheeks anyway. I haven't cried this much since my parents passed away. Trey plucks the empty milkshake cup out of my hands and places it on Van's desk. Then he slides his chair over and puts his arm around my shoulders.

Van blows out a breath and watches Trey console me before handing me a tissue from his desk. "He really is doing the best thing for you. You might not understand it now, but when you're selling out arenas and touring Europe, singing to screaming fans, you'll understand why the two of you won't work."

"I can set you up with Tyler Vaughn," Trey says. "He's kind of an idiot, but you two could collaborate on a song or something."

"Griffin doesn't like Tyler's song," I manage to get out, remembering Maverick's words.

"Yeah, well, there are two artists who kind of screwed Griffin over. Tyler Vaughn and Cammie Sanchez." Van rounds his desk and sits in his chair, tapping his pen.

"The two of you are on different paths right now. Who knows? Maybe something will happen one day, and your paths will merge again, but he did the smart thing for now," Trey says.

"Where the hell did you get that?" Van asks Trey.

I slide out of Trey's hug and steal another tissue before blowing my nose.

Trey says, "What? I'm the creative one out of the two of us."

"Yeah, but usually you'd say, 'Shit happens, get over it.'"

"She's crying, man, have a heart." Trey smiles at me.

I can't help the laugh from bubbling up my throat. "Thanks, guys."

Van's eyes shift to the Post-it note. "I'm serious. Meet with her. Get a lawyer if you have to."

"Are you guys always this nice?" I tuck the contract in my purse.

"We're not into screwing over artists to get them to sign with us. We want our deals to be beneficial to all parties."

"I like my sleep at night," Trey adds, and I laugh.

Van rolls his eyes.

When I leave Aces High, I call the woman on the Post-it—Jannie Reider. She was expecting my call, so I make plans to meet with her in the morning. In the meantime, I take pictures of my contract and send them to the best businesswoman I know—my sister Savannah.

THIRTY-TWO

Griffin

Maverick slams his bedroom door when we return home to Lake Starlight. The trip being cut short isn't what he's upset about. I had to sit him down and tell him Phoenix wouldn't be coming back.

I take in the kitchen. The faucet not on the sink. Her hair tie on the counter. Her keys in the dish. She's everywhere. Even her scent still lingers.

Heading from the kitchen to the garage, I grab the last Amazon box that was delivered. Back in the kitchen, I toss her ponytail holder in the box. Then I pick up the candle she bought at the farmer's market and add it to the box. The book she finished with her head in my lap while I watched the Dodgers game is next. Another hair tie. In the box. The deodorizer she put in the bathroom. In the box. I didn't realize how much she had saturated our lives.

I finish collecting her things then head to her bedroom. After grabbing a few suitcases, I put them on her bed and fill them with the rest of her clothes and jewelry.

I drop onto the mattress and the box spills over onto the floor, all her belongings now laid out in front of me. I run my hand through my hair, repeating the same shit I've been telling myself all weekend. This is what has to happen. I can't keep her. She's meant to fly, not be caged in with an eight-year-old stepson in the small town she has a love-hate relationship with.

My doorbell rings. I stand up and stop in the hallway, hearing Maverick open his door.

He stares at me, hopeful that it's who I hope it is too.

We both head down the stairs.

I look out the side window and see an Uber pull away. Could it really be her?

Maverick swings the door open, and we both step back.

"Not much of a greeting." When we don't say anything, Maggie walks in, leaving her luggage on the front porch.

"What are you doing here?" I step out and pick up her suitcases, bringing them inside.

"I'm here to see my son. Come here, Maverick." She opens her arms, and Maverick steps into them, allowing her to hug him. "Why is everyone so glum? Helloooo? I'm here after filming two movies back to back." She looks at Maverick and grabs him by his chin with her thumb and forefinger. "Aren't you excited? I flew directly here."

What would she have done had we still been in LA?

"Is there a hotel I can call for you?" I ask.

She rolls her eyes. "I'll stay here. You have plenty of room, and I'll make myself scarce you know from"—she covers Maverick's ears—"the nanny."

"Maverick knows, and she's not here." I head into the kitchen because a beer sounds good right about now.

"Oh. Where's the nanny?"

"Her name is Phoenix, and he ruined everything." Maverick points at me.

I crack open a beer, ignoring the wine that Phoenix left in the fridge.

"Break up already?" Maggie lifts her wrist as if there's a watch there. "Faster than I figured."

"She's signing a record deal right now and I don't want to live in LA. Not that any of this is your business."

"I'm going to get my phone." Maverick leaves his mother's side, but she grabs him again.

Maggie pulls him into her chest, swaying them back and forth. "I missed you so much."

When she releases him, he pushes down his misplaced hair and runs upstairs. I bet we don't see him for the rest of the night.

Maggie joins me in the kitchen. "I don't get offered a drink?"

"What are you doing here?" I lean against my counter, arms crossed and my beer dangling from one hand.

She glances at the sink and laughs. "Still think you can work with your hands, huh? You're not your father." Making herself at home, she opens the fridge and takes out a water. "I have to say, it's disappointing that you went with such a cliché relationship. I mean, an aspiring singer? Really, Grif?"

"The last person I'm talking about this with is you."

She sits at the breakfast island, soaking in my house. I'm thankful I already removed all of Phoenix's stuff. I don't want or need her judgment.

"Oh, we can talk about your relationship problems," she says. "We haven't been together for years."

"Not happening."

She blows out a breath. "You're so black or white. Live

in the grey once in a while. Or hell, live in color and enjoy life."

I push off the counter. "Are you taking Maverick for the weekend?"

"I thought I'd stay here. Now without the nanny in the way, you can show me around." She smiles and sips her water.

"Not gonna happen. You're not welcome in my home. So I can call a hotel for you if you'd like, or you can use the visitation you're owed and take Maverick somewhere. He'd probably enjoy a hotel so he can swim."

She laughs. "Want to wallow in your heartbreak?" She makes her voice babyish-sounding, and the urge to physically remove her from my house is fierce.

My phone dings in my pocket, and I welcome the distraction.

Van: *She signed this morning. Jannie will be representing her.*

Me: *Thanks.*

Van: *You sure about this?*

Me: *Yes. This is the right thing to do.*

Van: *I get it, but I miss you. I can't lie, I'd hoped she was the reason you'd move back.*

Me: *This is home for the foreseeable future.*

Van: *You're already back in Alaska?*

Me: *Arrived this morning. No reason for me to be there anymore. Just... look out for her, okay?*

Van: *Don't worry. Trey's mothering skills are top notch and he's on the case.*

Me: *Thanks.*

Van: *That's what friends are for.*

"Is that her?" Maggie interrupts me.

"You need to go. Make your plans now because we're divorced, and I don't need or want you in this house."

She stands. "You're so welcoming. Jeez, she really did a number on you."

Yeah, she did, but my ex-wife is the last person I'm going to open up to.

A half hour later, an upset Maverick hops in a car with his mom to go stay at the Glacier Point Resort and I get to sit in my house filled with memories of Phoenix. I'm not sure I got the better end of the deal this time around.

THE NEXT AFTERNOON, a familiar truck pulls up my driveway. I'm in the garage, trying to keep my mind off of Phoenix by being somewhere she didn't spend time. But having a new SUV means I can't pretend to fix my vehicle, so I'm installing shelves. To hold what? I haven't figured that out yet.

"You going to hide out indefinitely?" Denver walks up the driveway. He pulls out a large bucket of paint the painters left behind and sits on it.

I don't look over. "I'm installing shelves."

"I see that. They're crooked."

I step back, and sure as shit they are. "Fuck." I throw my wrench and it hits the drywall, leaving a huge hole. Just like the one in my chest.

Denver slides over another bucket of paint and slaps the lid. "Let's have a chat."

"Is this where you're nice before you kick my ass?" I sit down beside him.

"Why would I kick your ass?"

"I broke up with your sister."

When I texted him to tell Sedona to call Phoenix, he didn't say anything other than "Done." I feared a late-night knock on my door once I returned.

"You're forgetting one key thing. You selflessly broke up with my sister."

"What are you talking about?"

He laughs. "You love her, don't you?"

I say nothing but stare down between my legs. I should own the feeling, but somehow, admitting it out loud feels like it will make the heartache that much worse. "It doesn't matter."

"It kind of does."

I pick up my head and look at him. "Why?"

"Well, you're making the decision for the both of you."

"Please don't."

"Don't what?" he asks, leaning forward to rest his forearms on his thighs.

"Don't try the reverse psychology thing. I'm older than you, remember? I did what needed to be done and it's over. Your sister has a great career ahead of her and I have a great life here in Lake Starlight. This is where our story ends."

He stands and blows out a breath. "So that's it? No talking you out of it, huh?"

"It's done. Believe me, she'll find love again. Not that she necessarily loved me. But she'll recover from the hurt once she sees her name on a billboard or hits number one on the charts."

Denver smiles and puts his hand out between us. "Then I guess there's only one more thing to say."

I shake his hand. "What?"

"Thanks. Thanks for helping Phoenix get the opportunity to shine."

I huff and stand. "My pleasure. And to think you were worried about her being my nanny."

"I guess it turned out okay, huh?"

I shake my head. "Stop it."

He laughs. "Okay, but you know I won't be the last Bailey to visit you, right? There are two more."

"Am I in the *Christmas Carol* movie?"

He walks backward to his truck. "Remember, the Ghost of Christmas Future is always the scariest. I think we both know which Bailey that will be." He opens his truck door.

"Who?"

Laughing, he sticks his head out the window. "G'ma D, of course."

He pulls out of my driveway and I can still hear him laughing. When he reaches the end, he waves goodbye and speeds down my street.

I pick up the wrench and start disassembling the shelf so I can start over. No way he's telling the truth. Why would the Baileys care whether I date Phoenix or not?

THIRTY-THREE

Griffin

Two weeks later, Maverick and I have avoided downtown Lake Starlight, but in the process, we've discovered other parts of Alaska—like I'd hoped to do with my son. We've hiked trails, discovered waterfalls, and he was in awe when we saw our first moose.

But even though we're moving on, it still feels as if something's missing. I can't find anyone to watch after Maverick—at least not anyone who feels right. I'm not sure if it's because Phoenix was a part of our lives from day one or if her presence left a lasting impression we just can't fill, but I lie awake at night, wondering what she's doing. If she's okay. I trust that she's strong and independent and can get through this on her own. Besides, Van and Trey are there as her safety net.

My doorbell rings in the middle of the afternoon while Maverick is in school, and when I glance out the side window, I see an auburn-haired girl at the door.

I don't get the door all the way open before she pushes her way through.

"Juno?" I say, recognizing her now.

"So you're over her now, right? I gave you two weeks. That should be long enough." She pulls a bunch of papers out of her bag. "This is a standard contract, and don't worry, I would never give you a crazy date. You'll only get the best ones."

"What?" I shut the door and run a hand through my hair.

"I'm a matchmaker, remember? And you can't be alone forever. I figure you should hop back on the horse, as the saying goes, and get fixed up with a new woman. We don't have a lot in Lake Starlight." She pauses, hopefully to take a breath. "When I say a lot, I mean we don't have a huge selection. It's Alaska. The male population is naturally higher than the female one, but I can ask you a series of questions to narrow down your options."

I shake my head. "I'm not looking for anyone right now."

"Yeah, you told me that once before and then you nailed my sister and left her in LA with a broken heart." She waves me off. "But no worries, she's doing great there. Denver thanked you for all of us, right? We all appreciate what you did."

"Uh-huh."

She grins. "So I have this one woman. She's a bit older and just lost her husband. Is fifty too old?" She's dead serious.

"Well—"

She waves me off again. "Phoenix was young, and you seemed to like that, so I have this one girl—technically, she's a senior in high school, but she's already turned eighteen and she graduates in a month."

I stare blankly at her, and she smiles.

"That's a no. Okay." Digging through her papers, she pulls out one. "Do you like strong women?"

"Sure." Why am I answering these questions?

"This one is a homesteader, which means she lives off the land. She doesn't have a ton of time in the summer months, but all winter she's yours. It might be a little bit of a trek for you."

"I appreciate the offer, but I'm not interested."

She sits on the couch, finally breathing. "Why? I'm a believer in true love, so I want everyone to be with someone. No one wants to live their life alone, right? One day Maverick will move on from here, go to college or something, and you'll be sitting in that chair, wondering when he'll return. But he'll have his own life and the visits will grow further apart and soon that gorgeous hair of yours will be white and who knows, maybe you'll even be balding. It'll take you a little longer to get out of the chair. Then he'll marry and have a family of his own, probably down in the lower forty-eight. During our long winters when it's hard to visit people, you'll grow isolated and lonely and probably start having conversations with yourself."

"Um." I clear my throat. "Okay?"

She shrugs. "Love makes the world go around." She nods and her eyes are wide.

Looking at her, you'd never guess she was Phoenix's sister.

"How about I'll think about it?" I say.

She stacks her papers in a neat pile. "Yeah. This isn't a decision to rush, but the quicker you get out there, the quicker you can live a fulfilling life with a partner. Plus."

She leans in. "When the arthritis sets in, it's harder for you to... you know..."

"Okay, Juno." I take the papers from her with no intention of looking through them. "Sorry to rush this visit, but I have to install the sink."

She circles around and heads into the kitchen.

I blow out a breath.

"Is this *the sink*?" She inspects it. "You know, one of our brothers could do this for you."

"I'm almost finished."

She leans her hip on the counter. "Yeah, Phoenix told us it was important for you to do it on your own. She made Denver take it apart when you two went to Anchorage and he installed it. Luckily, she called and told him, otherwise you'd have a usable sink and wouldn't have to go into the bathroom to fill your pots." She laughs, patting my shoulder. "I'll leave you to it."

"Wait."

Juno twirls around with extra flair. I'm sensing that she's the dramatic one. "Yeah?"

"So Denver had the entire thing together and Phoenix told him to take it apart?"

She nods and shrugs. "None of us understood it, but Phoenix was adamant that you'd get it done and didn't need anyone's help." She waves. "Bye, Griffin. Let me know who you choose, and I'll get the women lined up."

I wave back. "Yeah." My voice is barely audible.

The slamming of the front door jars me back to the present. I look at the sink.

Today, this bitch is mine. If I accomplish nothing else, I will fix this sink.

THIRTY-FOUR

Phoenix

"Sedona Bailey."

We all stand and cheer when the dean calls her name. Jamison whistles with two fingers in his mouth while Sedona crosses the stage, shakes hands with the men and women there, and accepts her diploma. She leaves the stage with red-tinted cheeks, never one to want too much attention.

"She did it!" Savannah wraps her arms around me. "My two little sisters are getting everything they ever wanted."

Hearing someone in my family say how happy they are that things are working out for me in LA is surreal. I secured the agent Van told me about, and he was right, she's great. I ended up signing the contract as it was written. Jannie told me that Van and Trey included some things they wouldn't normally and was curious why they were being more generous with me than some other artists. She even asked if I was sleeping with Trey. I guess he's got a reputation in LA.

"I was thinking about coming down in a few weeks so we can look for a place. You have your advance now. You shouldn't be wasting your money on rent," Savannah says on our way down the stairs of the auditorium.

"Maybe. We'll see."

"Can you at least get an apartment? I mean, you're still staying at a hotel!"

Savannah doesn't get it, and I can't blame her. The thought of making LA so permanent that I have my name on a lease—or god forbid, a mortgage loan—feels suffocating. I'm not ready. I'm still hoping Griffin will change his mind. We've been in New York since last night and I haven't had the guts to ask if they've seen him. It's probably better this way. The last thing I need to know is that he's living it up in my old town.

"I know. I don't have a lot of time to look though."

She glances at me.

"How are you enjoying your soccer career?" Liam asks Jamison from behind me, and I stifle a laugh picturing the cringe on Jamison's face.

"Call it what it is, football." Jamison laughs.

He's been on his best behavior, as have I. Case in point, I pretended to be happy when I went to their apartment last night and saw all my sister's things mingled with his.

Griffin sent all my stuff to me in LA. Well, he sent them to Trey and had him deliver them to me. At least I never have to go somewhere we've been together. I dodge the restaurant we almost ate at and the sidewalk where he broke up with me. It's easy enough—only a mile out of my way.

When we reach outside, Juno comes to my side, shivering. "I think New York is colder than Alaska."

"How do you think I feel? My blood is already thinning in LA." I shiver along with her.

Liam wraps his big arms around Savannah. I bet she's warm. So is Brooklyn, who's wrapped in Wyatt's. We had some last-minute guests crash our girls' trip. Harley couldn't come because Phoebe has her first cold, and Holly is absent for unexplained reasons. Reasons we didn't ask about. No one wants to broach that subject, especially with Austin.

"Trey says hello," I tell Juno.

And he did. When I told him I was going to New York to see my sister graduate, he said he'd fly me on the record label's plane and be my plus one. I informed him it wasn't that type of event, but I'd take him up on the offer of the private jet. It's like a whole new way of flying, and since being in Griffin's, I didn't want to go back to economy class.

Juno knocks her hip against mine. "Shut up. No one knows."

"We all know," Brooklyn says. "Hard to miss you on the back of a guy who looks like he should be on the cover of *Extreme Sports Weekly*."

"It was one night. Nothing happened," Juno insists.

Lucky for her, Sedona emerges and comes right into a huge hug with all of us. We congratulate her, hug her, and kiss her cheek. Jamison kisses her and whispers something before we all decide we need to warm up.

"Isn't it spring? Damn it," Juno says.

Wyatt laughs. "Here I thought you guys were all tough being from Alaska."

Brooklyn slaps him on the stomach. "You're from Alaska now too."

He swoops her up in his arms. "I know. Happy to be a resident of Lake Starlight."

I watch them with awe and envy. They came from two different places but made it work. Wyatt relocated to Lake Starlight from Manhattan.

He lowers her back to the ground in a true prince move, and Brooklyn smiles at him as if he's her world. Which I know he is and for good reason.

We all file down the street, and Wyatt flags down one taxi and puts as many of us as he can inside before grabbing a second one, the true New Yorker in him coming out.

Jamison ends up next to me in the taxi. I really need to stop disliking him. I think I hold some resentment because in a way, it feels as if he took my sister away from me. But I can grudgingly admit—at least to myself—that she seems happy and he appears to take good care of her. Maybe now's the time to make amends.

"So do you ever play in LA?" I ask him.

He looks my way, appearing surprised that I'm talking to him. "Aye." He clears his throat. "I do. I'll check the schedule."

"Do you think you could bring Sedona with you?"

"She can't go with the team, but I can ask Coach if I could travel separately. Maybe if we have a few days between games, we can stay a while." He smiles.

I remember back to our childhood home, when he'd always be on the couch next to Sedona. Maybe some people just find their person young, and for others, it takes a while.

Brooklyn was engaged before Wyatt. Surely she loved her first fiancé? Maybe that's what Griffin was to me. Just my first real relationship before my forever one. Though I feel as though I'm breaking apart every day I'm without him.

"I'm sorry," Jamison whispers. "It sucks. I know."

"You do?" I look at him as though he's lying.

"When I went back to Scotland and your sister was in New York, we couldn't make the distance work and it was horrible. That's why the minute I got back in New York and knew we had a chance again, I called her. Missed her like crazy. I know we haven't always seen eye-to-eye, but I do love her. I love her so much sometimes it hurts."

I like the way the word hurt sounds when he says it with his accent. It sounds less painful.

"Love isn't supposed to hurt." I sigh.

He smiles. "I worry one day she'll wake up and say, 'I deserve a guy who doesn't travel all over the world for his job. A man who will be home to cook me dinna every night.' That's why it hurts. Like I hurt for heartbreak that has yet to come."

I had no idea he had this side to him. I always thought he was a cocky, self-assured soccer player with the looks to match his confidence. "My sister loves you so much. You have nothing to worry about."

"I hope not."

Before the taxi pulls up to the curb of the restaurant, I share a moment with who I suspect will be my brother-in-law one day.

"I get it though," he says while we wait for everyone to get out.

"Get what?" I ask.

"Why Griffin broke it off. I wouldn't be able to live in a different city than your sis. It'd make me crazy, loving someone from so far away. Too much can go wrong. Too many misunderstandings. Too much missing one another."

I get out of the taxi, and Jamison reunites with Sedona before I can respond. Everyone files into the restaurant, but I hang back and think over his words.

He's right. I couldn't be in LA knowing Griffin and Maverick were in Lake Starlight. I would miss them too much. It would've killed me.

When I join my family, I sit at the end of the table.

They've allowed me to wallow thus far, but Sedona knocks me with her knee. I look up and she's smiling, telling me in her nonverbal way that it will all work out.

I nod, although I have my doubts. Because if this is what I really want—the singing career—then why am I so unhappy?

My phone dings with a text from Jannie after the waiter has taken our drink orders.

Jannie: *Guess whose song is being considered to be in a new movie?*
Me: *Who?*
Jannie: *You, silly. This is huge for you! I'll email you over the details.*

See? That news alone would usually have me hijacking this dinner to tell everyone my news, ordering shots for everyone to celebrate. But the one person who deserves to celebrate with me doesn't want anything to do with me.

So I sip my wine and listen to my family badger my twin with questions. What will Sedona do now? Does she have applications out to any companies? I watch Jamison stare at Sedona, Liam's hand on Savannah's shoulder, Wyatt's hand threaded through the hair at the back of Brooklyn's head, and jealousy stirs inside.

I shake my head. Griffin wants it this way. This is the way it has to be, whether I like it or not.

THIRTY-FIVE

Griffin

Two months, and my biggest problem is I have to hear Phoenix's voice and the song I wrote for her all the damn time. I thought the Tyler Vaughn thing was bad, but this is ten times worse. Especially since the song is for Maverick's mother's new movie.

Yeah, welcome to hell with me.

"Can you please turn it off?" I ask Maverick.

"Can we go to the movie when it comes out?"

"No. It's inappropriate."

Phoenix was nice enough to send me a message before it got announced though. I thanked and congratulated her and didn't say anything else.

I turn on the faucet, installed by my own two hands last week, and fill a pot with water. Took a little longer and a lot of YouTube videos, but I did it. The shelves in the garage are another story though. One fix-it project at a time.

The doorbell rings. For the first week or so after Juno, I worried whenever I went to answer it, but I'm over that.

Opening the door though, I almost shut it in The Ghost of Christmas Future's face.

She smiles and steps into my house with Ethel behind her, talking to someone.

"Welcome," I say.

"Hey, Mav," Dori says. "I'll be on once I finish this."

He sighs, not bothering to correct her anymore with the name thing. "Awesome. This is my last bit of homework and then summer vacation."

Dori lifts her hand for a high five and he slaps it.

"You play online with him?" I ask.

"Yeah. It's really fun. Ethel's still getting the hang of it, but the whole retirement place is starting to pick it up. We used to do game nights, but this is much more fun than playing gin rummy and holding your nose. You know old people just blow wind whenever they want."

I nod.

"Oh great, you fixed the sink. So you're ready?" She pats Maverick on the back. "Give us a minute with your father."

He hops down, taking his homework with him, and disappears upstairs. She certainly has a way with him.

"Ready?" I ask.

"Gotta go, Muriel." Ethel presses her finger to her Bluetooth and concentrates on me.

"Yeah. You've proven you can fix a sink, so go get your girl," Dori says.

I shake my head. "I have no idea what you're talking about."

"Let me tell you a story about me and my late husband, Albert. He wanted to be a fisherman, but he had this obligation to his father. For the company. Now, unlike you, he didn't go buying a fishing boat..." She looks at

Ethel then at me. "Hold on. I think that was for someone else."

We sit in silence as she thinks a little longer.

"Did I ever tell you I was an ice skater? Probably could have been in the Olympics." She stops again. "No, that's for someone else too." She scratches her head.

"Dori, you don't have to give me some story that somehow relates to my situation with Phoenix. I love your granddaughter, but it's just not the right time. I'm fairly sure since you and Albert lived in this town until he passed and you still live in this town with your nine grandchildren, that the two of you were happy in the same zip code. I don't believe love can mature and blossom in two different states, let alone two places as drastically different as Lake Starlight and Los Angeles. So I appreciate you coming here to convince me to run off to LA and win your granddaughter back. I do. But it's over, and she's going to meet a guy—"

"A guy who'll treat her poorly," Ethel interjects, and Dori and I turn in her direction.

"What?" I demand.

"I saw her on a magazine cover with that Tyler Vaughn. I guess they might collaborate. There are rumors they're a couple now."

I shake my head. "No. Tabloids rarely tell the truth. I doubt Phoenix would involve herself with a guy like Tyler."

"Men can have screens over their true selves," Ethel says.

Dori pats Ethel's hand. "Do you really want to leave Phoenix out there to men who don't love her? Only want her for her body or her voice? Sleazy things happen down there."

"It's not all bad."

Ethel's eyes widen. "You moved from there. You didn't

want to live there anymore or have your son grow up there. But you're willing to leave the woman you love down there? And she's heartbroken, which means she's vulnerable."

I stand up straighter. Damn if Ethel doesn't have some sound advice. But I can't protect Phoenix. She has to live her life and make her own choices.

"I just don't understand the youth today," Ethel says, looking at Dori. "How come everyone just gives up? If my Frank had given up on me, he would have buried me first."

Dori pats her hand again, and I'm pretty sure Ethel has quite a life story.

I shake my head. "No one is giving up, but there are obstacles."

"Obstacles are meant only to steer you another way, not to block you," Dori says.

Am I insane or are these two ladies making sense? I have to be desperate for any reason to run to her.

"If everyone stopped at an obstacle, I wouldn't be able to vote," Ethel says.

"There are ways around everything," Dori says. "You just have to find what works best for you. People overthink everything."

Did I give up too soon? Do I not have to sit here by myself? Could Phoenix allow us to work somehow? For her happiness, maybe I could spend some time in LA during the summer or Maverick's school vacations.

"Oh, we're here because Ethel's granddaughter just got divorced and we're looking to set her up," Dori says.

I shake my head and look between them. "I thought you were here to get me back with Phoenix?"

Dori laughs. "No. You said you were done with her, so we figure let's fix you up. She's a sweet girl. She talks a lot but means well."

"Dori?"

"What? I have a picture here. It was right on my phone."

How can they even think I'd want to be fixed up? I just told them I was in love with Phoenix. "I love Phoenix."

"Then why are you here?" Dori asks.

I look around as if an idea is going to form. "I have no clue."

"All you have to do is go get her," Ethel informs me, and she's right.

"Maverick!" I yell.

"Relax, we have him. I'll call one of the girls to watch him." Dori stands.

I grab my keys, my wallet and my phone, stuffing them into my pockets.

"Come here first," Dori says. I walk over to her, and she hugs me tightly. "Welcome to the family."

Stepping back, I'm still confused by what transpired in the short time they've been here, but my mind is set on getting to Phoenix as fast as I can.

THIRTY-SIX

Phoenix

I wish Jannie would have told me the movie was Maggie Cooperton's movie. The man I love's ex-wife. I might not have agreed to it.

But I didn't know, so I stand in the back of a promo night with exclusive invites, waiting for my time to sing. I never even knew they had these but being asked to perform the song that's suddenly on everyone's television in a movie trailer is nice.

It would be spectacular if I didn't have to think of Griffin every time I sing the lyrics about finding love in the most unusual of places. About disappearing from your life and finding a love that intoxicates you. About losing that love. Living without that love. At the time he wrote the song, I felt the lyrics because I felt the heartbreak I would feel if I lost him. But after singing them so many times, I've realized he wrote the lyrics for how I would feel. After he left me on an LA sidewalk in broad daylight.

The first time I figured it out, I was so angry. I wanted to call him up and tell him off. Tell him he's an asshole and I never want to see him again. Then... I wanted to thank him because as the words slip from my lips, there's truth to them. I feel a deep connection to the words, and it produces a more powerful song. Griffin Thorne is truly a genius. A stupid genius, but a genius.

"Phoenix, right?" Maggie Cooperton peers backstage, her elaborate cocktail dress showing off her amazing figure. Her hair is perfect. Her makeup flawless. Why did Griffin divorce her again? Oh yeah, she cheated.

"Yes." I smile politely because she's the actress starring in the movie that my very first song will premiere in.

"Griffin's Phoenix, right?" She steps closer. She might be the most beautiful woman I have ever been this close to.

"Yes."

I want to ask her how much she knows. Are the rumors true? Are they back together? Is that why she's seeking me out? As some tit for tat? Then it all rushes forward. He could be out there past the black curtain. He could hear and watch and criticize me singing.

"I had to meet the woman who roped Griffin. I mean, so few of us have done the job."

I smile. Truthfully, I didn't think it was that hard of a feat.

"You made the right decision though. Us women have to let our careers take the reins because no man will step back for us."

I continue to smile politely while my fingernails dig into my palms. I feel lost most days without him and lately putting my career first hasn't felt that rewarding. It's as though my world is off axis and I'll never again feel normal. How could she leave Maverick, a boy so young and full of life? She barely sees him.

"Was it easy for you?" I ask.

The look she gives me makes me want to crawl under a rock and say sorry for talking. Then she smiles. "It's never easy, but we have to do what we do if we want to be successful."

"But isn't it our choice?"

"Excuse me?" She places her hand over her chest. Each nail is painted to perfection. What must it be like to keep up her appearance all the time?

"I mean, why can't we dictate when we'll work, where we'll work, and what we'll do? Why can't a world exist where you can be a mom and a movie star?" I fail to mention that there are actresses who do just that. Sure, they take their kids with them or turn down movies or shows to spend time with their kids, but they make both work.

"I guess it depends what is most important to you. I'm not sure what Griffin told you, but Maverick was a surprise. And Griffin was more than happy to take the reins on raising him so I could pursue my career."

"Because Maverick was more important than his own," I say more to myself, a giant lightbulb going off in my head.

"What?"

"Griffin moved out of LA for Maverick. He uprooted his life and gave up his career for his son. Not because of that stupid article. Not because of Cammie Sanchez or Tyler Vaughn. He did it for the most important person in his life—your son."

She inhales deeply. "He left LA because of rumors. He left because he couldn't handle the criticism. Because he's such a perfectionist that someone thinking he's a sellout hurts him, so he takes his toy and runs away."

I shake my head. "No. That's not it."

"What are you, twenty-two? What the hell do you know

about life?"

"He didn't give me up. He picked Maverick." My eyes widen and I look around, but just as I'm about to find Jannie, the person in charge approaches.

"You have it wrong," Maggie says. "Maverick is first priority for both of us, but Griffin left you. I know it might be hard, but Griffin isn't a man who is supposed to be nailed down."

"I have to go." I try to push past the man holding a microphone for me.

"*No.*" He shoves the microphone into my hands. "You need to sing. The band is set. Let's go."

"I'm sorry, I have a plane to catch."

The guy stares at me. "Your plane can wait the four minutes while you sing this song."

My shoulders slump.

"I guess Griffin Thorne will have to wait four minutes longer to be told how he feels," Maggie says behind me.

I turn around to face her with the microphone in my hand. "No. This is me having both. Because I'm going to go out there and sing my song, then I'm going to cut out on the cocktail party, find Griffin, and tell him how much I love him."

She laughs. Hollow and empty. "Good luck."

She turns around and disappears through the curtains backstage.

"Are we finally ready?" the man snaps.

"Yes."

A different man announces me, and I step onto the small makeshift stage, looking forward to getting the song over with. When I'm midway across the stage, I realize there're no drums, no electric guitar, no bass. It's just one man with an acoustic guitar.

I smile and he smiles. He nods toward the crowd, but I only want to stare at him. Griffin Thorne, music producer. Griffin Thorne, ex-husband of Margaret Cooperton. Griffin Thorne, father of Maverick Thorne. Griffin Thorne, my boss, my boyfriend, my lover, my everything.

He strums his guitar and I clear my throat to get rid of the large lump that's resting there.

"Our love lit up my soul and the world as I knew it disappeared..."

I lock eyes with him as I sing the beautiful lyrics he wrote. Words that, after this moment, will never fit us. Because our love is about to be what dreams are made of.

When the song ends, Griffin puts down his guitar, and I run into his arms and cling to him so tightly that he can never slip through my fingers again.

"I love you," he says.

"I love you."

"I'm sorry. I shouldn't have assumed. I shouldn't have decided for us both."

I draw back and put my finger to his lips. "Relax. Breathe."

He smiles.

"Let's start over," I say.

"Great idea. I'm Griffin."

"I'm Phoenix."

"Can I kiss you?"

"You better before I kiss you and then you're the hero who waited for the heroine to kiss and—"

My words end with the smash of his lips. Applause commences, and the curtain falls.

I was so wrong. Sometimes you get exactly what you deserve.

Phoenix

"Are you sure about staying home?" Griffin hands me and Maverick the bowl of popcorn and slides under the blankets with us.

Maverick clears his throat and I dump some of the popcorn into his bowl. No need for all of us to get sick.

"My date got sick. It's a great excuse."

We both look to Maverick who has a stash of Kleenex next to him.

The video music award show comes back on and we all quiet.

"Stop playing with Grandma," I tell Maverick and he slides his phone onto the cushion.

Our song is up for Best Music Video from a Film. They speed tracked it by using mostly clips from the film which, luckily for us, we get to see Maggie with my vocals behind her. I don't truly care if we win or not.

"Here it is." Griffin turns up the volume.

"It's Mom." Maverick points. Maggie was going to be

the one to take Maverick. It was going to be a surprise, but when he got the fever Thursday night, we decided it was better to cancel.

I'm not sure if my words resonate a little with Maggie or not, but she's made it up here once a month and took him on vacation for two weeks. I hope for Maverick's sake, she continues to make him a priority in her life.

"It is."

"And you're singing, Phoenix." He laughs and I join in because it is oddly funny.

Thankfully they go to the next video after only seconds and once this is over the television is off and we're going to get Maverick to bed and have some alone time together.

We're in the middle of building a studio because I convinced Griffin that if I can have it all, he can too. So far, he's only got one artist to work with him—me. Truth be told I take up a lot of his time. But I won't be the last artist willing to come up to Lake Starlight to work with him. He really is a genius.

"Hey," I whisper. He turns to me. "Thank you."

"If you win, this was you. I'm not busting out those vocals." He kisses me briefly and I linger longer than I should.

"You need to take more credit."

"I love you," he says.

"I love you, too."

"Stop kissing, they're picking," Maverick says, and we turn to the screen.

"And Tyler Vaughn wins for Bombshell."

Griffin inhales a deep breath and I laugh, grabbing the remote and turning off the television.

"You didn't win?" Maverick says, his frown growing deeper.

I bend down and pick him up, falling down to Griffin's lap where he tickles Maverick as he begs for mercy.

"Oh Mav, I won. I won big."

Griffin looks down at me and his fingers stop tormenting his son.

"We all did," Griffin says.

Maverick slides out from between us and runs out of the room. Griffin bends down and gives me a very PG kiss with the promise of an X-rated one later.

Then the doorbell rings...

"I'm going to disarm it." Griffin nudges me up and stands before Maverick can answer the door.

"Remember, we live in Lake Starlight."

He laughs and barely beats Maverick to the door where my entire family is waiting outside with balloons and cake.

"You should have won." Holly comes in with a huge bouquet of congratulations balloons.

"Tyler Vaughn. Ugh." Brooklyn sticks her finger in her mouth.

"It was totally rigged." Harley lets Dion down and he runs over to Maverick.

"Watch out, he's sick."

Harley waves me off. "Oh pity if Dion is too tired to run around non-stop."

Everyone laughs because the kid is kind of a terror. High energy as Rome says.

"Next year it's going to be yours." Savannah comes over and kisses me on the cheek. "Your voice was amazing."

"And I say group vacay to LA next year," Cleo says.

"Hell ya." Denver joins her with the cake in his hands.

"Sorry girl." Juno hugs me but there's something majorly off with her.

"Kingston sends his apology, he was sent to a fire this

morning." Just as Austin says that, my phone dings with a sad emoji from Kingston.

Kingston: *Should have been yours. Sorry sis.*

"I'm really okay, guys. I mean it's been a whirlwind of six months."

Griffin comes over and puts his arm around me, kissing my temple. "There's a lot of years to come, everyone."

Griffin's words get them all to agree loudly and say of course, definitely, she's a star.

Sedona's text comes a second later.

Sedona: *Love you. I'll kick Tyler in the balls if I ever see him in NYC.*

I laugh and everyone stares at me.

"Sedona?" Rome asks.

I nod and catch him looking at Denver. Sometimes twins just get one another more. Sedona doesn't have to apologize, I already know she's sorry and wishes I'd won. She'd rather me laugh.

The next text surprises me and it's from a number not programmed into my phone.

UNKNOWN: *Who wants a video music award? Hold out for the Grammy - Jamison*

I smile down at it. Maybe I do like that guy now.

"Let's cut the cake and pop the champagne," Grandma Dori says.

Griffin digs out the knife and the plates. Maverick plays

with Calista and Dion, Phoebe standing and falling but trying to keep up with them.

Rome's busy ensuring everything is child-friendly, shutting doors and telling Phoebe 'no.' The girl should be in one of those blow-up sumo wrestling outfits.

Harley is telling Rome to relax and finally gives up, enjoying her own adult time.

Austin can't stop touching Holly and they're sharing so many smiles and kisses, it's obvious something is going on.

Juno is busying herself with cutting the cake under Grandma Dori's direction.

Brooklyn and Wyatt are busy looking out Griffin's window to the lake discussing if they should have bought property here. I love my sister, but I don't really want her five chickens.

Liam opens the box for the shelving that was just delivered. "You want me to put this together?"

Griffin almost runs over there, and everyone screams. "NO! He'll do it himself."

Liam holds up his hands and drops the box.

Oh they already know my boyfriend so well.

Savannah hands a champagne glass to Liam. Their wedding is set for next month in the gazebo, much like Austin and Holly's.

They share a weird smile too and then Harley hands a glass to Savannah. Savannah discreetly passes hers to Liam, and he quickly swallows it and returns the empty glass back to her.

"UH!" I cover my mouth. The only person who saw me is Brooklyn. She turns beet red and a soft smile comes to her lips. I look down to find her glass is empty as well, and Wyatt is swallowing a mouth full although his glass is full.

You've got to be kidding me.

Grandma Dori takes a knife and stabs one of the congratulations balloons. Okay then, she's letting her feelings be known.

Austin stops her before she kills another one. "Hey, everyone." He stands up. "We have some news."

I swear even Phoebe grows quiet as we all give them one hundred percent attention. I catch Harley's fingers crossed under the breakfast bar. She might be the most hopeful of all of us.

"Holly can't have the champagne."

"Why?" Harley asks.

"She's three months pregnant!" Austin kisses his wife's temple.

We swarm them, hugs and kisses, suffocating them to the point Austin pushes people back. Oh this is going to be a long pregnancy for her.

Holly beams. "Where's Dori?"

I catch her in the hallway, and she is wiping tears from her eyes.

When Holly finds her, she pulls Dori into her arms, nodding her head that it really is true. As they move apart, I see how worried Grandma was. Austin seeks them out and the three of them hug in the hallway.

"Um... Everyone." Brooklyn looks to Wyatt, and he shakes his head. She looks harder and he shrugs. "Wyatt drank my champagne."

"What?" Juno says. "Both of you!"

Brooklyn nods and we all swarm her. Grandma Dori, Austin, and Holly coming out from the hallway.

"We're going to be pregnant together?" Holly asks and Brooklyn nods, tears falling down her cheek.

"You're not the only two," Savannah says and all of our heads whip in her direction.

"NO," I say.

"All three of you?" Grandma Dori looks pale.

"Someone watch her, she might pass out." I point to Grandma.

Austin takes responsibility for her and we all wish our congratulations to them all.

"I can't believe this. The one time I'm not pregnant and you three are all pregnant. ROME!"

"No. Absolutely not," he says.

Denver looks to Cleo. "No jealousy here."

Griffin approaches me, putting his arms around my stomach and resting his chin on my shoulder.

"What about you? Jealous?"

Maverick definitely makes me want a child, but I'm far from ready, so I answer honestly.

"Not yet."

He squeezes me. "Good, because I want just us for a little bit longer. Only a little longer though."

I laugh, understanding what he's really saying.

"Well, aren't I just the loser sister." Juno shocks us all out of the cake and champagne.

"You're not a loser, Juno." Harley puts her arm around her.

"I don't have anyone."

We all stare at her. "Maybe it's time to start matchmaking yourself." Brooklyn pats her hand across the island.

"I think I know the perfect guy," Grandma Dori says.

"We all know who the perfect guy is." Rome sighs.

"The question is, does Juno?" Denver adds in his two cents.

Juno breaks down into tears and we all swarm her now.

"What's wrong?" I ask.

"I'm the world's worst matchmaker." Her head falls into her hands.

"No, you're not. Why would you say that?" Savannah comes up on the other side of her.

"I matched Colton up."

"Uh…" everyone groans in unison.

She lifts her head. "And now he's engaged."

Another round of tears and sobs escape and she disappears into her hands again.

We all look around but most of us look to Grandma Dori. Even she can't fix this one.

The End

COCKAMAMIE UNICORN RAMBLINGS

The obstacle of plotting nine books out at one time means that you might think something sounds good initially and then when it comes time to write the book you realize your initial idea won't work. Especially when you title the stories more than a year before you're going to write them. LOL Back when we first came up with Phoenix's book her hero wasn't going to be Griffin Thorne. At one point it was just some construction company owner who had a kid and she was going to be his nanny because her singing career wasn't panning out.

Funny thing is when Griffin Thorne emerged on the page in Advice of a Jilted Bride we still didn't have him in mind for Phoenix. Denver's plane going down with Griffin was strictly for Rome and Harley's (Birth of a Baby Daddy) storyline. We weren't even thinking of how it might fit in with Phoenix's book at that point.

In the end, the decision that Griffin was made for Phoenix was final when we were plotting Falling for my Brother's Best Friend. Phoenix returned back to town and had to make some tough decisions about pursuing her dreams. We love when it all comes together in the end! Who would have thought that the seventeen-year-old girl who gave Austin so much trouble in his book would be a natural step-mother to Maverick? Now we look back at our original storyline and think how boring anyone other than an older, hot music producer who's at his own career cross-roads would've been.

We hope you're enjoying watching the Bailey clan grow like we are. There are so many more fun surprises in store!

SUPER HUGE THANKS to our team who if not for them, we'd never be able to finish these books!

- Danielle Sanchez and the entire Wildfire Marketing Solutions!
- Cassie from Joy Editing for line edits.
- Ellie from My Brother's Editor for line edits.
- Shawna from Behind the Writer for proofreading.
- Sarah from Okay Creations for the cover and branding for the entire series.
- Sara from Sara Eirew Photography for the super sexy picture of Griffin and Phoenix.
- Bloggers who consistently carve out time to read, review and/or promote us.
- Piper Rayne Unicorns who shout from the rooftops about our new releases and love our characters like we do.
- Readers who took a chance on our book with so many choices out there.

And for what's next... we know, we know. And we wish we could apologize for leaving you with that massive cliffhanger with Juno and Colton. At least you'll get a little more information in the novella, Operation Babies (releasing on April 21, 2020). It's going to be raining Bailey babies!!

XO,
   Piper & Rayne

ABOUT PIPER & RAYNE

Piper Rayne is a USA Today Bestselling Author duo who write "heartwarming humor with a side of sizzle" about families, whether that be blood or found. They both have e-readers full of one-clickable books, they're married to husbands who drive them to drink, and they're both chauffeurs to their kids. Most of all, they love hot heroes and quirky heroines who make them laugh, and they hope you do, too!

The Baileys

Lessons from a One-Night Stand

Advice from a Jilted Bride

Birth of a Baby Daddy

Operation Bailey Wedding (Novella)

Falling for My Brother's Best Friend

Demise of a Self-Centered Playboy

Confessions of a Naughty Nanny

Operation Bailey Babies (Novella)

Secrets of the World's Worst Matchmaker

Winning My Best Friend's Girl

Rules for Dating your Ex

Operation Bailey Birthday (Novella)

The Greenes

My Twist of Fortune (FREE)

My Beautiful Neighbor

My Almost Ex

My Vegas Groom

The Greene Family Summer Bash

My Sister's Flirty Friend

My Unexpected Surprise

My Famous Frenemy

The Greene Family Vacation

My Scorned Best Friend

My Fake Fiancé

My Brother's Forbidden Friend

The Modern Love World

Charmed by the Bartender

Hooked by the Boxer

Mad about the Banker

Complete Set (all 3 books)

The Single Dad's Club

Real Deal

Dirty Talker

Sexy Beast

Complete Set (all 3 books)

Hollywood Hearts

Mister Mom

Animal Attraction

Domestic Bliss

Bedroom Games

Cold as Ice

On Thin Ice

Break the Ice

Complete Set (all 3 books +)

Charity Case

Manic Monday

Afternoon Delight

Happy Hour

Complete Set (all 3 books)

Blue Collar Brothers

Flirting with Fire

Crushing on the Cop

Engaged to the EMT

Complete Set (All 3 books)

White Collar Brothers

Sexy Filthy Boss

Dirty Flirty Enemy

Wild Steamy Hook-up

The Rooftop Crew

My Bestie's Ex

A Royal Mistake

The Rival Roomies

Our Star-Crossed Kiss

The Do-Over

A Co-Workers Crush

Hockey Hotties

Countdown to a Kiss (Free Novella)

My Lucky #13

The Trouble with #9

Faking it with #41

Sneaking around with #34

Second Shot with #76

Offside with #55